by Philip Wylie

THE END
OF THE DREAM

THE END
OF THE DREAM

Philip Wylie

1972
DOUBLEDAY & COMPANY, INC., GARDEN CITY, NEW YORK

Designed by Wilma Robin

PROLOGUE:
AN IMPOSSIBLE TASK

The date (Old Calendar) was June 6, 2023, and the place, Faraway, New York, again in the Old Geography.

Faraway, a twenty-five-thousand-acre stand of largely virgin timber, lies in the Adirondack Mountains somewhat to the north and west of the familiar Placid-Saranac vacation region. It was owned by Miles Standish Smythe and his sister Nora, and had been in the family since 1854. It had been the hideaway of a group of Eastern millionaires who had constructed a huge central lodge and a number of cottages together with service buildings and homes for guides on the northern shore of the largest of three bodies of water within its fenced boundaries, Lake Enigma. The other two were less than a mile at their widest points: Big Panther and Little Panther ponds.

Originally, the only means of reaching the "camp," as its owners called it, was by rail, a spur fifteen miles long served by a single small locomotive and a rolling stock of three baggage cars and one very elegant private car. Massive iron gates barred the spur, which was, by intention, seemingly blocked by a hardwood scrub. Behind that barrier and invisible from the main line was a guard's house, initially occupied by a dull-witted chap named Seth Bartlet and his more capable wife, who had seen to it for more than a decade that none but club members and guests entered the property.

A fire in the winter of 1853 had destroyed the lodge and several cottages, after which the aging members decided to sell the tract. It was purchased by Daniel Smythe, who built a lodge of modest proportions and new cottages. Faraway then became the summer resort and hunting preserve of Daniel Smythe, his family and their descendants.

Early in the twentieth century that lodge had been replaced by an immense clubhouse of fieldstone, and over the years various members of the family and numerous friends had built elaborate summer places along the shore of Lake Enigma. The property included several mountains, and through the uncut forest ran the Mystery River and several tributary creeks. The Mystery fed Lake Enigma and flowed from it, underground, for some miles, which presumably accounted for the names of both the lake and the small, clear river.

There were, of course, other private holdings as fast in the Adirondacks. But more of them had repeatedly known the ring of axes and later the snarl of power saws. None had maintained through the twentieth century a comparable stand of virgin forest. Not surprisingly, Faraway had been the last northern refuge of the ivory bill and was, still, one of the few places in the Adirondacks populated by otters, fishers and martins. In very cold winters it also became the range of wolves, driven south from Canada by hunger.

The rail spur had long since been replaced by a fifteen-mile graveled road still guarded by descendants of Seth Bartlet.

When, on Miles Smythe's twenty-first birthday, it came into his and his sister Nora's possession, he maintained it in the customary way, security measures included. In his boyhood he had spent his summers and many a winter vacation at Faraway. In the long and the shorter periods one of the resident guides had trained him and his young friend Willard Gulliver in the northwoodsman's skills. But, though he accepted his heritage with aplomb, he did not visit Faraway for several summers. He had graduated from Princeton magna cum laude, and immediately launched the Foundation which had begun in his precocious teens as a response to anger in the form of a creative dream. The Foundation for Human Conservancy made Miles a world figure but failed in its purpose as Miles had surely expected from the start.

When he could, in the ensuing decades, Miles got up to Faraway from Manhattan or elsewhere. He loved the place. His boyhood chum, Will Gulliver, after finishing his graduate work in ecology and becoming Miles's right-hand man in the Foundation, usually accompanied him. He had married Miles's sister Nora. Little by little, as both men perceived the approaching ruin of the civilization they had dedicated their lives to trying to rescue, they began to prepare Faraway as a retreat, a place where, if all else gave way, their families and those of selected friends and colleagues might escape any ultimate horror and, hopefully, survive in that guarded wilderness with the makings—or remakings—of a viable society. By 2010 a miniature, self-sustaining city had been quietly constructed on Lake Enigma and, five years later, wives, children and elderly folk were being quietly assembled there. The others were to come later. Not all of them made it.

Now, on a day in what once would have been June 6, in the year A.D. 2023 by Old Calendar reckoning, this nucleus of forest-bound civilization served a purpose for which it had not been designed. Faraway was the "Central City" of District Two. It lay in Area Six.

That meant it was the capital of what had been the United States and Canada.

District One was now Europe, Britain and Soviet Russia.

Area Six was that part of USA which had been New England and New York State along with Canada's Maritime Provinces and Quebec. The New Calendar described this June day as 6/17/23, since the year had been divided into thirteen months of twenty-eight days and an Added Day, yearly, and two in each fourth year. The extra month followed December and was called Aurora by people who still used the old system. But children of school age were already puzzled by the Old Calendar, which they found absurd and confusing.

A day, then, in late spring.

The time, midmorning.

The sky was quite blue, bluer, many were saying, than it had been since it became gray all over the world.

The population of Faraway had just passed the four-thousand mark, a new high. It was a busy population. The children were in school, the older youths taking accelerated courses at college or on graduate levels. All able adults were occupied in servicing what Miles called the "habitat" or in its two major undertakings.

The first of these involved the recovery and reorganization of human beings in District Two. As of that June date 2,310,-065 survivors in the USA and Canada had been registered. Many were aged or ill and many, young children. They were being assembled in suitable towns and in a few cities according to their needs, desires and skills. That number could be said to have at least minimally adequate shelter, enough food, limited communications and basic transportation.

It was estimated that a half million persons in District Two were still "at large," and an unknown but plainly considerable fraction of them were willfully so, and in violation of the New Laws. During the years after 2011 when civilized nations faltered and fell, a shocking percentage of once satisfactory (or once criminal) human beings regressed to banditry and barbarism. In mid-2023, such bands were still being located and dealt with in ways as humane as circumstances permitted. Many of these wild folk could, with treatment, be reclaimed as useful citizens and their professional skills thereby recovered—in a time when skills of all sorts were precious. Many of these bands contained numbers of children, all of whom were regarded as salvageable.

As rapidly as possible, then, the survivors in District Two were being settled and were both supplying and being supplied with essentials. Similar procedures were taking place in District One and in Three through Seven, though the pace of recovery was slower and the degree less well known for Five (China and India), Six (Africa) and Seven (Latin America). District Eight (Island Communities, Atlantic, Pacific and Other Seas) was still unformed.

The second major activity of the Central City was the integration of District Two with the others for the establishment of a world government. Toward that end the Third World Congress was now in session in Paris, attended by Miles Smythe, who was director for District Two, and a score of his associates.

This endeavor was difficult, owing to the magnitude of physical problems, and it was further hampered by language translation. No lack of will and no national fealty or political dogma appreciably interfered with the work. In three generations genus *Homo* had been reduced by its own acts, and in spite of every possible warning, to an estimated fifty millions from a peak more than a hundred times as great. One person existed in 2023 for every hundred-plus alive at the century's turn.

That was a sufficient reduction and it had happened in a sufficiently short period to make mandatory the need for a central government (and a totally different way of life from the recent and most "highly civilized" sort). Even that stubborn breed called mankind got the point. It had taken a ninety per cent extermination, in a series of incalculably grim calamities, to shatter man's deluded attitude toward his special nation and its political and economic system and, above all, to erase man's near indelible idea that he existed above and outside nature and could do with and to nature as he pleased.

The First World Congress was called in 2020. Between them and the Third, present, Congress (2023) nine out of ten in the residual world population perished and in 2023 there was still no certainty that the efforts of a world government could save humanity. That uncertainty was well understood by all literate people and most others. The past half century had shown that, however fast the scientists exerted their efforts toward anticipating new perils, others of unknown deadliness were overlooked or even not detectable.

The havoc man had wreaked on his planet was so immense and of so many sorts that assurance of safety had become absurd.

All that remained was *hope*.

If man could reorganize, if he could continue to live with minimal damage to his ruined environment, if no future catastrophe of a sort and scope he could not manage were to occur, then, at some future date not soon expectable, he could say with modest confidence that he had succeeded and could look to a future of open-ended duration. But even hope was exhilarating after the past decades.

The opaque and usually densely clouded sky itself was turning pale blue again. And, everywhere else on the depeopled planet, nature showed signs of recoveries of greater or lesser magnitudes. The seas were slowly returning to their pre-inundation levels. The Antarctic ice was building up anew and ice was forming in the northern seas. Pests and plagues were under control or had burned themselves out and so vanished. And, almost anywhere, there could be found evidence that the titanic "vengeance" of nature which had left few people had also allowed tiny samples of uncounted life forms to persist. These were becoming the "seed beds" of regeneration and redistribution. Upland brooks were often as pellucid as those at Faraway. Many rivers were becoming almost as clear. Birds, mammals, insects, reptiles and plants that had been thought extinct, or had vanished from huge regions, were beginning to reappear or return.

Hardly a day passed that the Central City at Faraway did not receive reports, often a number of them, of such welcome

14

surprises. A pair of nesting scarlet tanagers was reported from what had been Pennsylvania. A school of bottle-nosed dolphin was cited off the eastern tip of Long Island. A black bear was photographed in former Wyoming. A man in Texas was bitten by a rattlesnake. After several unusually heavy and unusually uncontaminated rains in the vicinity of Palm Springs, California, six species of desert flowers bloomed and a rare species of desert shrimp hatched in standing pools.

Each such "bulletin" was an excitement for all. The fact that the snake-bitten Texan died was not nearly so cogent as the fact that another and supposedly extinct reptile had lived and could perhaps take its place again in the ecological life chains so hideously interrupted. And man's powers of recuperation surely are no less than those of other living creatures!

The four-thousand-plus citizens of the Central City, Area Six, were undoubtedly the most nearly optimistic group in District Two. What all but a few young children had experienced was so appalling that, had they not been chosen for their condition and characteristics, all might expectably be mad: husbands without wives, wives widowed by disasters, orphaned youths and only a few complete families, most people at Faraway went about their work with a visible if understated joy. Why?

There was hope.

Not long ago and for a long while there had been none.

Life, even at this odd capital, was not luxurious. Working hours were unlimited and the work was never finished. There was no "America" any more, and most of what had been that was still devastated. Less than three hundred remained in hospitals, maimed, ill or still suffering mental collapse. For everybody's loved ones and friends were lost in their majority . . . dead by ways known or unknown and ways all too easily envisaged.

15

Nevertheless they had elected representatives to a government of all humanity and it was in its third session. As the New Laws were passed by the Congress they were universally accepted and with only occasional, usually technological debate. The ancestors and even the parents of these survivors would have called the New Laws intolerably confining, even dictatorial. Such was not the case. People in the organizing and differently governed world were free in the fundamental sense and the tasks they performed were executed voluntarily, however stringent and demanding they might be. Their privations—or what would thitherto have seemed that, and intolerable in degree—were welcomed.

It was, all over the recovering world of man, "good to be alive" for the one, real and unchanging reason: each individual's aliveness meant that *humanity* lived and it meant that humanity had a hope of going on, even of biological immortality, all man ever had the sane right to hope.

At Faraway, on that morning of June 6, a man sat in a singular building among the ultra-modern structures on or near the shores of Lake Enigma. This extensive structure was underground and reached by a covered stairway. Over its massive portal chipped letters described its function:

RECORDS BUILDING
The Foundation for Human Conservancy

The heavy, power-swung portal gave on a set of business offices, artificially lighted, air-conditioned, luxurious even by the highest-achieved standards. It housed business machines and other equipment developed before the End. There were six offices opening off a wide hallway but only one was occupied by a single man, Willard Page Gulliver, Miles Smythe's lifelong friend and his second in command while the Foundation was viable.

The structures and technical facilities at Faraway anticipated the world calamity that had taken place. It was Miles's belief that by using the two immense fortunes he and his sister had inherited it would be possible to unite every individual and every organization with an interest in saving the environment, so as to form a giant body dedicated to the rescue of man from himself, from his environment-despoiling "technology."

What Miles considered the vital needs, as he rapidly built up his ultimately world-renowned Foundation, consisted of a galaxy of acts and of things. One such effort concerned research. For, as Miles used to state at every opportunity in the early years (the early seventies), "Until we know exactly what threatens us, our planet, its life forms and ecology, we cannot know what priorities to set for escaping doom." The Foundation backed a research program in order to find the most imminent threats.

His second effort was to set up a clearinghouse for all relevant scientific data as such data existed and were developed. At one time (1989–95) the Foundation employed more than twenty thousand persons in those two efforts alone. The material thus gathered had been shipped to the Records Building at Faraway and filed in auto-retrieval banks in an atmosphere of inert gas, for its preservation. Thus there was stored here an almost complete history both of the facts relating to the environmental debacle and of what mankind said and did in the increasingly dreadful decades.

This was now Will Gulliver's "library," a repository of 3,900,000,000 catalogued items.

Alone in the edifice, he prepared to dictate to a computransor a letter to Miles, or what would have been a letter in his younger years and what he still thought of as such. Actually, his words would be stored electronically on a single "chip" which would be lasogramed in "open" periods to a satellite and thence to a sister copier in Paris at the rate of a hundred and eighty thousand words per second. From the Paris recording Miles could play back Will's "letter" while noting, as he listened to this "audio," any portions he wished transcribed for later, careful perusal.

The day before, Miles had requested from Paris that Will forward by computransor all he had thus far done on what Will had, from the first, called "an impossible task."

This task had occupied him for more than half his working time in the past eighteen months. It was, in so far as the directive went, simple-seeming. Will was to gather and annotate a selection of material from the fabulous stores in the Records Building that would show how the world had come to its present state in the half century just past.

This project was not to be formal history.

On the contrary, it was to serve as a collection of the *sorts* of calamities that had brought man to his knees and as a varied exhibit of how individuals and groups, eyewitnesses, governments, committees, in effect, *people*, had reacted to those events at the moment . . . or soon, or finally.

Such a book, or set of books, the directive observed, would be invaluable in the decades ahead as a general text designed to instill in readers, from high school age on, a wide, emotionally effective sense of how it was *possible* for a species that considered itself rational, civilized and self-ordered to pass through so many and such diverse catastrophes without taking effective steps to prevent or even diminish the impact of most, until too late.

Willard Page Gulliver was, as even he acknowledged, the best possible person in former USA, at least, for that effort. As second in command at the Foundation he had stood on that pinnacle where the over-all view was most knowing and broad. He had lived through the period, all of it, and had been in the midst of far more of the events he was to choose from than almost any other man.

But that June morning, as he moved with his long-legged saunter from the White Pine Dining Hall and breakfast to the Records Building, he had felt ashamed of the results of his long and very arduous efforts. Looking at Faraway and thinking of it as the capital of ex-USA, then looking back at that nation and at others in the 1970s, '80s, '90s, it seemed to him that nothing, no collation, not even the billions of documents available, would accomplish what the directive asked.

The differences were too gigantic. The events too many and too diverse, too complex in cause and effect. They would seem alien, in the main, even to the children of this day and so, for the hoped-for future generations, even less credible. On a planet now largely reverting to wilderness, or the equivalent, even the old cities and their throngs would be unimaginable.

Indeed, Will had often observed, as he labored over the anthology, that *he* sometimes found it hard to recall exactly how it was, even in Manhattan on Fifth Avenue at Fifty-seventh, where the Smythe Building stood from the late seventies, "evolving" eighties and most of the "triumphant" nineties. The tremendous buildings and dazzling, decked thoroughfares on Fifth Avenue, the sounds and smells of the great towers and the light patterns beneath, and of the weather changes above the plastic roofs over the avenues, or, again, the effects of the plastic domes covering many neopoli (commonly, "newburgs") were almost unreal to him even as memories.

His back-dreaming mind would recall a period of rainbow-hued street lighting as the usual thing—only to remember, later, that it had been a feature of special occasions. He would think the piny scent of Fifth Avenue had been per-

19

manent and suddenly realize it had not. "Scented city air" in Manhattan and elsewhere was a delight (or vexation) to millions until it was suddenly found that the perfumed additives, volatile essences, were slowly breaking up the molecular chains in plastic canopies overhead. That sybaritic gambit was swiftly abandoned when the snow load on the weakened "lid" over Chicago's Loop crashed down, like an instant avalanche, and buried a noonday multitude on the sidewalks and in the traffic under ten to fifty feet of snow, ice and jagged debris.

No one man and no number of men, he felt, could possibly choose the proper material to reproduce even a partial sense of what those who had lived through the events themselves often recollected incorrectly . . . often had forgotten, and always looked back upon with reluctance if not in curling horror.

Will Gulliver did his best, knowing the reason for his appointment.

What was it? Who was he?

The poor lad who met Miles Smythe at a special school where only a few students were poor and on scholarships. This boyhood chum of Miles's became not only second in command at the Foundation but also Miles's brother-in-law. He became famous as well.

Who's Who in America gave Will's birth date (May 12, 1953) and the record of his academic career: Princeton, Cornell and MIT, an M.A. in literature and a doctorate in biology. It stated that he had married Nora Van Dyle Smythe on May 12 in 1974, that they'd had two children (dec.) and set down his present title as assistant director of the Foundation for Human Conservancy. The entry continued with a two-column sketch listing his various intervening posts, honors, etc., club memberships, directorates and publications, both

scientific and popular, including his best-selling books on conservation, pollution and other environmental topics. This
précis—since Will refused to do so—Nora had compiled and
sent to the editors of Who's Who, after Miles damned Will
for his "modesty," calling it "false" and "sheer hypocrisy,"
to Will's concealed amusement. Miles's vanity showed, there!

What did Will look like, as he prepared to dictate his
"letter" to Miles in distant Paris, at his age of seventy
and as one of the beneficiaries of the Lupotte-Carson lon-
gevity treatments?

Like, people said, a philosophy professor: tall, thin, angu-
lar, loose-jointed, long-faced with recessed eyes under black
brows and heavy near-black hair in which two white streaks
ran parallel; big-nosed and wide-lipped; a man who spoke in a
resonant bass that was, often, a mumble; a shy man, to most,
but an eloquent speaker and a man with an eerie sense of
humor. He had a poetic feeling for humanity and a tran-
scendent sense of nature—both held to realism by knowledge
and by a mind of tremendous force and scope. On his long
face were chisel marks of regret and grief that, by sudden and
minute shifts, became the crow's-feet of mirth. Will dressed
neatly and well but wore his clothes as if they were old bath-
robes. A philosopher-professor type to the casual eye, but also
one born for adventure, a spellbound man, and spellbinder, a
being intended for learning and understanding, a man whose
laughter on a still night carried a mile.

His enemies—most of them Foundation foes—called him
an alarmist and said he spent his life "standing on the panic
button." He was called a "scientific scarecrow," "an erudite
wolf-crier," "counterprogressive" and "anti-productive." But
no one said his data were in error—just his conclusions. And
he was never, anywhere, judged to be mean, cruel, stingy,
selfish, or even . . . unkind.

21

It was his obvious kindness and known generosity which bent the points of most such efforts at disparagement. For the world knew from the early days of the Foundation that most of its spectacular and successful efforts to encourage mankind were promulgated by Willard Page Gulliver. Miles used the cudgel.

In another age he might not have attained so much power, wealth and eminence; but he would certainly have had more fun.

This man, who could not have been adequately characterized in the longest of biographies, was now trying to get across his thoughts and feelings to another, one whom he (and millions agreed) believed to be the greatest of the age.

"Dear Miles," he began, eyes scanning the pickup box on the desk before him, "as you asked, I'm putting what I've chosen for the book on chips, for you. Rather, Ethel is going to do it. The more I ponder the whole thing, the less hope I have of its effectiveness. And you will find you can skip many of my words, which, in the main, merely briefly introduce or invade these miscellaneous chapters. And what a miscellany! Much of it you can skip, to get on with the stuff less familiar to you from experience.

"As an introduction, I have drawn heavily on the opening chapter of G. W. Packett's 1975: *Date of No Return*. You may have forgotten that best seller of the late nineties but it remains a fairly adequate and certainly the most outstanding discussion (of many) of the exact time beyond which man was without hope of salvation. Packett put it at 1975. I'd have perhaps set it a little later. No matter. *Something* is necessary as a lead-off to explain the now nearly incredible fact that there actually was a time, some fifty years ago, or thereabouts, when man might still have been able to prevent his near extermination."

22

He switched off the instrument and pondered. Then continued:

"I agreed with the general view that we must henceforward rely on printed words rather than 3D-TV or motion pictures and other graphic forms of education. I agree that no networks of the old sort, no such general systems of audiovisual broadcasting, must ever be resumed. Such media ruined the perceptions of the masses, their sensitivity, humanity, and their capacity for the evaluation, application or use of the disjointed information these old networks did scantily provide.

"Even so, as I have gathered this material for, now, a year and a half, I often think, *If only I could show the pictures!* Say, then, I've done what I could with the one medium we agree is basic: the printed word."

He hesitated and his tone changed as he departed from that subject. Miles would want, as he knew better than any other person, all the news of local interest, trivial, novel, routine, whatever. So he began to supply it, free of the hesitancy he'd previously shown and, instead, genially, often with a wide grin.

"First, about the fusion reactor in the Hudson gorge. I flew down in the electro-chopper last week when we had word here they were ready for a trial run. It has been quite an operation! The reactor, you will recall, was set in ooze at two thousand feet. But your suggestion of trying to use a work-sub was good, and once they got the plant cleared with remote-controlled hydraulic hoses it wasn't too difficult to engineer a tunnel with that equipment. In three days, Ellison and his people had the plasma flow-swell—at the lowest level, pro tem—and, of course, the underground lines were ready. We expect to have the plasma on 'regular' and more juice than we need for everything, very soon.

"We took a short, spendthrift cruise over Manhattan before

returning here. Our approach was spotted and signs of life were largely concealed before we were very near. But there are dozens of boats, maybe scores, using gas motors, I'd bet. At night, as many as a thousand lights are said to be visible. There have been more fires. Two or three more of the older skyscrapers, none of more than eighty stories, have fallen. I suppose, winter storms. The water level is down some three centimeters if the Orange Mountain recording gauges in Jersey are correct. And I have reports from the automatic station in Antarctica. New snow and lots of it, which is great news.

"Things are normal here, to strain that adjective.

"But bizarre events are diminishing. The latest of that sort, since it verifies one of your predictions, will fascinate you. The victims of it—and their end—are of interest, especially as it suggests a situation that may be commoner in all uncontrolled areas than even you had hitherto thought.

"Shortly after my return from the Hudson Fusion Plant the chemo-monitors here showed a sudden rise of noxious fumes. After a quarter hour of high readings on a twenty-one-knot westerly, we felt we should check. Cahill and Blaine went out with the smaller electro-copter, trailing standard sensors. What they found was a private golf course that does not appear on the last geodetic maps of USA. Even more odd was the fact that, as our people came in, they realized the course was in good condition: narrow fairways, not badly weed-grown, and one or two shady greens still nearly in shape for putting.

"Camouflage nets still hung over some stretches and it had evidently been constructed—at what a cost!—to look from the air like patches of pasture and of woods, the netting serving to disguise its actual nature. Also, it had been built, like so many late twentieth-century developments, over massive areas of solid-waste fill, layered with bulldozed earth, as usual. We guessed that it was about twenty years old, that is, from the last fill and cover to the present. Around it were several low residences, tree-hidden in most instances and, where in the open, partly disguised to look like abandoned farmhouses and barns.

"We believe the fill came from the new city, North Iroquois, which you will remember went up on an abandoned military reservation, Fort Drum, I believe, in the late 1980s. Anyway, the road from the hidden residences around the very carefully concealed course led off toward that general area.

"Our crew didn't land—the area was still toxic as hell. But they got a shift of wind that permitted some low-level reconnaissance. So they can make a guess about what happened and this is why, really, I send the story. Perhaps as many as a dozen families or groups, since there were six large houses and all of them may not have been spotted, had been living there until, probably, summer before last. With servants, plainly, owing to the kept-up course and several other, familiar indices.

"Forced labor, of course, possibly brainwashed but possibly willing, to some degree, simply for the chance of survival at whatever cost in slaving. The heavy equipment the crew saw was electrically driven, or the hide-out would have been spotted in the 2010s when the federal air checks functioned best, and last, too.

"At any rate, the usual had happened, summer before last, believe it or not. A golf cart had holed through. It went down about thirty feet, and by using the on-board spot the crew could see the cart on its side and not quite drowned in the usual soup, which was still bubbling. Three more recent cave-ins were found and there may be others. One is about a hundred feet in diameter and boiling hard—the latest one, probably, and so the one which presented us with the high reading.

25

"The crew took the usual measures, first collecting samples, then bombing in the craters till they were adequately sealed. We have an analysis of the gases and it's pretty much like many others: CO, CO_2, sulphur compounds, methane and nitrogen oxides and various organic compounds of heavy metals.

"Plainly, when the golf cart holed through to the subterranean mess that had been combining and stewing beneath the fairways for years, it started a gas and steam geyser that wiped out the local crowd, probably before they even had time to get clear. A lot of lower trees, shrubs, are dead, many of the taller trees show blighting and some of them are gone. What is left of a few bodies—all ages—can be seen here and there. Bones, and all scattered. Coyotes or timber wolves from Canada.

"All that, as it may interest one of the subcommittees in Paris. So there may well be, even in our area, other such hideaways established covertly by people with plenty of money, well-hidden spots where families survive, still in hiding, of the sort we had imagined extinct. No signs of life, of course. The crew flew around with a bull horn for an hour, calling, asking for signals. But since this group was alive, and even playing golf, two summers ago, it seems that we would be wise to keep an eye out, at this late date. With more power available we can get more 'batteries' charged, of course, and scout with greater care—world-wide, in the end—but we should consider more power allocation for the aircraft available, to make sure this sort of criminal isolation isn't commoner than the surveys have suggested, not to say as dangerous, possibly, as the Outsiders were and the Bandits are."

Will paused there, pressed a button, dialed an instrument with about fifty holes for the stylus he used, and waited, eyes on his desk. In seconds and almost without sound, a book

26

slid on a transparent, near-invisible chute to the spot where his eyes held. Its dust jacket was perceptibly faded but its title and the design around it still could be discerned clearly. The volume itself, cloth bound in red, seemed almost in mint condition. Around the title: 1975: *Date of No Return* and the author's name, G. W. Packett, was a line drawing of a supersonic airplane from which flames seemed to rip forth with a roar the somewhat dimmed colors could not yet quite subdue.

Will picked up the book, replaced it, shrugged and returned to his letter. This he did rapidly and with a faint look of amusement, for he knew Miles would care more for the "domestic" Faraway news than for anything he had said thitherto.

". . . we had two girls born since you left to Mrs. Cleveland and Martha Justanson. Great shape, all.

". . . one death, poor old Hinckle, just when the medicos were pretty sure his mind was coming back. It probably did—and so was the cause of death. Hinckle, you doubtless recall, was on the last vehicle to get clear of Marie Byrd Land. . . .

". . . and we have another geneticist. Oliver Hazard Perry Graves, no less! He made it on foot over the winter to here from North Dakota. Pretty exhausted and tattered, some nasty abrasions and cuts, his starting pack was stripped by Bandits along the way. Beard two feet long and the second thing he wanted was a barber. The first was a triple bourbon, if available. He's going to be a tremendous asset for us all.

"Now all we need are some more, or *some* molecular biologists, electron battery engineers, surgeons, theoretical math teachers, carpenters, masons, metalworkers, steamfitters, a plumber or two, etc., etc. ad infinitum. For one of any such I'd trade three of our clergymen, the lot, so far, praise God. . . ."

27

He signed off affectionately, shut down the recording device and immediately switched it on for postscripts:

"Your suggestion about the mass of stuff that's coming with this—the idea of choosing material as if for precocious teenagers in the nineteenth century—was exceedingly helpful. Thinking how stupefied a young person living in the late 1800s would be to hear what lay ahead for his heirs was a superb trick, or so I felt. However, it often led me to use the old names more than I might have—along with many other terms now gone, renamed or altered, and I haven't bothered to change those. Any of the secretaries can update them where needed.

"Also, the next (really, first) 'chapter,' the excerpts from Packett, may or may not be relevant, a thing I cannot decide. He was a rather stuffy writer, and awkward, but he's sounder even than some of the 'Hure' scholars and less fatuous than other 'popularizers.'

"I was about to sign off when Ethel buzzed to say I'll have to transmit this stuff in two parts, owing to official need for the equipment. So, in the time I now have for a first shot, I'm going to send you, Miles, *the final part of the book,* along with whatever else can be sent of the beginning, enough, I calculate roughly, to take you into the 1980s, somewhere. This, because I wrote the final section, Part VII, myself. And I cannot wait to know your (anybody's) judgment. If you or they don't like it, I must redo the book from 2015 to now.

"When I get a time opening, I'll send what I here omit, the 'middle' part of the book, from wherever cut off (so as to include my finale) on to the year 2018. After 1980, of course, the material gets grimmer, involves human masses and relates to some horrors science didn't understand. But from what there is here and the final piece by me, I hope people can get an idea of whether or not I was the man for this 'impossible' job. Four thousand people here, and I, send love. Devotedly, if nervously (like any prima donna), yours, Will."

TRANSPOSE LETTER, EARLY PORTION OF "END OF DREAM" AND LAST SECTION. TO GO AS SCHEDULED. OPERATOR TO REPORT DELAY, IF ANY.

WILLARD P. GULLIVER, Acting Director
District Two, Central City 6/17/23

THE END
OF THE DREAM

I
Selections from
1975: Date of No Return

NOTE: Part I consists of excerpts from a book published in 1995 by Doubleday and Company, in New York. Its author, George Washington Packett, a scholar with degrees in history and creative journalism, contributed many technical papers to appropriate periodicals but also wrote seventeen "mass audience" books about the "current" state of civilization in the years between 1964 and 1997.

The following excerpts from his most famous (or, to many scholars, most infamous) work are not always in the order in which they appeared. Some are reprinted here only in part. But Packett does convey, in the editor's opinion, something of the attitudes of individuals, groups, governments and the public, in the years he discusses.

What is important to bear in mind, here, is not so much that Packett's attitudes and evaluations are his own, but that his facts and his factual descriptions, his quotes and attributions are absolutely correct.

WILLARD P. GULLIVER, Editor

In 1970 the American public was exposed for the first time to an all-media warning of its environmental condition. Television, not then three-dimensional, the press, the mass magazines and the radio almost overnight began to discuss "pollution," "conservation" and a "clean environment as a right." These subjects had been more or less in the news and in hazy national consciousness for some years. But, almost with the first day of this special year, public concern was focused on the matter.

Within weeks an anti-pollution crusade became the major emotion of students and diverted their often mutinous attention and activities from such recently leading "causes" as the war in Vietnam, the draft, poverty, the low status of "blacks," the proper term at that time for Negroes, education and its administration, along with such broader matters as the "system" and "establishment" which many activist young people in numerous unruly organizations were then proposing to destroy.

The new and exploding concern soon became a political matter. It was said that all the members of Congress had become "instant ecologists," a remarkable—rather, a miraculous—achievement. The President, Richard Milhous Nixon, was among the early converts. Previously, he had not been interested in conservation or pollution save as throwaways in campaign speeches—promises of improvements in the American environment which, however, were non-specific and tendered offhandedly.

In early 1970, however, the President changed his mind and suggested five billions be budgeted in 1971 for federal aid in reducing air and water pollution, and similar sums in the years to follow. However, with that abrupt shift of view, he did not show any sign of understanding the actual problem. Congress was as uncomprehending, with a few exceptions.

Not more than one American in ten thousand had, in 1970, or later, for that matter, any true sense of the nature or the certainty of the coming calamities. Not that many, in early 1970, perceived that a tremendous and absolute shift in all dominating cultural concepts would be necessary for the mere hopeful beginning of environmental restoration and salvage. Those who remember the era now find it impossible, or nearly so, to understand why there was so little effective public response to a situation which already seemed crystal clear.

In years just past there had been many, many calamities that were pregnant of ill omen. One London "smog" had caused, in four days, deaths at the rate of more than a thousand a day. Los Angeles had been conducting a long battle against its still often contaminated air after the citizens had reluctantly, and following only unarguable tests, admitted their cars were the agents of their misery. Oil spills at sea and in harbors had occurred and the grounding and breakup of one oil tanker, the *Torrey Canyon*, had greased long stretches of shore in the English Channel. There had been a very serious spill or, more accurately, leak from at-sea petroleum wells off California with subsequent turgid incursions at and near Santa Barbara.

Every major river in America was grossly polluted, an "open sewer" even in current terms, and the overwhelming contaminants consisted not only of countless industrial wastes and effluents but urban sewage which often reached rivers and lakes untreated, as the same lines that carried human sewage served for "storm" or street waste. The latter frequently overtaxed such treatment plants as existed, and so emptied human wastes, fecal and all others, into waters, without prior chlorination or other processing.

That Lake Erie was "dead" had been known for years. That its sister lakes, Michigan, Ontario and Huron, were "dying" was also known. Superior was endangered though in a relatively viable state in 1970.

. . .

Americans were producing a daily volume of solid wastes at the per capita rate of between four and five pounds. "Garbage

35

strikes" had already revealed to the citizens of several cities what the scope of that single disposal problem was, when collection stopped for days or a few weeks.

The rat population of the nation was estimated as greater than the human, some two hundred million rats, give or take a million or two.

Many other dangerous contaminants were known to abound in the dust and fumes of cities and in manufacturing areas. The asbestos used in numerous major products was thought to be at least partially responsible for the rise of respiratory ills, especially those resembling the chronic and finally fatal lung ailments of asbestos miners. Lead levels were rising in human beings constantly exposed to automotive traffic and the tetra-ethyl lead then used to raise the "octane rating" of gasoline, or to reduce the knock characteristic of gasoline-using engines.

People by 1970 were fairly aware of many other and different toxins in local but often extensive regions. Nitrogen oxides, sulphuric acid, other acids, carbon monoxide and sundry gases abounded in urban air and manufacturing locales. In some cities and areas, moisture combined with sulphuric stack effluents became an acid strong enough to "dissolve" such fabrics as were made from certain plastics. Nylon stockings, a synthetic material closely resembling silk and more durable, at times literally "melted" on the legs of women on the street.

. . .

Perhaps the most startling, and certainly the longest-publicized, contaminants were the chlorinated hydrocarbons and, particularly, DDT. A scientist-author, Rachel Carson, had dramatized the perils these involved in a book called *Silent Spring* almost ten years earlier. The book had been ridiculed by innumerable colleagues, by pesticide chemists, manufacturers and persons with interests in agriculture.

By 1970 it was known that DDT and its relatives had entered the seven seas, via rivers and rain, and now were found in measurable amounts in the fatty tissues of birds, mammals and other orders of life, the world over. In addition, a plastic widely used as material for liquid containers of household and other substances produced, when burned, a toxin resembling DDT and having the same effect. Since such "disposable" material was usually burned, in backyard trash piles or municipal dumps and incinerators, it added a bizarre quantum to the DDT peril. Several species of birds on the Atlantic coastal areas north of Florida had become extinct, or doomed, as these DDT and allied chemicals affected their enzyme systems and prevented the formation of shells for their eggs.

DDT was concentrated in human fatty tissues, too. By 1970, mother's milk contained from twelve to thirty times the amount of these toxins that the federal bureaus allowed as the limit for interstate commerce in cows' milk. Observers had grimly predicted that in twenty more years, at the current rate, Americans who were grossly overweight would have, in their fat, such an amount of the material that reducing would be impossible. In other words, any effort to shed excess fat would pour the poisons, DDT mainly, into their systems and in fatal amounts.

Even so, it was argued that the massive production and world-wide distribution of DDT must not stop. This pesticide was the cheapest for mosquito control and the control of other bearers of disease. Without DDT tens or hundreds of millions would be stricken with malaria and other ills, including dengue or breakbone fever, yellow fever, certain forms of encephalitis, and so on. This mercy-need took no cognizance of the fact that where DDT had been used for some years the insects it was expected to eliminate had become or were becoming resistant to the poison.

37

President Nixon had in 1969, by executive order, decreed that the DDT group of pesticides was to be phased out and, meantime, used only where "necessary." The public thus assumed that proper measures were being taken in the matter. Actually, the use of DDT and its deadly associates was nowhere prevented for any individual or company.

As one looks back at countless examples of that common act of seeming validity but no actual force, it is impossible to judge whether or not the administrators and executives who employed it were aware of its perfidy. Checking to find the truth in the environment was possible only for specialists, or teams of specialists. Checking for nationwide response, if any, was even less feasible, owing to the scope and cost of such a project as well as the need of know-how.

. . .

The land of the United States was being skinned and gutted by thousands of business and engineering endeavors. Roads, railroads, power lines and rights of way along these had been and were being kept free of brush by the use of various chemicals, some of them enormously toxic, as cyanide, and others, complex hormones that had a deadly effect on the green plant spectrum. These, of course, drained in rainstorms from their place of application into the surrounding ecosystems. The extent of that menace can be imagined when it is known that, by 1970, these mere sides of roads and rail beds, power-line paths and the like had a total area greater than that of the New England States.

A newscaster, Walter Cronkite, for Columbia Broadcasting System, a major TV network, disclosed in February of that year that the total amount of annual pollutants in the United States was 25,000,000,000 *tons*.

Even so, up until 1970, there had been less total concern and protest of the general public over that immense amount

38

of contamination than over the allegedly controversial fluoridation of water supplies to reduce dental caries in children.

Again, there was far more anxiety, nationally, over the carcinogenic and other ill effects of cigarette smoking than over the sum of water and air pollution.

It will seem difficult to understand the public's lack of balanced reason about the massive threats it faced. A nation, stinking from border to border, its lakes dying, its rivers the national slop jar, garbage pail and factory dump, would be convulsed by the finding that sugar substitutes, cyclamates and saccharine, were "carcinogenic" and, then, federally banned. Few citizens would trouble to note, even if they had the competence, that the attribution of cancer-causing properties in these diet sweeteners and sugar alternatives for diabetics was based on mouse research, or that the amount required to cause some mouse malignancies was, by weight and cost and for the equivalent of a normal adult, about three hundred dollars' worth a day.

• • •

Strip mining was denuding and destroying enormous areas. Open-pit mines and quarries gutted ever more and more extensive regions. New roads, airports and car parking spaces removed a million acres or more from use as plant cover, annually.

Estuaries and river mouths along seacoasts, including immense stretches of marsh and swamp, were being filled at a tremendous rate though these were known to be the mating and/or breeding and rearing grounds for scores of valuable crustacea, bivalves and fishes.

• • •

Of course, in 1970, the public had not grasped the simple fact that its sudden interest in environmental cleanup was on a collision course with the goods and services or Gross

39

National Product which it bought or used at an ever rising rate, one it had not the slightest intention of curtailing.

There was talk about "sacrifices" necessary and "passing the costs of cleanup on to the consumer." There was, however, far more talk about inflation and recession, the seemingly paradoxical condition in the nation at that time. Economists were sure the Gross National Product would soon hit the trillion-dollar figure it had approached in earlier years. It did so. The census would be taken, as usual, in 1970. At the year's start it was estimated that the population would number two hundred and four millions. Welfare programs on every level, medical care for the aged, schemes for a guaranteed income and other such paternalistic, sometimes decent, often expensive and wasteful endeavors and plans were constantly launched, or in long-term being, or contemplated, all with one aim:

America and its affluent society felt it must and would assure every citizen of an education to any level desired, or its semblance, a sufficient income to purchase those goods and services that represented "un-poverty," every modern medical and health advantage, in effect a "packaged" life, birth to death, and more than seventy years between the two, then a national average.

None of the major corporations providing the basic goods and services of the nation had any thought of reducing its production in the decade ahead, or ever. Instead, various underestimates of demand had caused countless minor and many serious dilemmas and mass discomforts owing to corporate blunder and underpreparation. Strikes, the delays inevitable in manufacturing processes, the managerial errors noted, and other factors resulted in telephonic foul-ups and inadequate electrical supply for growing numbers of communities and cities.

There was not enough electric power to keep New York

City air-conditioned in the summer of 1970 and not enough to keep its refrigerators going. Brownouts were common in dozens of areas owing to power shortage. The New York telephone system was similarly inadequate and for the same cause, underestimate of demand. Postal service, nationwide, was close to collapse owing to obsolete equipment and procedure.

So a public that was at least nervously informed of certain of its more visible pollutants was also one that raged for and expected quick and great increments of needed services and goods. The corporations supplying them were more than eager to expand.

Electric power was produced in three ways, by burning fossil fuel, by hydroelectric generation and from nuclear reactors. Coal, gas and oil, the main energy sources, were, of course, contaminating. Nuclear reactors were proliferating, although not as rapidly as had first been expected.

All such plants produced fantastic amounts of heated effluent, the coolant for the "boiling water" systems that powered turbines and generators. Two to three million gallons a minute were raised by ten or more degrees when returned to their sources, lakes or rivers or bays on the seaboard. Other problems with these power sources were subtler, not yet understood, or, if understood by experts, still unheard of by the average citizen.

He—and she—would come to know them the hard way. Whether a general effort at educating the public in reactor liabilities would have led to political pressure and foresighted alterations of reactor planning is undeterminable. That sort of "pressure" would have been necessary. It never was encouraged by the corporations, of course, or by the Atomic Energy Commission, and not by any other federal or state body. In 1970 it was predicted that within a decade, or at most two to three, uses of water would exceed the total available rainfall on the nation. The demand for reactor-cooling water, alone, would soon amount to more than half the flow of all rivers within the bounds of the country. The resulting heat rise would, of course, do vast ecological damage, but of sorts not really known or much discussed. That such torrents of effluent were also slightly radioactive, and that the hot isotopes would in some part be precipitated on riparian, esturial and lake bottoms, was not even noted publicly. The high-level radiation of stack gases—again, a matter not yet of general concern—was an unknown.

What was known, though not with any public anxiety in scale, was that the need to change fuel rods in reactors, and to replace radioactive parts of the assemblies, involved transport of "hot" material to sites where fuel-recovery plants retrieved the unexpended uranium or plutonium for reuse, and that the hot junk was also shipped to remote places where it was retained in boiling-hot "tank farms" till its isotopes should lose energy enough for less costly storage. Fuel rods and other metal machine parts were moving across US by truck and rail in special containers with individual cooling systems and lead casing to keep their thermal and radioactive violence under wraps till their destinations were reached.

Few people knew that the overradiated junk required *centuries* of boiling, of decanting and other careful control before being safe to package and move elsewhere, underground in some presumably safe geological region. That every rail line was measurably "hot" from such haulage was not widely appreciated as significant. That this extensive and costly series of processes and of transport would rise exponentially as reactors proliferated, again, was knowable but not even dimly grasped by the vast majority. Problems of that complexity and sophistication were far beyond the public grasp —and of the grasp of Congress or state or county governing bodies. It was assumed that people who did have the knowledge were managing the situation well.

Nothing could have been more mistaken.

Nobody, or almost nobody, had enough knowledge to contemplate usefully the present situation, not to mention the future. In 1970 there had as yet been no transportation or other *known* disaster of a sort even to start the public worrying about the growing risk from this single source. Reactors were believed to be the best possible energy suppliers of the future, the least polluting and, in fact, the only visible new sources in a nation using up finite fossil fuels.

. . .

Americans were fed a stream of corporate "information" about various resource exploitations that sounded satisfactory and in many cases were lies.

Lumber companies took advertising space in the mass media, for one example, to point out proudly that they were "planting" more trees than they cut. Statistically, that was correct. However, it did not note that where they had cut, and where they then replanted, trees a century or many centuries old were destroyed. The new "crop" would be "harvested" sooner, at a smaller size, and after a half century's wait! Also, the harvesting of a natural forest resulted in the ruin of the ecology of the region to a massive and permanent degree. Before lumbered areas could be replanted, the very soil was often eroded away and what remained was bare rock or hardpan. America's wood supply was, in fact, vanishing.

. . .

A different procedure, largely the work of the Army Engineer Corps, was scraping and raping the land in the name of "flood control," the provision of "navigable waters" and the erection of immense dams for several other alleged purposes, including the provision of hydroelectric power sources and the making of lakes for "recreation," irrigation and pollution management. The last meant water-impounding to enable sewage and industrial pollutants to be pushed along, downriver, faster, at peak-load periods.

"Navigation" was often meant for barge haulage, and in 1970 some ditches for that kind of use were being dug to Tulsa, Oklahoma, and to Dallas, Texas, making them "seaports" and using waterways that, in dry months, were themselves near dry. The stated use for such multi-billion-dollar follies was gravel transport, since little other cargo could be found for those two vast canals. Gravel and "pleasure boats" would travel to the sea from cities hundreds of miles inland. The minute slope of those and many other such Army Engineering Corps jobs—and the locks essential in most of them—guaranteed they would become near-stagnant filth traps for their entire lengths.

Rivers were straightened, and streams and creeks were turned into chutes and their banks steel-faced, stone-lined or cement-paved. The flood-control philosophy did not take into account years of abnormal rainfall because it could not. But the act resulted in extensive industrial and real estate development on sites safe from flooding in normal or subnormal years. In the others, unpredictable and yet sure, these new areas were drowned, resulting in devastation and economic loss to individuals, corporations and whole communities. Turning rivers and tributaries into paved chutes brought such waters downstream at accelerated rates.

Water-hungry industry was attracted to the lakes made by the Corps and other such agencies. Humanity followed: the jobs were there. Hydroelectric plants rose below the giant dams. But this nationwide situation had one disadvantage. The impounded waters were rapidly silted up as they blocked previous flow and caused formed runoff to be precipitated behind the dams. A lake built and presumed to be viable for

44

a century and a half might reveal that, in fact, it would be mud to the surface in twenty or fifty years. The response was, often, to build many more dams upstream as, mainly, silt traps.

Silt, in general, is topsoil. The escalation of industry to provide an exploding population with goods and services, the agricultural pattern of "mining" soil, the tree-denuding practices, the paving and covering of the land for more homes, roads, factories and so on reduced the arable land rapidly, and although, in 1970, a surplus of such potential food source existed, the surplus would not last long, clearly. What was deposited behind the thousands of dams was food of the future. No means to reclaim it existed.

. . .

As 1970 matured the suddenly alerted public realized it had, indeed, a problem. Before that year was out new and unexpected risks were found for the first time . . . by the average voter.

Years earlier scientists in Japan and Sweden had grimly realized that certain lakes and salt-water bays were heavily contaminated with mercury. Until then it had been casually assumed that in its metallic and other industrial states mercury, being heavy, would sink to the bottom of any body of water, soon be ooze-covered and then remain there, unmoving and harmless forever. Deaths in Japan and other odd phenomena led to the finding that anaerobic bacteria in all such waters could and did convert mercury into organic forms—forms, in short, which could and would enter the life chains, the ecosystems.

For several years federal authorities in USA ignored the ever more frightening data being received from abroad. But, as is so common in such affairs, almost overnight the government experts, along with various private investigators,

45

discovered that literally hundreds of streams, ponds, lakes, bays and the like were inhabited by a mercury-loaded biota. And soon it was learned that some of the most prized food fishes in the seas were mercury-bearers.

There had always been a trace of mercury in sea water and in many fresh waters. How much of the metallic taint present in fishes and other sea and fresh-water foods was owing to a buildup that had gone on for eons, and how much was due to the mercury added by man, was not easily determined. And how much organic mercury man himself could tolerate without harm was unknown. The point where harm might begin, and even the nature of what such possible, chronic symptoms might be, was unknown.

The civilized world stumbled into 1971 determined to ascertain these plainly vital bits of information.

. . .

But though few laymen were concerned even in early 1971, some additional numbers of scientists began to wonder, at least, about other toxic metals that were being added to man's water sources in quantities exponentially greater than those naturally found there. There was selenium; cadmium, known to be harmful in small doses to the liver and other organs; beryllium; plutonium.

Quite a list, since most of the elements were being used in some or even many industrial processes, and a great many elements are hazardous or even lethal to genus *Homo*, in very minute quantities.

. . .

As the more literate members of the cultures of the West began faintly to realize the theoretically possible peril in the simple elements, a far, far more appalling truth was called to the attention of all who could and would heed.

By 1970 it was estimated that industry and allied human

46

activities were dumping into the environment at least *half a million chemical compounds,* many of incredible complexity, of which tens of thousands were known or could be surely predicted to have toxic effects on some species.

None of these five hundred thousand diverse chemicals was of a sort that existed in nature, so that all life forms encountering any *one* of them would have no genetic or inherent capability for managing to co-exist with the substance. These additives ended up in the seas, brought by rivers, runoff or rain. And while some of them were small in quantity, thousands upon thousands of them went to sea by the thousands or *tens* of thousands of *tons.*

Finally, not only were their effects unknown, though sure to be deleterious in some mammoth, undreamable degree, but the seas themselves were a chemical factory. That is to say, these alien materials were certain to be intermingled and to form "x" thousands of different, *additional* compounds unknown to science. What these were, of course, nobody had attempted to imagine. Funds for research into such rarefied areas simply didn't exist, and were not appropriated in the years beyond 1970.

What finally was done was a mere stopgap: the planet's seas, by 1980 carrying more than a million new chemicals, were monitored. When some harmful *effect* became detectable (or happened to be detected) a study of its cause was undertaken. Myriads of these statistically predictable eco-calamities were not monitored soon enough, of course.

• • •

Since those and many other similar circumstances were known at least to relevant experts, and since those noted here had been repeatedly described by all the mass media, the author feels justified in the choice of 1975 for the title of this volume.

The year was, surely, that last at which mankind, had he owned the will, reason, sanity, logic and the mere "instinct for self-preservation" he boasted of, might have faced about and begun to undertake to live realistically in the real world as he was then able to know it.

A later date was too late.

However, in 1971, the first (and inevitable) reactions to the "environmental scare" appeared.

For some fifteen months there had been a surge of concern. But this was followed by growing resentment, ennui and boredom. From the first, ecologically informed citizens had feared that reaction. Editorial writers began in '71 to complain that there was an overemphasis on "environment." TV networks found that their presentation of the ever growing data about the crisis was causing millions to switch stations —and that, of course, was not to be permitted. It "lost viewers": cost money. Other factors began to militate against the brief time of sanity. Industry capitalized on the changed mood by increasing its disastrously untruthful pretense that it was taking the costly and correct measures to reduce its contribution to the filthy earth. And the public, no doubt, began to realize in its deep unconsciousness that any genuine effort to halt destruction of the earth's life-support systems would put an end to "progress," "affluence"—almost everything men thought of as civilized.

Again, by 1971, so much data about the general peril had been proffered to average persons that they surely knew the subject was too vast, various and specialized for broadly useful thought by them. It thus became an area of responsibility for somebody else, the scientists, in sum. And since the "scientists" had provided the wonders, comforts and miracles of their age, it seemed reasonable to most people that they would eventually take care of the unhappy spin-off.

The trouble was ignorance.

In 1970, not two Americans in a thousand could have defined "science." It is, of course, knowledge, pure knowledge, with its teaching and the means to add to its sum. But what was regarded as "science" by nearly everybody in that period, many scientists included, was the material *result* of *applications* of knowledge. And all these were made for special ends that were achieved with little or no reference to the vast remainder of science (of knowledge) wherein lay, or could lie, information as to what dire results might accompany the one end gained.

The men who used scientific theories to make automobiles did not consult biology to learn what horrors that achievement might carry. In 1970 it can be safely said that only a few thousand, or perhaps not even one thousand, men and women in the entire USA had a sufficiently wide understanding of science, together with the essential breadth of imagination and also the inclination or motive, to think about their world and its near future with any relevance whatever.

So it is that by hindsight alone this author can set forth where the massive blunders occurred, what they were and when they became irreversible, leading to the shocking condition of us all in the year of this writing (1994) and the dismal prospect some foresee, still.

If the first sufficiently telling alarm sounded in 1970, it was being ignored widely in 1971—and a turning point was thereby missed, the last, as I shall here attempt to prove, available.

For in 1971 people switched off the grimly growing news about their endangered environs.

They were sick and tired of it.

Being tired of it was infantile.

What came later, when an effort was made to compel

49

industry and cities to stop polluting, was worse. The effort meant temporary shortages, and that the people, led by labor, would not endure.

An infantile majority became lunatic.

II
"Vengeance is Mine,"
sayeth Nature

A note on the following section by its editor, Willard Page Gulliver, and some examples of early disasters.

1. *Editorial and Personal Note*

In Part II of this collection the reader will encounter numbers of real persons. Among them will be Miles Standish Smythe, and it will be gathered that this man was among the great figures of all time, a twentieth-century Leonardo in mental stature and a prophet with no front runner—the convention for a historic or legendary herald.

Miles Smythe was born on January 1, 1953, the son of Jason Smythe, an exceedingly wealthy man and a renowned or—to many—notorious physician, psychiatrist and author. Miles's mother was Amy Gorham, a beauty of international fame, a talented musician and the sole heiress to a second, equally huge fortune. She died when her daughter Nora was nine and Miles seven. In 1963 Jason remarried. Patricia Hunt Collier Evans was a leader of the feminist (and, later, the "women's liberation") movement. Patricia Smythe was also a celebrated beauty and almost as well known (from nearly as diverse viewpoints) as Jason Smythe.

The doctor was a huge, powerful, extroverted, unique and difficult man. His concepts of the nature of human sexuality and of the effects of man's long-standing taboos were a cause of controversy that raged from the mid-fifties through his lifetime. His second wife, Patricia, supported his ideas. The theories, however, were a cause of great humiliation to the Smythe children, and perhaps explain in part their often unconventional ways of behaving.

Miles attended the Fifth Avenue Special School in Manhattan from grade one till he went on to Princeton University. He and his family lived in a two-story penthouse on Park Avenue. Dr. Smythe had his offices in a facing but otherwise identical penthouse. Fifth Special was experimental, advanced, highly unconventional, and yet its basic curriculum was designed so its students were among the highest-scoring college applicants every year.

Because Fifth Special students came largely from families with money, status and power the trustees (Dr. Jason Smythe was one) still followed a program of "student balance" launched by the founders. A small number of boys and girls from poor families, Negroes, Puerto Ricans, Orientals and others, were admitted on scholarships. The scholarships were generous, and any child admitted that way to Fifth Special was enabled to maintain face with his classmates owing to an ample allowance. The father of such a student might be a plumber, a Bowery bum or unknown and the mother a whore —but (theoretically) any youngster admitted to Fifth Special (in grades three to five, only) would presumably enjoy equality with the others from then on.

These "free students" made up less than a tenth of the enrollment of about three hundred for the twelve "grade equivalents."

52

I was such a fortunate one.

My Scottish father, George Gulliver, was a dye and pattern maker and an alcoholic. He was seldom seen in our railroad flat on East Eighty-third Street in Manhattan. Mother was half Irish, and never admitted the other half was Indian. She claimed it to be Spanish and we five youngsters were reared in that belief. As a grown man and long after her death I learned the truth: her father had been a member of the Mohawk tribe, one of that strange clan of nerveless men who did most of Manhattan's high steel construction in that period.

My first years at Fifth Special among largely wealthy and highly privileged children were almost too hard to bear and only my mother's pride, together with the open resentment of my young chums (which I met with a rage faked to hide my fears and inferiorities), kept me struggling to remain in Fifth Special.

Here it was, of course, that I met Miles, and was unwittingly instrumental in his choice of a career.

At that time we had a class in something called introductory sociology taught by a martinet (one of the very few members of that faculty who was not a superb teacher) named Elroy Corddy. On a day in December of 1965, Mr. Corddy used the recent New York blackout as a sociological theme. Elroy Corddy was a member of the National Guard and a volunteer air raid warden. His harangue—and he was given to harangues—on the topic soon began to irritate me.

The incident had taken place that November, in the evening, and it was merely the first of what became a succession of blackouts and brownouts common there, as elsewhere. But Corddy's analysis of mass behavior under those conditions grated on me. It was, however, the most common attitude, one taken by editors and by nearly everybody else.

Light and power were cut off that time on a clear, cool

night with a full moon. In the ensuing hours of dark, public behavior was surprising. Crime dropped to a low level—not the seemingly more likely opposite. People spent the night trapped in high buildings and in stalled elevators, where panic could have occurred. But there was little or none. Ordinary citizens went into the streets and became self-appointed traffic directors. Cars and trucks, using headlights, continued to move everywhere under such amateur policing. Police cars and fire apparatus got through when and as needed.

In sum, the New Yorkers behaved magnificently.

Corddy's next deduction from that was what irked me most.

"It simply shows," he said to the class, sniffing, "that even under nuclear attack the people of this city would remain calm and levelheaded, helping one another in parallel degrees, thus frustrating major enemy expectations in his use of such weapons." (That may not be verbatim but it is the way the little, red-bristly man spoke.)

I snorted after containing myself as long as I could.

"You disagree, Gulliver?"

To my own astonishment, I not only answered that I did, but I stood up and said, in a manner I'd never remotely thought I could or would use here, "It's crap."

"Perhaps you'd add to that—ah—rather plebeian and—ah—inadequate comment?"

By then I began to regain my senses. So I tried to get off this unprecedented hook. "I sort of think people might react differently in a nuclear war. The first bomb would maybe level Manhattan. Start the place in fire storm."

"We hadn't realized your military competence, Gulliver. Proceed."

I sat down, however, palms sweaty. Corddy addressed the class. "Gulliver's remark is based on information that is not supplied in any Civil Defense manual," he said, smirking. "Perhaps he has sources other than federal? Sources I lack?"

There were some sixth-grade, teacher-polishing sniggers.

I had sources and I was angry but I knew Corddy wouldn't accept my information about hydrogen bomb effects so I switched, saying only, "Suppose there hadn't been any moon, in the blackout?"

"So it was Luna, not human character, was it, that saved the sum of things?" He erased me with a small-eye stare and began explaining how wonderful people would be under all sorts of bad conditions, blackout and so on. I shriveled.

That was when, in mid-flight, Miles's voice rolled over the twenty kids. It was a deep bass in childhood and merely grew a little deeper and more resonant when Miles reached adolescence. His peroration was one word: "Shit!"

It was not a permissible classroom expletive, where manners were required.

Corddy sucked in a breath. Miles then stood—he was enormous for twelve and would become a giant in the following few years. His blond hair fell over his brow, which, even then, was lined. His blue-gray eyes had a burn that meant "disaster en route." His hands were fists. He started bellowing in a sort of restricted fashion, and Corddy couldn't shriek loud enough to stop or even to drown it.

What Miles said was elaborate, lucid, terrible and true. The adults who were then going around boasting of how well they and everybody acted that November night were "horses' asses." To assume that one incident on the moonlit night would characterize behavior on a dirty night was insane. To imagine it would reveal anything about conduct involving a nuclear weapon was mindless. Close to nuts. He, Miles, for one, was not going to spend one more minute in this class listening every day to an alleged teacher doing what he

55

considered an act of pedagogy when it was, in fact, mental buggery.

It went on till teachers and pupils rushed in from other rooms to see what caused the clamor, thunder over squeals.

Later that day Miles asked me to his home.

I had never even seen anything like it even in movies or on TV.

Or anybody like Nora.

Or like all the other Smythes.

And that same afternoon, as Manhattan hazed up for night and got its trillion lights on, I wandered around Miles's room looking at his trophies and stuff while Miles sat watching me but, plainly, thinking hard about something, so hard I was afraid he had regretted having me over.

Then, suddenly, he smacked his thigh hard enough to break mine, nearly, and began to talk.

"God damn! You know what? It's not *only* blackouts! It's just about everything! People think of nature and the planet and science and themselves just the kook way old Corddy thinks! Somebody has got to start straightening them out. I mean, we're crazy. Our water's filthy, air's hard to suck in, we're covering terra firma with poison and paving over or scraping off the soil. Our whole species—is flying on a bum gauge. Some guy should start a reorientation course and, damn it, Will, *I'm that guy!* And *you're* going to help me."

Just like that.

I was asked for supper—dinner—and there was a butler.

Looking from this vast journey's time span to that, for me, nervous yet glorious day, I realize how subtly I was informed and how deeply changed into somebody else.

Jason Smythe, the psychiatrist, would become a father figure for me. Nora would be my wife. Miles a greater friend than most men ever know. The doctor's second wife, Pat, and her then absent daughter by a first husband, Zillah, would teach me many things, and some I didn't want to learn. I'd be a guest here often in the days ahead. I was on my way to summers and winter vacations at Faraway, where the guides would turn Miles and me into "first-class north-woodsmen" by a long and often painful schooling up where there still was real wilderness.

That night at dinner Miles was voluble about his decision to lead the world in a fight for survival. Oddly, I felt, the doctor apparently accepted that career decision as fact and with approval. What I deemed a whim the doctor saw as a culmination. He often had insights of that clarity and from as little evident cause.

So that is how and when I came to know Miles and the way my life was altered. He became a great man, some said, the greatest of his age, the "last of the Florentines," an admirer wrote, and it fits well enough. But Miles Standish Smythe was a human being and it would be an error to suggest he was not just a superior person, which he was, but perfect, which he was not.

Far from it, in certain obscure ways—and visibly, even spectacularly, flawed in a few others. He was deficient in ego in an odd way. He had a volcanic temper seldom out of control, but when Miles lost that temper he was dangerous, even deadly. His "sex morals"—his phrase, again—were unconventional, but that certainly was owing to his father's psychological theories and to the conflicts they caused in Miles—and Nora too. He was a prodigious worker, prodigious in whatever he did, but he sometimes worked to a point where his effort was wasted owing to sheer exhaustion. In such a state, he could be absurdly petty.

From the age of twelve on, he followed the purpose he announced at the time. His father had been right about that. His studies were chosen, in the main, to that end. His adult friends were often picked because they could augment the biological, ecological, scientific or technological memory bank his big skull housed. He grew up to be taller and bigger than his huge father and he was probably among the strongest men living. That giant size and that awesome power he took for granted as one accepts blue eyes or long arms.

Many people thought of him as fanatical or obsessive. But the line between obsession and devotion, or dedication, is not easy to draw and perhaps not susceptible of drawing. To me, neither term fitted, for a fanatic is emotionally unstable, and obsessiveness is related to a narrow concern. His tragic flaw, in the view of those who know and knew him best, was that habit of self-deprecation, a way of acting that seemed to mean he felt, somewhere, somehow, so inadequate or guilty that, despite the tremendous good he did, his "sins"—his word—could never be atoned for.

We all tried to help him be rid of that. And he did learn how his self-deprecation hurt his public "image," so he quit showing it to the world; he was objective enough to understand his image was germane to and had an effect on his life aim. But he did not exorcise his demon. With his family or intimate friends he and that compulsion often took charge. Self-belittlement sat ill on him even for that group, of course, and Miles's displays gave rise to many private analyses.

Miles's behavior, some said, was owing to an unconscious or else inadmissible superstition: that, in effect, he derogated himself so his achievements could go on without "punishment." That idea is absurd. So is the notion he played introvert to oppose his father's blazing extroversion.

And my own theory about my friend's strange habit of downgrading himself may be wrong. But there was evidence to sustain my kind of idea, in psychology, before the final times. That evidence showed human "personality" to be, in a major part, not acquired in life but genetic, innate, inherited.

Among Miles's forebears were some pretty withdrawn people, hermits, nearly, not anti-social but loners. One of them was the founder of the Smythe fortune in pre-Revolutionary times, Elias Smythe, who supposedly named the lake and river at Faraway, where, legend says, he was not only a trapper but found gold. No one else ever found gold in the region, though many tried. And the fact that old Elias Smythe had trapped in the general area in the 1700s perhaps influenced its purchase by the family, much later.

In our teens Miles and I used to go prospecting for gold at Faraway, if we could sneak away from our training schedules. We never found any, but we learned a lot about geology and geophysics. Miles didn't need gold, anyhow. I could have used a few buckets, as my education and other expenses came from "loans" the Smythe family advanced, which ultimately, to their chargrin, I paid back, with interest. For I began to make money at Princeton, and by the time I finished my graduate work I was quite well off. It's not as hard as those who make it try to make others believe. I was a pretty cute market speculator and I began to buy a few things that were cheap at the time and yet certain in my mind to become valuable. I gambled, of course. But the whole thing was not my main interest so I didn't sweat out my risks. Owing the Smythes so much, together with a passion to be financially independent, drove me, if you could call my operations driven.

But it was Miles whom I wished to sketch here. He is still, at our age of seventy, almost the colossus and powerhouse he was as a younger man. Like many super-size males, he is graceful—has to be, perhaps, as clumsiness would be disastrous. He's handsome as hell though he does have one incongruous feature, a relatively small nose, flattened slightly and uptilted somewhat. His brow, eyes and jaw would be ideal as models for a Da Vinci sculpture of God or Solomon or, perhaps, Samson. Pat, Dr. Smythe's gorgeous wife, once said, "When he enters a room people ought to be frightened, but nobody is."

Thinking of Miles's nose, it occurs to me that the organ would be ideal for a circus comic, one big enough. His nose may be the physical sign of the imp, the comedian, the clown Miles loves to be. Even now, at seventy, with his history of mighty efforts that failed, as head of what's left of a nation that thought itself the earth's most "powerful" and that truly was the most "advanced" in technology, even after the near extermination of the human species and after being witness to the unbearable events that led to it, even in the year 23, or A.D. 2023, the fun in the man erupts, quite often at the bleaker moments.

Another Smythe forebear with this same instinct for solitude was the great-grandfather who disappeared after a banquet to celebrate his sixtieth birthday. His sons spent a fortune trying to locate him, but in vain. When he died at the age of eighty-six it was discovered that he had gone to live in the wilds of British Columbia, where his "friends" were wolves and bears and bobcats, as he explained: not any of that "mostly evil breed called man." There he had lived, a happy man, and there he had died. Miles even found that there existed a clan remnant in remotest, mistiest Scotland, some "MacSmiths" or near to that, who were known in their scantily peopled hills as "the sky folk."

Extreme shyness, as psychologists know, is usually an acquired pose, real enough but unconscious, cloaking an ego too arrogant to show its bloated condition.

No such inward distortion fits Miles.

In my view, and as he tried to explain it to me, obliquely, his self-deprecation and the periods of intense depression that sometimes followed came from a gene; the cause was inherited. He dealt as best he could with something common in children but, in him, innate and not open to maturation or other remedy.

Miles is bashful.

2. Black Valentine's Day

One man ultimately learned the cause of Black Valentine's Day besides the agent. He eventually told it to another who passed it on to a few more in the certainty that it would be entered on the record. For a long time, however, events made any such historic notice impossible.

The man responsible confessed as he was dying. His name was Elliot Brown and he was in St. Anthony's Hospital in Newark, New Jersey, when he finally told his story. A fattish, bald man now thinned by terminal cancer of the then rare sort that could not be arrested, son of a morose architect whose great expectations had not materialized, one of six children, Brown grew up in the environment of hate, self-pity and world-blame that is common in the home of a disappointed father and, in this case, of an embittered mother too.

Elliot, who inherited the most meager genetic strains of both parents, was granted a degree in a junior college, night school division, and became what his diploma permitted, an electrical technician. He was also a racist, a member of local chapters of secret organizations dedicated to the extinction of—or, at least, the final resistance against—numberless anti-American traitors which such groups perceived everywhere, Reds, kids, criminals, non-whites, liberals, the lot.

At the time of his confession Elliot Brown was a skeleton covered by skin, a living thing with sunken, pale gray eyes and lips on which metastases grew like halves of strawberries. After employment by three major power companies

61

he had given up work to live on relief. He would never have divulged his tremendous secret had not his physician been Jewish, a young resident named Stern whom Elliot was unable to have replaced.

Even so, he would not have talked had he not heard from a well-meaning nurse a fact about Dr. Stern offered as an effort to lessen this detestable but dying man's prejudice. The story was simple and true: Dr. Stern had watched his mother burn to death in a tenement window when he stood below, helpless, on that Valentine's Day.

The date of that anguish sent Elliot's thoughts whizzing back to his years of labor under hated bosses. For the last ten years of employment he had been a district inspector of the power transmission system of New England, Canada and Erie Power and Light Company, or NECE, one of the biggest. The sophistication of these systems had increased with the growth of the great power grid that finally stretched from New Brunswick to Florida and west into parts of several states adjoining those on the Atlantic coast. Elliot's duties involved an extensive territory, to cover which required four weeks.

Just when he first realized that, if he wanted, he could easily and without personal risk cause a massive power failure he never confessed. Some germinal idea may have been latent in him for a long time but it became a thriving fantasy that Elliot amplified as a sort of quid pro quo for his immense grudge against society.

It must have developed slowly if for no other reason than that its accomplishment involved literally hundreds of steps, and these would have to be designed so they would remain unsuspected before the critical moment and afterward. What matters is that Elliot finally carried out his scheme, with elaborations that took him, in the guise of a fisherman or bird watcher, into areas served by NECE but not in Elliot's own territory.

On a cool April morning Dr. Herman Stern, a dark-eyed and dark-skinned man with a mournful profile and an honest face, looked in on Elliot while he was alone in a treatment room.

"Well, fellow, how're you doing?" His smile was intended to diminish the daily whine. But the whine wasn't tried that day.

Elliot was hooked up to tubes and needles and half sitting. He did not seem cheerful but he did not look as usual, on the short-term edge of new grievances adduced and readied for immediate listing. He even seemed a little—not roguish, exactly, Stern thought, but something like it which the patient enjoyed and others would surely find malicious or unsavory.

"I hear," Elliot said, "your old lady burned alive."

"Oh." The face-on expression was sadder, now, even than the long and drooping profile.

"That true? The Black Day?"

The doctor nodded. He didn't want to think of it, even less to talk of it, but the man was dying and knew it and his offer of communication on any level but that of beefing was novel, even interesting. So, quietly, in a few sentences, he explained how and why he had had to stand helpless while flames poured out of a sixth-story window and incinerated his loved, screaming mother.

Elliot listened—avidly. He was going to get his back from this yid. When the doctor stopped, he said, "I done her in. Murdered her, me. And maybe like about a hunnert thousand more people like her. Yids, a lot of 'em. Like her. You. Niggers, thousands."

Stern made the only sane appraisal. Some wandering bit

of cancerous material had been carried to the man's brain and grown there till the man's mind had been its victim.

"You think I'm nuts? It's God's truth! I rigged two sections of the NECE grid to blow—and it went off bigger than I had even expected."

"You what?" Stern remembered this living residue of a man had been some sort of high-tension line inspector. "Tell me about it."

Five minutes later Stern felt that one of them was mad. Ten minutes later he phoned from the room that he must not leave the patient for at least half an hour.

He was there for an hour.

He came back for more the next day—bemused, horrified, driven against his will to learn more about this incredible act of one man that had ended so many lives, ruined more and was remembered, nowadays, only as a minor vicissitude of the nation.

That second day Elliot, with excessive pride, gave the physician a few details of his treachery. As Stern was to reflect in later months, the size of the fiend's ego, his megalomania, his sense of justice and vindication were psychologically classic—the perfect image of the assassin: weak, mindless paranoids determined to make their mark, however contemptibly.

It was not until Stern was a general practitioner in the town of Lake Placid, where he had gone with his wife and new baby, like many, to escape any further urban disasters, that he repeated the tale. He did so after he had been made chairman of a local sports and conservation group which Miles addressed one afternoon. Stern, like all the world by then, knew a great deal about Miles Standish Smythe and his Foundation. He liked Miles at once, and told him about Elliot's deed because, he had long felt, *somebody* besides himself ought to know, just for the record. And who was better able than Miles Smythe to understand the fantastic revenge on society of a once fat, bold, nondescript, invidious and finally skin-and-bones fiend?

Even so, Miles was shocked more than the physician had expected. Stern was in turn stunned. He had taken the world's view of Miles, the image, a Hercules tramping unmoved and resolute through the horrors of the past and present. As he stared at Miles's broken features, his stiffened hands, disciplined not to clench, and at the changing shape of his shoes which revealed the curling toes, as he saw the light in the man's eyes switch out, the young doctor regretted his act. Miles had proven to be one who never could become inured. Suffering made him suffer. So his career had a cost in courage the doctor could not bear to contemplate. Stern began to apologize for burdening the man.

Miles halted that and smiled. Then he spoke—his voice like the first sound of thunder.

"There was some inside discussion of the possibility that the Valentine's Day thing was due to sabotage. One of the men in my Foundation told me about it. There was some evidence of tinkering at several points where safety equipment hadn't been damaged, burned up. A group of men could have done it, he said. But the signs weren't conclusive and the blackout could have been due to systems failure."

Stern nodded when the voice trailed into silence. "One man did it, though. I'm sure of Elliot's story."

"Sabotage." Miles seemed not to have listened to the comment. "Funny how nearly everybody, even then, was under a compulsion to believe what was happening must be the result of Communist action. And even when the USSR began to suffer identical or similar calamities. The Red mania did a lot of damage to our own work. Gave people a whipping boy—and so, a rationalization for that endless

65

notion they could eat their cake, have it, feed it to their kids, and the kids would still have it too."

Stern smiled. "Human, though."

The other looked up quickly, his eyes blazing and blue again. "What we used to *call* human."

"Right." Stern accepted the rebuke with a sigh.

The "Valentine's Day thing," Miles had said.

Miles's sister Nora was and had for a good while been Mrs. Willard Page Gulliver. His father was then recovering from his first heart attack at the new Harkness Pavilion on the Hudson, that February night, the thirteenth. Miles had long since forgiven his father, if that is the way to say it, for Miles's youth-long shame. He had come to understand the old man and admire him for all that was admirable in the man—not the sum of him, but a large part. When I dropped in on my father-in-law I found Miles there. Old Jason was out of his oxygen tent and able to get around his rooms a little.

The door to the suite was half open and as I came along the hospital corridor I heard them laughing. Laughing in a certain way, one that indicated they were busy with, and enjoying, their still new relationship—going over the old hurts and misunderstandings with the happy aim of increasing its intensity and, so, clarifying the old pain to solidify the new regard.

Before I rapped on the door I heard Jason say in his light tenor voice with its numberless modulations that gave his meanings special patterns but patterns the listener, granted some acuity, could clearly discern, "You mean, Miles"—this pattern made of wonder and a more usual ingredient, curiosity —"you felt duty-bound to tell Will about Nora and yourself before they were engaged?"

Miles must have nodded because I heard no sound from him and his father continued as if there had been a signal.

66

"Strange. Ever since you told *me*, I've been baffled."

"Rare thing for you, Dad."

They both chortled briefly.

"Here was I"—the psychiatrist sounded reflective and also still puzzled—"taking the stand I did, aware, too late, how it affected your mother—and completely unaware that my own son and daughter—acting on my apparent advice, call it speculation—*Lord!*"

"I don't think we did. That she did when she first—well —or I, then or later. It does happen, you know. And did, before you wrote your first book. Before books existed."

Jason gave a title with questioning warmth. *The Oedipal Myth and the Human Reality*. Lot of errors in it. Some truth. Did your sister want you to tell him? Ask you to?"

"No."

"You did it for your own sake?"

"The sake of the three of us," Miles murmured. "Or so I believed, then."

"A terrible risk—"

"See what you mean. Did, even then. It could have busted them up. And Nora wouldn't have told him. Not, anyhow, till some exactly right time came, later, years later, maybe."

"Maybe she already had."

Faintly, I heard Miles take in a breath. "Maybe," he said after a pause, "you're right, at that."

Jason chuckled. "So, now, I know how Will took it. Which is what I wanted to know, it appears."

"To hell with all you probing, cheating psychiatrists!" Miles was laughing as he spoke.

"Was I right?" the older man asked after a time. "Am I?"

Miles snorted. "So, add us to your computer punch cards. For us, sure. I think. It cost something—secrecy. Maybe that's why I eventually brought it up. To shake off some lingering sense of the need to keep it hidden."

I was about to tiptoe away and make another, louder approach. Eavesdropping isn't my commonest or even frequent vice. But I'd done it! Stood there listening to them discuss my wife, their daughter, sister. One more, slow, easy yet considered speech held me in spite of my shame. It was Smythe's.

"I think I better break a confidence, son. You wouldn't like it any other way. When Nora told me she was in love with Will and wanted to marry him if, as she expected, Will was near to the asking point, she also told me she was doubtful about what she wanted to do if he did—say a tremendous 'yes' or a gentle 'no.'" The older man sniffed—a nervous habit of his later years—not a sniff of superiority but one used for punctuation in a tense moment. "When I asked what her reservation was, she told me."

"Oh." Miles thought that over. "Good for Nora!" A quiet ten seconds passed and Miles chuckled again. "The offspring of psychiatrists must all be busybodies, confiders, tellers of needless truths, I guess. The home conditioning." Both men chuckled.

Then I knocked, and was told to come in, which I did, but before I took off my coat I said, "I've been standing outside listening to you two somber oafs exchange guilty knowledge about my wife. I trust candor will haunt you both."

That fixed up my prickling conscience.

What, exactly, they were discussing may be inferred. If not, no matter. I had married into a tabu-freaking family. And they were people of shatterproof will.

"How's it out?"

Miles asked that. I said, "Wild." For the three previous days it had been very cold. Now the blizzard which had been foretold by the weather people was building up as expected.

"Didn't have Les drive you up, I see." Smythe was looking at my coat to show how he knew. It was damp with brilliant

68

drops on its collar of synthetic fur. "Les" was the Smythe chauffeur.

"No. Came on the Whistle."

"Did it?" Smythe asked and both were interested.

"When it got to cruise speed, yes. And how!"

I described my ride from the station at Fifty-ninth and Central Park in the recently opened Whistle. Essentially, it used a tube bored beneath the maze under Manhattan, through solid rock, mainly, and sheathed, where the rock wasn't solid. "Trains" were air-propelled through the tunnel, air-cushioned so as to touch nothing. The trains were like segments of one long car, jointed to allow for easy curves and level-changes. Each train seated a thousand persons. There were three stops in Manhattan, a dozen more, to date, in the branches that went on to Westchester and out to Connecticut. The trains cruised at seven hundred miles an hour at this time and were expected to reach their design speed of a thousand by summer.

Cheap electro-cabs operated in fleets from the stations, and people either used them or walked, unless they had a license to drive a gasoline-powered vehicle in the region or, of course, owned one of the new electron-battery cars. Many already did though they were still expensive.

"Fun?" Miles asked.

"A little surprising. And they better do something about the squeal. It's deafening, almost—would be injurious, if you traveled the Whistle regularly, I'd think."

"I'll send Arthur back and try it with you. Okay?" Miles said. "Haven't had time."

Soon we left Jason and walked away. It was getting on toward time for dinner and Nora and I were to be at the Smythe apartment for cocktails and dinner. When we stepped from the hospital, wind and snow came "like BB shot in a supersonic wind." Miles said, "Wow! Maybe I shouldn't have phoned Arthur to go on along!"

Even those words, yelled, were ragged and hard to interpret. I nodded, and we bucked into the white, loud craziness. It would have been a hard walk had not Miles spotted an empty electro-cab and roared, as few others can.

The driver heard it or, perhaps, like most, glancing a second time to make sure the man was as big as he'd thought, he saw the open mouth and my waving arm. We had a slow ride in heavy traffic that skidded and sluiced into the storm. The dome of the uptown entrance of the Whistle appeared abruptly—and unbelievably near, since it was brilliantly lighted. Soon we were on the elevator, brushing each other.

In a car that halted where we were placed, according to marked squares on the platform, Miles began to talk cheerfully about his father's recovery. Then the Whistle rose and Miles covered his ears, grinning. We reached speed and began slowing in a minute or two.

There weren't any cabs at Fifth and Fifty-ninth or in the blocks we pounded through, beyond there. When we reached Park Avenue at Sixtieth the wind was shoveling north to south at hurricane speed. Snow came down as if Antarctica was being dumped. Wind made the building corners and irregularities scream, moan and bellow. Our eyes stung and we couldn't see anything across Park except, now and then, in some wind-carved cave in the avalanche, a glimmer of lights. Once we realized that we'd lost track of the cross streets and had to wait for a chance to be able to read the sign right over our heads. After we did so, we started counting.

I knew that we were going to be frostbitten if we didn't get out of there soon—if, as seemed likely, we were held up by a stoppage of traffic. We counted off cross streets and had reached the middle of our last block when the lights went out.

70

We didn't realize that for a while. It seemed to us only that some of the lights in the apartment houses at our left had been switched off. But the next block looked dark and by then changes were taking place. We were still on the west side of Park when southbound vehicles turned on high beam and made a dazzling confusion of what little could be seen at all. Both rivers of machinery started braking, and cars around us began to skid. There were several collisions. From near and far came crashes and glass shattering. Then the horns began.

It was Miles who first recognized the truth and bellowed it into my ear. "Power failure."

I nodded and went with him.

There were people on Park Avenue in cars with splintered windshields. At some intersections the drifts of snow were already so high we went around. People passed us, bumped into us, muttered and vanished. The temperature was falling swiftly. We watched several people, including two or three drivers of the big rigs, leave their stalled vehicles and flounder to the sidewalk. Ordinarily, Miles and I are both given to lending a hand to strangers in difficulty and once or twice I made a spontaneous quarter turn with that aim. Miles did too. Neither of us did more.

Why we didn't help is understandable, though I doubt either of us figured it out then. We had made three quarters of our own trip. We wanted to check on our families. And there were so many "problems" on every hand that it wouldn't have meant much if we had stopped to help a few people. Nothing we could do that they couldn't, plainly.

At last we made it, climbing over engine hoods and forward battery covers of vehicles to cross Park and tramping through drifts to the apartment house marquee where a doorman should have been standing and was not. A head-high pile of snow, part shoveled, the rest drifted, indicated that the apartment crew had been trying. But the snow was a foot deep where they'd quit. We got inside.

"Hello, Bill."

"Mr.—" and the doorman stopped there.

The lobby, or "rotonde" as it was called in that building, was a big one with marble, gilt, lemon and black upholstery and mirrors in about equal amounts. I saw myself and realized why the doorman had balked. Like Miles's, my eyebrows were white and thick, there were ice crystals on my face where a beard had gathered them one by one on the growth since a morning shave and my hat was heavy with icy snow so that its brim hung partly over my head, all around.

We began defrosting as the doorman recognized us.

"Almost gave you a bum's rush," he said in a slightly over-hearty tone. "Had to throw about two hundred strangers out, so far. Everybody wants in—in, *any place*. Lot of our own people haven't showed up, too. Lord knows where they got settled, or stuck."

"Big area—power cut?" Miles asked him.

"Big? It's the biggest in history. New England, part of Canada, west to middle of Ohio, and down past Washington, D.C."

"Jesus."

Bill assisted us in beating, rubbing and brushing off the now melting snow and ice. The size of a dark puddle on the floor and its extent on the carpet showed that this operation had been standard for some period of time.

We went to the elevators when we were free of the stuff, leaving Bill to mop at the water and slush we'd contributed. I rang. Bill had to charge the main doors and do verbal, then some physical, battle with three boys of about twelve who wore jackets and looked to be getting waxy cheeks. Miles rushed back and ordered him to let them in.

I heard a few sentences from the radio in the rotonde:

". . . the same procedure as a Condition Red. Again. Attention, all air raid wardens, auxiliary police, National Guard members. Report for duty at stations assigned for Red Alert. If not feasible, assist authorized personnel wherever encountered. This is a major emergency."

The elevator hushed down and the door opened. On the way to the high Smythe floor it hit me. "How come?"

Miles was distracted from some concentrated effort of mind. "How come what?" Then he grinned. "Took it for granted, didn't I? The building has auxiliary power for the elevators and central heating, air conditioning. Not anything else, though."

"Oh."

He had that scowl back again but it went away swiftly. "Corddy," he laughed. "Remember?"

I repeated what I'd perfectly heard. Then I did remember. A long time ago and a pompous sociology teacher who had given us a sermon about another blackout—as faulted and groundless as all sermons are, or nearly all.

The Smythes were living in a tower penthouse now, near the pair of duplexes they'd called home and offices when I met Miles. Horicon, the butler, was old but very able still and unwilling to retire, for which all were grateful. He greeted us as if nothing had happened and then Nora was running to me, in my arms, and saying after a kiss, "I'm so relieved."

She kissed Miles's cheek and added, "Twice relieved."

We went on to the drawing room. Both Pat and Zillah, Pat's daughter by a former husband, were in the front room. A fire muttered on the hearth, and drinks were being made by Zill, who'd heard us come in. Pat was displayed by a chaise beside the fire, and I was struck as always by the fact that she had not let time manage things. Rather, the skill of her plastic surgeon, and her own determined efforts to supplement

73

that skill, had succeeded so well that it took bright daylight and a close scrutiny to see her years.

Zill, of course, had the advantage of twenty years. But the same skills and arts kept her looking twenty—after two husbands, two babies, one war in which she'd served as a Red Cross something, two divorces and probably a hundred lovers. She looked as ready for the hundred and first, as eager and as relatively unselective as she'd been in 1965 when I first beheld the golden witch.

Pat greeted us. "Hello, darlings."

Zill said, "The world has almost ended, again."

Miles sipped the drink Zill handed him, and then took a call on the building phone.

The doorman asked for aid in the lobby—three car smash victims had come in and the situation on the door was tight. Miles turned down my offer of aid and asked Zillah to go with him. With that I learned more about the blonde engine of sex. In the Desert War she'd driven an ambulance—after completing a course on the care of battle casualties. News to me; but people were always learning more about Zill, and that more in various areas.

When they'd gone I turned on the radio, and soon we knew that New York was in bad shape. The radio announcer was good; cool, quick and lucid. These days, too, the new disaster policy was in effect. As much information as possible was broadcast. For a while, and after certain prior disasters, the authorities had tried the opposite method, keeping most of the worst news secret. It merely increased fears and led to more extensive panic. Not knowing is worse than knowing . . . the worst.

After the great Harlem Fire that nearly sent Manhattan into firestorm and total destruction, politicians came to their senses and switched the orders. Trying to keep that blaze secret had stampeded tens of thousands, since it was visible

74

for a hundred miles. These people fled and made bloody shambles in the streets, in tunnels and on the bridges.

Now we were given the truth:

". . . warehouse on fire at West and Franklin. Do not attempt rescue. Get as far from warehouse as time permits. Dangerous chemicals in storage there. Will explode. Noxious gases already issuing from site. Acids will flow. Keep clear. Do not approach for any reason. Evacuate all dwellings within ten-block area. Repeat . . .

"Third Avenue not yet open! This route must be cleared. No regard for vehicular property to be taken. Persons still in vehicles will leave them as bulldozers are in use to clear lanes. When you leave your car or truck see that your neighbors are out of their vehicles."

Next came a staccato series of commands which were largely "clear" and, if abbreviated, only for speed. These went out to trained groups, ordering them, by number and name, to special emergency areas.

A hospital's stand-by generators had gone out and a team of electricians was urgently needed. Hundreds of thousands of persons were trapped in elevators in high buildings, of course, and almost as many in the reconstructed but conventional subway lines. As the pressure blowers of the Whistle failed, one train lost way beyond an injection point but a second, behind it, crashed at full speed. The fact was known, not the consequences, easily envisaged.

One of the reports from people in a high-rise building was especially shocking. This was the recently completed and fully occupied Regent Towers on Fifth Avenue some distance from the Smythes' building. Its elevators, banks of them, were, of course, stopped where the blackout affected them—many between floors. It was a cooperative edifice and its tenants were still squabbling over the cost of a stand-by power plant. Few of the tenants had left the luxury apartment. The lobby was packed with refugees from the blizzard. Servants and service people had stayed in, waiting for a lull. But recently departing persons told of a gas leak and of gas permeating the structure.

The radio station was informed and now advised complete evacuation, with the warning that a used cigarette lighter, a struck match or even a spark might result in an explosion. Now and then this alarm was repeated. The leak was located in a main, but repair would take time. Gas pervaded the structure, rapidly. Its windows were the new plastic like those in the building where we sat, and unopenable. The doors at street level closed automatically behind those few tenants and people admitted from the street. Many people rushed out into the storm as the grim implications of the bulletins struck home. Most did not.

When the building exploded, the colossal firework was visible from our tower windows and the shock wave cracked two picture windows in the Smythe drawing room, letting in a thin, screaming blast of icy air and snow, though the plastic panes were supposedly unbreakable. Nora and I tried taping the long rents from the inside but the pressure of the storm ripped off the silicone adhesive tape. In the end, I got a door open and went out, in my wet overcoat. There I managed to close the tape Pat and Nora heated and handed out. The driving wind held it in place.

When I came back, half frozen, the radio was saying something new:

". . . this channel will handle only emergency news and orders from now on. All information on weather will be transferred to Station 8018. . . ."

Pat was already turning the dial. "Some friends of Zill's were due in from Paris about now," she said. "At Kennedy—or Cranberry."

She looked at my wife and me questioningly to see if we objected to the switch. We didn't, of course, and it was with a shock I recalled that several Foundation people, among them Dr. Davies, the ecologist, Plantley, the demographer, and Zanley, the plant biologist, with some of their assistants and secretaries, were also expected to fly in this evening, from Vienna. No use mentioning it, I thought.

Pat tuned the set and we heard a talk by a man with a voice both brazen and emotionless about the weather: the blizzard would not likely end until early morning, though from now on it would tend to become squally with briefly diminished winds and an occasional lessening of snowfall.

While that word was studiously stated in its flat, harsh announcer's tones, Miles and Zill hurried in. The rotonde was full of people and locked against others trying to enter. There were people down there with burns and cuts and frostbite. We offered to help but were told the place was already packed and a pair of trained nurses had managed to get in before Bill locked up. He'd done it at Miles's command when the vast, ornate lobby was packed. By then most people outdoors had found shelter somewhere.

I helped fill a wastebasket with such medical supplies as Miles's father kept on hand. When he left the penthouse with Zill I realized I was looking at a Zill I'd never known. She'd always been offhand about her wartime ambulance driving. "I probably drove fewer casualties from the lines in that ambulance," she'd said, "than the number of guys who used it with me, and a couple of other Red Cross gals, for a love-wagon."

That, I thought, might not even have been exaggeration. But the Zill I briefly saw now was the one who drove the wounded. Calm, hair tied up under a scarf, swift and busy as she gathered a load of edibles, eyes very clear and purposeful, blood on her hands and arms, bare now, with the scissored stumps of an evening dress showing, and in flat-heeled shoes to which she'd just changed, making her seem very different.

77

THE END OF THE DREAM

Calm and calming, competent, efficient, her sex-smolder subdued, making her a *person* only.

They went out and I returned to the big room where tall
candles were burning, logs blazed evenly, and my wife and Pat
were listening to the damned incessant horror coming from
the new channel.

". . . I will repeat the information we have, as of now,
8:17 P.M. Eastern Standard Time. Air traffic is stacked up
over most east coast areas. Planes able to reach airports at or
beyond Columbus, Ohio, and points west, or the border of
North Carolina and on south, have landed in those areas or
are proceeding to them. Planes destined for the blackout region but not yet airborne and flights short of their points of
no return have remained grounded or are en route back. None
of the fields serving the New York area is open. Everything
from Maine to southern Virginia and west to central Ohio is
shut down."

It was a woman's voice. I realized this only after hearing
that much of the news. Quiet, but very clear, calm, with no
sign of stress or even its repression. What it said flung the imagination into horror before it made that horror specific:

"The newly opened Cranberry Airport in New Jersey is not
in use. Equipment meant to permit landings in all weather
has failed. Kennedy is under ten-foot drifts. Dulles, also supposedly immune to any storm, went dark twenty minutes ago.

"Flight SST-S 108 from London attempted ditching off the
shore of Delaware. The Coast Guard has not returned from
its effort at sea rescue. Flight SST-S 1119 from Rome made a
safe landing on the frozen surface of Greenwood Lake in New
Jersey. Bulletin. All planes running low on fuel and able to get
this message are urged, if no better landing facilities are
within range, to make some similar attempt. The official order
follows."

What followed was a long list of lakes, and of some river

78

stretches possibly usable by lighter aircraft, along with various extensive flatlands including, even, swampy regions I knew to be spottily clear but patched with small tree clumps and heavy brush. The very mention of those swamps and their precise locations showed the desperation of Flight Control everywhere.

We were listening to that list when Horicon silently materialized and said in his standard register, "Dinner is served, madam."

Pat stood slowly. "We better, I guess."

But we didn't, right then.

The reason was Nora's cry, "The storm's dropped down."

We looked out the windows and it had.

For perhaps a quarter mile we could see through the diminished snowfall and what we could see was illuminated by dozens of fires, large and small. Some were in the streets nearby. Some apparently were consuming lower structures. The greatest one soared from the remains of Regent Towers, which we couldn't see because the buildings between us and that mass of debris cut off our line of sight. What still became shakingly evident was that the upper part of Regent Towers, visible before the explosion, had collapsed. About thirty floors.

But we remained there for a time for another reason.

Commander Emmet Buckley had kept his ship at cruising altitude for nearly an hour now, hoping and, until recent minutes, perhaps even believing his communications officer would get through to Flight Control somewhere. The solar flares that had caused this mess were growing larger. His crew and passengers, four hundred and eight people all told, were getting some extra radiation but not a dose that couldn't be borne in this emergency.

The passengers knew they were stacked up. Some probably knew, or guessed knowledgeably, that it wasn't usual for one of the new, "silent" supersonic superliners to remain at seventy thousand feet when over the continent and, so, above their destination.

Emmet Buckley was a powerful man, not tall, wide and thick, forty-one years old with a record for hours aloft and miles logged as near to perfect as any. He'd flown SST-S's for three months before he made his first commercial run—on this same trip, Berlin to New York—rather, Jersey and Cranberry. He wished, now, that his kids could see the grandeur of the Aurora Borealis, pale and sweeping rays, red, yellow, purple, green, sliding silently across the sky. Solar wind transformed to light. Invisible from the ground—air too dense, now.

His communications officer, Billings, called sharply on the intercom, "Plane closing on our orbit, approximately same level." Why another ship, another SST-S it must be, was "closing," the commander didn't know. Coming around the opposite way. He moved the controls to climb, which was standard operational procedure, but Billings cut in with two words: "Com's out."

Buckley had no time to be glad there had been a brief moment when the communications worked. The double-belt warning had been on for some time. He made swift movements and the huge ship slipped on its side, righted and shot out of its circling course at a sharp angle after it leveled off. A moment later the closing SST-S was briefly visible before it passed—a shimmering form against the Aurora, port and starboard lights glimpsed, gone. Their combined speeds were nearly three thousand miles an hour. The flight deck and the steamlined passenger-striped tube shivered briefly in the thin air that brought vibrations from the other craft's passage.

Buckley swore. Why had the pilot gone counterclockwise?

A Soviet ship? With a pilot who forgot the stackup rules were opposite, everywhere else? Probably.

A stewardess came through after she unlocked the doors. "Captain?" She remembered. "Commander?"

"Yes, Olive?"

"A passenger failed to clamp his double," the girl said with a breathlessness. "Hit the opposite seats and he's screaming his ribs are broken."

"Maybe they are," Buckley said, aware his flat tone was a sign of nerves. "Why isn't Lea seeing to the guy? She has the training."

"Lea didn't hitch. She had a sick baby. She's unconscious. Dead, I think—neck broken, it looks like."

The commander frowned. "Okay. Jim, go out and pacify the cripples. If Lea's dead, or even out cold, bring her up here. Suggest we have facilities for taking care of her. I mean—stop the sweat, if possible."

Jim unhitched and followed Olive into the first-class cabin. He had a glimpse of white faces, smoky air and the shimmer of the extra drinks he'd ordered as they were shakily sipped or held in tight hands; light caught the cocktail glasses and flickered.

When the door slammed and the bolts automatically slid in place, Norman Dover, the flight engineer, leaned over Buckley's shoulder.

"Just thirty," he said quietly.

Buckley stared at him. His sense of time must have gone haywire. He'd thought they had a good hour's fuel left. He called Billings and spoke tersely. "We're going down, Bill. Tank's going dry. You have got to get through and find us a field."

Billings tried, tried as sweat began to bead his forehead, as it ran to his chin. He kept manipulating dials with long, sensitive fingers that did not quiver because he dared not let them. As he listened, called, changed frequencies and came back to standard tuning, he knew the ship was coming on down and finally, with a porthole glance, that she was leveling off just above the overcast. He heard shattered parts of many sorts of talk and realized from those bits that controllers were suggesting frozen open lakes, even fields.

He hurried to Buckley.

The commander at first was incredulous. He turned the controls over to his second, Ames, and checked.

When he took over again his face was ashen. Jim turned keys, entered. "Lea's dead. I brought the body in. The guy with the smashed ribs is in bad shape."

That was as far as he got. Buckley explained their fix. Jim took the seat beside his commander then without comment and waited, watching the square, steady face as it looked at the deck below, solid like the sea at thirty thousand. Twice Buckley's eyes ranged over the panels in a sweep that took in every one of the hundred-odd instrument dials and recorders. He stopped both times to stare at the radar scope which he then turned up to "full bright." Vague blips began to multiply on the tube.

"Billings couldn't even get dope enough for the crazy landing areas they're offering. But if there's one field I know blindfolded in total dark it's Kennedy. I ought to get enough outline of Manhattan coming in from the sea to pick a slot and one I can use for the rest of the trip. Any better ideas?"

"It's dark. Drifts. Closed."

"Yeah. All the better. This baby can knock the drifts apart. It will be rough. If there's a wreck on the strip I pick, that's a shame. You think of anything surer?"

"No."

A minute later and Flight SST-S 108 from Vienna plunged into the top of the tempest. As it let down the storm tossed it like a kite without a tether. They sloped through ink, through the roaring, buffeting, snow-thick dark just beyond little areas of semi-visibility made by the glaze of landing lights. Buckley soon cut them in order not to be blinded.

He swiveled his eyes to the radar as often as he could and, finally, as he made a third sweep, caught a trace he recognized—a stretch of the south shore of Long Island. Then he looked at the altimetric gauges and back. The known line was gone. But he had a heading. At two thousand the air was incredible. He was aimed toward Manhattan but the ship behaved with such sluggishness he had to increase speed for the sake of control. He'd heard other pilots complain of this model and its slow responses in very heavy turbulence. They had said the Soviet SST handled better and so did the American plane. But the American airlines had been forced to buy foreign supersonics to compete; their own country's SST was still being tested. The public hadn't wanted the noise or the air pollution at high altitude—or low, for that matter. Well, they were getting it anyhow, and the profit was going to France and England.

Buckley did not think that out clearly but merely had a flash of feeling that passed in a second and left a sense of vague grudge that he was not flying an American-made ship. His eyes skimmed dials and his hands moved swiftly from point to point as he descended, shunting and bucking, below two thousand feet, below fifteen hundred. At that level he had to know exactly where he was: a number of buildings were as tall as his plane was high. So his was now an emergency procedure and it recalled the words of a long-ago instructor when their trainer was flying blind in the mountains: "There are rocks in these clouds!"

There were rocks in these, too, man-emplaced.

"You're low!" Jim screamed.

It distracted him for an instant. "Going between 'em," he

said and nodded slightly at the scope, which gave a picture of what lay below and ahead. It was his decision as commander and he based it on the reasonable belief that the turbulence above was too intense to fly through, while there was space enough over Manhattan to cross safely.

He was going to come down at Kennedy, closed or not.

A tremendous cross wind hurled the plane sideways. Then, abruptly, Buckley saw a great area of radiance ahead and in another moment the plane emerged into that opening where fires in buildings furnished the glare and the white world was blinding. Dead ahead stood a tremendous tower. It was almost dark, which seemed odd, till he realized the faintly glowing windows were lit by candles. There wasn't time to change course or even to scream, he thought, if you were that type.

We saw that collision. The pointed snout of the plane hit the building at an angle, hit the Regina Arms Hotel Apartments. The impact speed must have been near five hundred miles an hour, for there was time only to draw a breath between the plane's emergence from the wall of snowflakes to its shattering penetration of one wall and its still sliding appearance as it came through the other on its diagonal course. Steel beams and a great blast of bricks came out with the now demolished and compressed nose and the beams stopped the plane, soon and savagely, then held it so the forward part and the stern were suspended over the avenue and the side street. Part of a wing dropped into Madison. There was an avalanche of masonry that thudded and roared and bounded to the white streets and walks where few people, surely, were in the path of that cascading murder.

The noises seemed to go on a long while and they were loud even in that insulated apartment. Silence came slowly but finally as the movement of metal and masonry stopped.

The plane stood out from the corner of the building it had pierced, looking like a ruined javelin.

The nose was a stump clamped in the fingers of steel beams but more than half of the other end stood out over the street, wings crumpled, two engines swinging loose and, inside, three decks of people. I thought the people would have been killed by the G-forces at impact. My eyes were on a dangling engine as it snapped free and fell toward the street far below. A gout of oil squirted from the engine socket and splashed the building. There was a bright flare as fuel caught and dribbled, blazing, down the walls.

"My God," Pat groaned, "they're alive!"

Of course, some of them and maybe a great many. This was the new type of SST-S with Harmon swing-slip seats and Grogger bags. Passengers with double belts hitched properly would be automatically whirled around to meet the crash backward. Each seat would slide a meter on braking rails, and plastic sacks, instantly inflated, would surround everyone with an air cushion. Even such deceleration as we'd beheld could be survived.

As the drooling fuel and spurting oil mixed flames we could see quite clearly the movements of human figures in the ship and, soon, the violent opening of a hatch followed by the swift extension of a chute from the wreck to a window. There, hands from within caught it and presently, fantastically, people were moving, crawling out on that bridge, high above the avenue.

The flame of oil and fuel lengthened down the wall, its course wind-slanted, so it was twice delayed by high balconies where it fed pools to overflowing and continued its burning descent. We soon saw people in the glass-paned, opposite corner of the building where there were staircases. A few people appeared and, in moments, throngs, so the stairs became crowded and the descent was slowed. From the summit for forty stories that thickening snake of humanity corked down and over landings around and on down, more gradually all the time, with greater jamming as floor after floor of tenants tried to escape by that one remaining route. The puddle of people at the street exit grew swiftly; many were getting out safely and many times their number seemed for a while to have a chance, including, doubtless, some of those still crawling from the plane to the window.

"They've panicked!" Nora said quietly but bitterly.

"It's inevitable." I showed them why this sudden rush to evacuate the building had occurred: the irregular stream of flame had heated and splintered windows as it coursed downward, and then fired draperies and curtains. The wind had fanned those blazes into apartments on a dozen floors, setting them afire. From them, heat and smoke were rapidly filling the colossal tower.

Soon that opening in the storm either closed up or was carried away and the gale resumed, skidding and twisting where the skyscrapers shunted it and bringing back the white, high impenetrability of snow.

Later that night the blizzard ceased. Early in the dark of February 14 a warm wind rose and carried rain to the area in torrents. It put the fires out.

3. Comment

The estimated death toll for Greater New York was one million one hundred thousand. For the area from Maine to North Carolina and west to Ohio the estimate was five million. About one fourth were burned. Approximately half the victims froze to death. When traffic and transportation ceased to move people perished where they were or in search of some heated place. Homes and apartments dependent on electricity for heat became the tombs of myriads. Rich and poor, adults and children, they perished on the drifted highways, in halls, in neighbors' homes, in churches and schools they became ice blocks.

This Black Valentine's Day calamity has been given detailed attention and chronologically displaced for cause. One obvious reason is that I experienced the event. But there are better reasons.

The combined blizzard and blackout was the first blow to strike a great number of American cities. There had been shocking one-city calamities in the previous decade (1960–70) as will be shown here. But none was so massive, so lethal to so many and so costly in property. None, in sum, had been so absolute a proof of man's dependence on technology and his consequent vulnerability. That Black Valentine's Day inflicted a psychological wound that did not heal.

An immense but incalculable toll of injuries occurred. Its final total has been variously estimated. Conservative figures state that some thirty million people of all ages were injured or became ill owing to the blackout, the very low temperatures and the blizzard.

Another reason for giving the disaster special attention will be obvious. It was caused by a single man of mediocre intelligence, a victim of an undiagnosed paranoia. If that fact had been known at the time or in the months following, it might well have had a different effect on the public psyche. If one man could slaughter millions and put a third of his fellow citizens out of action for a time, that flaw in the system might have been inferred and acted on. The one-man cause might even have suggested what harm a single microbe, at its mutant appearance, could do, or one anything else, one more gadget or one more technical "breakthrough."

No such reaction occurred because no such information

existed. In the end, it was acknowledged by the spokesmen for the power industry that the failure was due, in so far as it could humanly be traced, to a combination of human errors, human carelessness, oversight, possibly even some malicious tinkering, together with an incredible flaw in the transmission system—"the best extant." The grid had not reacted as its designers expected when the evening's local failures began to multiply—in micro-seconds. Somewhere there had to be an overlooked bug in the grid.

The experts were going back to their drawing boards, as always, in such cases.

For the next example of the innumerable events that led to civilized disintegration, a seemingly minor and local dilemma has been chosen. It occurred in the summer of 1976.

The account that follows has been taken from the pages of the Olean (N.Y.) *Times-Harbinger*, an excellent small-city (or, nearly, big-town) newspaper. The *Times-Harbinger* energetically supported progress of the western New York area but it also undertook bold and well-informed crusades for improvements and attacked without fear those situations and activities in the area that its editors regarded as unprincipled, deleterious, dangerous, foolish or the like.

Had it not been for the effort of members of the staff, made after the blight was history, to find out how many sorts of similar but smaller-scaled happenings had previously occurred in the area but without public notice, the initial and dramatic failure of one crop would never have led, as it did, to a national scandal.

For three summer days a bluish haze accumulated over a part of the historic Genesee River Valley in western New York State, acrid-smelling, eye-smarting, nauseating where most dense. Superb journalism led to the unmasking of "blue-haze equivalents" in great numbers, all thitherto kept secret by big business pressures. There were many consequences of the exposé. For one, scores of top industrial executives went to prison, a minor result.

Between the 1976 episode and 1979 more than twelve billion dollars were spent by industry and government to curtail those "blue-haze type" situations. But it wasn't enough money. A new Administration soon pardoned the imprisoned executives. And the billions hastily spent on averting similar disasters in the future merely served to postpone them and make them ultimately more formidable.

Another result of the "Olean indictment" may best be stated here and now. When the nationwide menace was uncovered it became necessary to halt more than two thousand industrial plants and facilities in USA for periods of a year or more while their waste-disposal methods were revised. This meant that American consumers went on short rations for that length of time. Steel manufacturing was gravely curtailed. Automobile production was stopped entirely. Building construction was severly limited. Petrochemical plants were forced to cut down many processes to a small fraction of normal production and to stop many others. There were other reasons for the industrial "recess."

The world situation in 1976, '77 and '78 was alarming, especially in the Near East. War was feared at any time and only desperate efforts of statesmen and leaders managed to stave off for years the expected conflict that became the Desert War. The claims of the Defense Department in the stoppage period on the Gross National Product had a compelling priority.

A society that still saw itself as affluent and still looked toward "abundance forever" was deprived, in peacetime, for a year or more, of new cars, any right to build a new home, all highway extensions, all new household equipment—and a host of other common possessions it had taken for granted.

Bitterness boiled up against the measures then taken, as mandatory for saving the environment.

The Genesee Valley crop blight did not lead to national surveys and reports until early in the following year. The nation spent 1976 celebrating its two hundredth anniversary. That festival was a multibillion-dollar paean, in all fifty states, to what America had done, was doing and would do, with emphasis on technical marvels, the GNP, and marvels to come. But since, by '76, people had frankly acknowledged that their "blessings" were accompanied by environmental curses, a secondary "theme" was set forth for the two hundreth anniversary of independence and progress. That was the promise of an all-out assault by science, industry and government on the causes of fear and wrath.

That secondary theme was a public relations fraud. But its massive presentation in all media and by brilliant audiovisual exhibits was telling. Even well-informed and highly skeptical environmentalists and other concerned persons were deluded. Only the coolest, most knowledgeable and stubborn citizens resisted the ubiquitous displays of the American future as purged of pollution. Thus 1976 ended on a note of national expectations vastly greater and more confident than any in the recent past—and utterly without substance in one main part.

For the second theme did not say or much reveal how the "glory of natural America" would be recovered, or who would do it, where the money would come from or what sacrifices and hardships would accrue to any such attempt. It merely displayed the *faits accomplis*, everywhere, clear air, clean rivers and deserts made green, with the endlessly hammered slogan, "America *can!* America *will!*"

Soon after the inauguration of the new President, what the staff of a newspaper in a small western New York City was uncovering and reporting began to be uncovered and

reported in other regions, in parallel if not identical forms.
The next few months brought forth suppressed information
which obliged the President and Congress to devise laws
that, by the following spring, had brought to a halt a vast
amount of consumer goods production.

Massive unemployment followed, as industry shut down
to reconstruct itself. Federal funds were appropriated to
meet such job loss but they met it only on a level of basic
needs.

The nation became angry, then hysterical. The behavior
of the frustrated consumers became so appalling that, in
June 1978, Congress and the President repealed the laws so
that the forbidden goods would begin to flow sooner than
planned and, in consequence, well before many of the major
alterations in manufacturing practices had been completed.
Haste and miscalculation, as has been noted, robbed even
the finished work of final efficacy.

What is important to know about America and Americans
at this time should now be manifest. It was politically impossible in the late 1970s to compel even part of industry to
suspend production for a mere twelve to eighteen months to
make essential changes in techniques. The American citizenry
revealed in its great majority that it was addicted to con-
sumerism, in effect, and the projected period of goods withdrawal resulted in mass symptoms not unlike those of a
drug-deprived addict.

What seems strange and very sad to some of us in the
Foundation was noted by Miles at about the time discussed
here.

The Industrial Revolution enabled most men in many
lands to enjoy benefits that no man had ever known before,
and to have other comforts, conveniences and luxuries
that only kings and courts and feudal lords had previously

possessed. For three generations the rise of technology increasingly provided that gigantic boon to most citizens in technologically advanced nations. The change in life was *that* sudden; the cornucopia exploded *that* abruptly; human hell was replaced by the new heaven of modern living *that* quickly. There was no time for men to adapt. There were not even enough data about the growing cost of this machine-made bounty until the machinery was in place and vastly producing. Man had too little warning of the self-limiting nature of his materialistic "spree," and that little came so late, and was so complex, man in general could hardly be expected to understand and act properly—halting work on what he believed the most glorious and rightful page he'd written in all history.

He blew himself up not by his explosion of knowledge but by the way he used it.

Man was still, then, a child.

Perhaps he can now achieve maturity.

And now, to the blighted potatoes. . . .

4. A Small Mistake

POTATO CHIP CROP RUINED
LOSS IN MILLIONS

Gainesville, N.Y. *July 7, 1976.* Yesterday's sudden alarm at the wilt of the main crop in this "potato capital" has overnight become a sad acceptance of disaster. The acrid haze noted in the area for the past days has completed its lethal work although traced to its source, distant industrial disposal wells. The famed Genesee River Valley annually produced a multimillion-dollar harvest of potatoes especially bred for size, texture and flavor to suit the requirements of the potato chip factories located nearby. But there will be no chips from this main source in the coming year.

"It's a total loss for everybody," declared Theodore Jedlovski, one of the leading growers, "and the fault isn't ours or nature's but Buffalo's and Lackawanna's. Whoever is to blame is going to pay!" "Ted" Jedlovski, a leading figure in Grange activities, was referring to the cause of the calamity, underground seepage from some of the many waste disposal wells serving industries in and around the manufacturing city on Lake Erie. It is now clear that a number of these deep bores were not "secure" as assumed.

Hundreds of them were used for the containment of industrial wastes after federal and state pollution laws prohibited their disposition in Lake Erie. Contrary to expert opinion, the liquids have seeped into underground strata and flowed long distances to form toxic gases which erupted in this region.

Assistant State Geologist Ormitt Calliday issued the following explanation at noon today:

"There is no longer any question about the cause. Toxic and corrosive wastes of many kinds have been pumped into such wells for more than a decade and even in the past there have been incidents of this sort on a minor scale. Areas distant from such dumpage have been plagued by venting of gases and noxious liquids due to thermal overflow or seepage through rock strata to points of issue.

"Heavy industry in the area, denied lake and stream disposal, has been forced to turn to wells as the only alternative economically feasible. It has been a calculated risk and while other somewhat similar problems have been encountered, nothing of the present scale or distance from the probable points of origin seemed likely.

"When yesterday's potato wilting was observed," the Assistant State Geologist went on, "an analysis of the haze was immediately begun. Preliminary reports, while not quantitative, show traces of a dozen possible plant toxins including arsenicals, chromates, fluorine compounds, cadmium and various particular and other substances. Many of the last are in complex chemical combinations which will require lengthy investigation before their molecular structure can be determined. The causal agent acts selectively on the potato and allied species such as 'deadly nightshade'—plants in the *solanum* family which have shown similar distress. This is seen as suggestive by the chemists and botanists now working in teams on the problem and may furnish a lead."

Asked, later, by a band of angry farmers informally gathered in the local inn who was to blame, the expert's answers did little to lessen the hostile mood. In effect, Calliday tried to explain that the "blue haze" resulted from an underground seepage from wells fifty miles or more distant which moved in a deep stratum combining with each other and with underground, natural materials on the way, so that their original sources would almost surely not be traceable.

Only one solid fact arises in the mass of mixed reports and of suspicion and efforts to evade blame: the great potato chip crop is ruined. Somehow, from somewhere, a highly selective but completely destructive chemical gas, fog or mist has issued from the ground in an area slightly more extensive than that in which specialized farmers raise the bulk of those potatoes that are made into the popular "chips," thin-sliced, fried, salted and packaged under a dozen brand names.

That industry is responsible is almost certain. No natural phenomenon on record has produced such a grim effect. All species in a great genus, including tomatoes, are completely ruined by exposure.

The *Times-Harbinger* is going to follow this story until the people and corporations guilty are located and named, or until it can be shown that the strange plague was not avoid-

94

able and that no human agent or agencies were the cause. If the Buffalo industrial complex is responsible for the extermination of a highly profitable food crop in the Genesee River Valley, the processes producing that kill must be learned and changed. The valley is an agricultural treasure of long-time renown. Industry must not and will not be permitted to devastate that rich, beautiful and productive freehold—or any other!

Olean, September 3, 1976. The *Times-Harbinger*'s pledge, following the potato crop loss of last July, to pursue every angle of that catastrophe led to a frighteningly frustrating effort. The editors have been promising a report ever since, and until last Wednesday, the first, there has not been sufficient material with adequate proof to justify such a report.

Today, there is plenty.

In a series of features the *Times-Harbinger* will run during the next six weeks these findings will be published.

As has been made clear by several interim editorials, both the minor earlier rumors and the recent, preliminary, scientific findings have been suppressed by means and in ways utterly unacceptable and shocking in a supposedly free and open democratic nation. It is, then, with a sense of deep shame that the *Times-Harbinger* opens its exposé with accounts of events prior to the Genesee blight which, in every case, have been thoroughly documented and proven but were kept from general knowledge. No means of silencing those who had the facts seems to have been too cunning, illegal or unethical, even criminal in many cases, for the "interests" and "authorities" determined to repress the truth.

In mid-January 1974, during a thaw, a toxic flood burst into the cellars of a block of newly built homes in the Wiggins-Heath development east of Clarence, N.Y. The flood carried

95

unidentified but nauseous wastes which forced the occupants of sixteen houses to evacuate them and they were not able to return to their homes until a team from a major industrial plant had "volunteered" as a "public service" to "decontaminate" the homes.

No compensation was offered, though householders tried to bring suit against the county, as it was believed the toxic or nauseous matter came from a leak in the brand-new sewers in the development. How such a bizarre substance got into the sewer lines was not investigated, nor was the motive that led an industrial team to decontaminate the homes ever questioned.

In March of that year a storm sewer in Depew "erupted" and overflowed sidewalks with a greenish and viscous liquid at a bus stop where about a dozen grade school students were waiting. Ten of these children soaked their feet in boarding the bus. All ten suffered delayed but severe burns. Some sustained crippling injuries. Angry parents made a very extensive effort to place the blame for the tragedy and to gain redress. They were not wholly successful. They failed to get the news of the severe harm to their children aired in any medium. It soon proved that radio, TV and the press had been warned by the Department of Defense (as the parents were also soon warned) to keep quiet about the burns suffered by the children. The families were promised modest sums in redress and these sums were paid after all parties concerned had signed pledges of secrecy.

On August 12, 1975, on a hillside behind the farm of Hernando L. Acosta, near Holland, N.Y., a small "geyser" or "fountain" erupted and flowed into the tiny brook that cuts through that property. Acosta had developed a large "egg factory" in the course of past years and the brook ran beneath the huge sheds where his hens were housed, which were held in place over belt conveyors.

He was proud of his latest factory, which produced a daily average of twenty thousand eggs of top quality. Finding his brook contaminated with a green slimy and stinking material, the "egg king" traced the source to the hillside "fountain" where he was nearly overcome by fumes. He had found on the way to the source that the small trout in the brook had been killed. He also came upon dead and dying birds on that walk.

Outraged, he drove to Holland to report the flowing pollution. He gave no thought to his hens, all of which were dead when he returned. His new buildings and equipment were heavily mortgaged. And, like others, his efforts to draw the attention of authorities to his loss met with disinterest and inaction. His mortgage was foreclosed in the fall. And his story of the poisoned fountain that flowed into his tiny creek and caused his disaster was widely discredited. The reason for that is suggestive: no one else ever saw the small "fountain."

At daybreak on the morning after his hens perished dynamiting began on the hill where it had appeared. A new quarry was being opened, it was said. For some weeks massive excavations continued on the hill site and reporters and others not engaged in the work were kept at a distance on the grounds that blasting made close approach unsafe.

Acosta took his loss and his subsequent frustrations in seemingly good spirit. But on November 19 of that year Mr. Acosta, an ardent sportsman, was killed in a hunting accident. It was assumed that he tripped and shot himself as he fell. But it is at least possible that his death was anything but accidental.

He was a cautious and experienced hunter, and no careful study was made to determine why he had, for that once, failed to carry his shotgun in the broken or open attitude. Apparently no ballistic check was undertaken to show his own gun was the death weapon. Mr. Hernando L. Acosta, in effect, could have been murdered as plausibly as he may have shot himself, and perhaps more plausibly. If so, why? Perhaps he knew too much, talked too much and kept digging into the cause of his miseries too stubbornly.

The following editorial appeared on the front page of the Olean *Times-Harbinger* on Thursday, July 7, 1977:

THE INDUSTRIAL "UNDERGROUND"

One year ago today this newspaper carried a front-page story with banner headlines on the "blue haze blight" of the potato chip crop in the Gainesville area of the Genesee Valley.

Every day last week this newspaper carried banner headlines and a front-page story about the sources of that blight, after a long and incredibly difficult effort by the staff to learn what the "hush-hush" facts were.

During the past week that *Times-Harbinger* "exclusive" has been picked up by every major newspaper, world-wide.

What the world learned may be summarized as follows:

The disposal of dangerous industrial and other wastes in deep wells has been a widespread and growing practice in USA and elsewhere for decades. With the development of machines capable of boring in hard rock holes of great diameter and at remarkable speed, this practice has become general. Wells twenty feet wide and as much as eight thousand or more feet in depth have been bored in thousands in recent years.

Geologists of high competence have been employed to select the sites of such drilling, in most instances. In many, these scientists have received payments far out of line for their assignments. Scientists are men, and even some highly trained men are open to corruption. Corruption was not,

98

however, an ingredient of innumerable choices of bore sites which have led to a fantastic variety of difficulties, tragedies, losses and calamities to hundreds of thousands of victims. The trouble was "the state of the art." Geology did not and still does not have a sufficiently detailed body of knowledge about the underlying formations of the earth's crust to be able, *in any instance whatsoever,* to say, "You can drill here and put anything you like in the hole and it will not escape for all eternity."

Furthermore, an unconscionable number of geologists, chemists and other scientists who served as consultants in site selecting were deliberately misled by management. A simplified parallel will serve to illustrate the method. Experts, if told to find a safe disposal site for caustic alkali, such as lye, could and did find such a seemingly proper formation. When, however, the industry had been hooked to the bore, it would pour down hundreds of tons of *acid.* Rock formations that would not be eroded by alkalis might dissolve rapidly when drenched in acids. And that *sort* of cheating was very common.

Even where there was no such hanky-panky the results were often grim. The very act of drilling often brought to the surface material that proved what had been deemed a single, unflawed formation was deeply faulted, cracked, filled by intrusive material of some other kind. Often, this intrusive layer extended for great distances and was permeable so that whatever waste might be dumped in the well would seep in the blotterlike layer for long distances, carrying the waste liquid to a point where it might emerge, as was the case of the Buffalo wastes in this area a year ago.

There are many other underground phenomena of nature which are very difficult or even impossible to ascertain from the surface or even from the careful study of a finished bore made by experts prior to use. What, again, in lay terms, seems

99

to be an ideal well in pure, granitic rock, without a flaw of any kind, may have been bored near enough to one or another such phenomenon so that, with use and in time, the adjacent material vents into the well. Hot water and cold, corrosive mineraliferous waters, steam and gases of scores of sorts have thus intruded on wells that appeared safe and sound. When such an event happens the results can be so varied as to make a complete predictive list beyond the competence of modern science.

These and other possibilities have been known for decades and they have given rise to the highly secret, federally sponsored Office of Underground Disposal Management, a bureau which, until the *Times-Harbinger* acted, looked to be a harmless body of inspectors and scientist-advisers but was, actually, a vast organization linked with industry and given free reign in its long-time effort to keep the public from learning about the true nature and the frequent disasters in well-disposal practices.

Even now, only a sampling of the actual calamities that were hushed up has been uncovered. At least a dozen disasters of some sort owing to well leakage have already occurred in every one of the fifty states. Towns and cities relying on wells for municipal water supplies have suddenly found their underground waters unsafe, even poisonous.

Several earthquakes are now surely attributed to the deep-well disposal of liquid wastes which, by soaking large strata of unstable material, sand, pebbles, shale and so on, have had a "lubricating" effect that allowed the strata above them to slide and slip, with resultant tremors. That particular hazard of such bores has been known since the sixties when Denver, Colorado, suffered several times the normal number of previously rare quakes owing to the quantities of fluid wastes dumped into deep wells by manufacturers of poison gases for the military.

There is good evidence to support the belief that the great quake of last April in the Middle West which sent the Mississippi River at La Crosse, Wisconsin, in a "tidal wave" was owing to shifts of deep strata lubricated by wastes of industries in an area of a hundred miles around the suddenly dropped and wave-shattered city.

There are many more horror stories to come. The secret endeavors of federal and state governments, with the connivance of industry, to keep sources concealed has stuck the American public with innumerable odd events of a large or smaller sort, all harmful, and all or nearly all, with an official explanation of a deliberately misleading sort, when, that is, such events could not be kept from general knowledge by any means.

At this moment no less than eighteen House and Senate committees are examining the previously "restricted" facts. No doubt legislation will follow, stringent and perhaps even adequate. For such craven secrecy is intolerable in America. Every top official in government and industry as well as every guilty scientist who contributed to this fantastic cabal must be tried and punished. The use of these bores for waste disposal must be stopped or at least permitted only for those wastes that cannot possibly create harm of any sort—which, perhaps, is no wastes at all.

What, then, shall we do with such wastes?

The question remains and it is desperate. Our rivers, still, after seven years of talk and even a good deal of action, are running sewers. The seas grow more dangerously polluted each hour. Science and technology are annually adding thousands of new substances and processes and artifacts to the list of our "achievements," all productive of wastes, and often of brand-new types of waste material.

Matter is indestructible. We say that—and skip the implications.

Men everywhere are trying to solve these problems and solve them we must—or vanish as a species from the earth.

We are told, daily, by Washington and in the advertisements of the great producing corporations, that the alternatives now being implemented for disposal seem to be as promising as they are titanic in design and construction. Great mountains of solidified wastes will rise in empty deserts under impenetrable cover, and so stand, far from human habitat, eternally, or near enough to that. There they cannot liquify, seep into the earth or evaporate into the air. Enormous tunnels are being driven halfway across the continent and lined with impermeable materials to carry those wastes westward and eastward for later solidification. Underground railways will transport presolidified material to the same areas.

We believe these measures will solve most of the worst of our industrial waste disposal problems.

But the *Times-Harbinger* promises to keep on with the watch and to assess all the new systems when they go into operation. People in Olean, people in western New York State, people everywhere are, we believe, as proud as we, the editors, of our achievement. One small newspaper in a minor American city has succeeded in launching, by itself, a worldwide awakening and a revolution in uncounted thousands of hazardous industrial procedures.

We are proud, of course. But we feel this is only in fact a typical example of the "American way" of acting. One man or one newspaper can change the sum of events. No American is "powerless" save he believes it!

5. A *Preface* to the Next Chapters

The "blue haze blight" seen through excerpts from a single newspaper was a local event with world-wide consequences.

The "chapters" immediately following concern some events of less magnitude. The first, about the Brownsville bees, is taken from press association reports. The two White House documents were "confidential" and meant to be burned. The peculiar account of the mishaps involving flatulence appeared in *The Manhattanite,* and the strange story of how the Mississippi Basin Horror began, and who first noticed the cause, appears in E. B. Black's *Popular History of Modern Dilemmas,* which was published in 1986. Records of the secret conclave on river use were taken from tape recordings made covertly by one of the men present. Other sources are shown directly.

The intention here was to select "typical" events.

However, as these choices indicate, no environmental mishap or ecological blunder can truly be called typical. Each is unique but many are comparable. Thus any of a hundred of other events, some hushed up, some given massive press and TV coverage, could have replaced those selected.

Chemical additives to foods consumed by Americans had many and far more dire consequences than the example given. The Cleveland disaster was the only one of precisely that causation; but similar wastes in other bodies of water had far more terrible and widespread effects. The President who received the "secret" memos here reproduced was not the first nor, certainly, the last Chief Executive to be furnished with such sinister counsel. Nor was he first to act on such advice.

It is expected that these samplings will suggest how increasingly *tormented* the public became in the seventies. Toward the close of that decade it was hardly impossible to listen to a news broadcast or pick up a paper without encountering word of some new woe. Most were minor and local but their sum, alone, had collective impact and the larger tribulations, obviously, created great dread. Readers must not overlook that last fact: however worrisome or even alarming the future may be or become it will never give rise to terrors in such abundance and of such shocking novelty. Man does not and will not have the profligate technology for that harm; man's numbers will not be great enough to have that impact on the biosphere; he probably lacks the mere resources to re-create that condition, even were he foolish enough to try restoring that kind of "civilization"; and surely he knows better now!

6. News Items

BROWNSVILLE FLEES BEES

APIAN ALAMO: TEXAS TERRIFIED

Brownsville, Texas, August 3, 1976. UIPA. The African bees have crossed the border early today near Brownsville and already several score Texans, mostly the young and a few elderly people, have been hospitalized. It is said that several hundred panicky citizens have fled this busy border city of seventy-seven thousand.

The invader, *Apis mellifera* (Gurgesson), is a mutant form of the "African" honeybee introduced in Brazil about mid-century. It soon escaped into the wilds and began moving northward, causing much pain and occasional deaths with a single sting, while multiple stings were often fatal. Thrusting into Mexico in 1974, its first mutant (Willard-Peccan) form became a hazard to man, greater than all other stinging and biting creatures including spiders, scorpions and poisonous snakes.

The new pesticide, Xano-Lethane, was massively air-sprayed over the infested areas and served to halt the northing trend on the Tampico-Mazatlan line by affecting queens of the subspecies.

The arrival of the almost equally dangerous Gurgesson mutant in Mexico City last spring has received world publicity. However, owing to the fact that Xano-Lethane had an unexpected spin-off in that it sterilized females in several species of insects responsible for the pollinization of a number of hardwoods and certain agriculturally valuable plants and commercially important flowers, the pesticide was not air-applied even though scores of deaths were occurring weekly.

Heavy and repeated plane spraying with Tri-Mort was begun in June and, according to announcements of last month, it had satisfactorily controlled the "death bee" in all urban and most other populous areas. The biospheric costs of that drastic method are not yet known. Heavy fish kills, massive tolls of wild life and considerable loss of cattle and sheep are expected and some have been reported.

Meanwhile, pandemonium in Brownsville and neighboring areas increases hourly. Supplies of screening and mosquito netting are sold out. Automobile dealers and used car lot proprietors report that there will not be an air-conditioned vehicle at any price by nightfall. Many of the winged invaders appeared in queen-led swarms, flying hordes in search of new hives or nesting sites. One swarm found its way into a supermarket and created panic. A stampede ensued with an as yet unknown toll of dead and injured. Another swarm set off the same reaction in a church where thousands had taken shelter owing to its great size and well-publicized air-conditioning system.

Serum is being flown to the beleaguered area, and local radio and TV stations are trying to halt mass panic. The broadcasters point out that only three victims per thousand are the least endangered and that those who are in danger can easily be recognized by a whole-body pink flush that appears within three minutes of stinging. The stings are admittedly agonizingly painful, but the pain recedes in a few hours and, for all but the peculiarly "sensitive" three per thousand, the effect of one or many stings is entirely local and not dangerous.

The city's mayor, in a broadcast made just before this dispatch was filed, called on the citizens to summon their "traditional stoicism and fortitude," and stated that ". . . already the numbers of dead and injured owing to traffic accidents, trampling, fire, heart failure and the many other causes than bee stings is great, growing and shameful. So far," the mayor went on, "no bee death has yet been reported. Not *one!*"

Several authorities on the insect have pointed out that the "Brownsville reaction" is "unwarranted, hysterical and incredible." As one of them comments, "The bees are, at most, a nuisance. They need cause no deaths and no protracted prostration. Sure, they can and do hurt like hell. But the risk of having a sharp pain is no excuse for roaring out of town by auto and getting maimed in the eighty-car crash just now reported on the Pan-Texas Throughway. What's wrong with those sons and daughters of the Lone Star State, anyhow?"

TEXAS SUES UI PRESS ASSOCIATION
Governor Calls N. Y. Times "Idiot"

Austin, Texas, August 4, 1976. UIPA Special. Governor of Texas John B. Cooker today ordered a damage suit for $25,000,000 filed against the Union-Interworld Press Association and member papers for publishing a series of reports by a local UIPA reporter of the sudden and appalling arrival of swarms of poisonous "African" bees in the Brownsville area.

After reporting what first seemed to be an amusing and not serious situation, the story continued with an objective and even technical account of the history of the stinging insect, its mutations, and the costly measures used to cope with it.

Early this morning Brownsville found it was under siege. Reported hundreds of swarms of the agonizing and sometimes deadly insects had crossed the Rio Grande, entered the suburbs and were moving on the downtown area. Scores of citizens, especially school children, had been stung and hospitals were overflowing as agonized people were brought to them from all points, often by drivers severely stung on the way.

Latest reports indicate that emergency measures are effective. However, the first news to reach the world strongly indicated widespread panic and chaos. Marital law and a communications blackout by the military prevent any word of the real situation from reaching other areas.

Speaking from the steps of the State Capitol at Austin to a huge, infuriated crowd of Texans, Governor Cooker expressed the mood now becoming state-wide:

"The idiot press had the nation and the world sneering at Brownsville while that stricken city's children were dying in dreadful pain. The idiot press speaks of an 'apian Alamo' as if the courage of Texan mothers who have given their lives in the streets to cover their babes and youngsters were a joke.

"The biggest press agency in the world, save one, and the libeling newspapers must pay for this unspeakable crime-in-print! For the idiot press caused thousands of amused and curious citizens to rush to the afflicted area—for, mind you —laughs. The result was a traffic shambles.

"Many of those people died laughing. Worse, these hordes prevented the rapid delivery of serums and spray materials to vital points. Had the idiot press not been the agent of this blockade, countless lives might not have been lost. And had irresponsible reporting not led to the blocking of highways into Brownsville, the present and admittedly more dangerous emergency spraying might have been avoided."

Bowen T. Willis, president of the UIPA, said in a preliminary reply, "The governor is understandably upset. It may have been somewhat poor taste of our Brownsville representative to take, initially, a slightly light view of what then was not yet even conceivable as the disaster it soon became. However, it is my belief that when communication is restored the world will find that a very serious panic situation did occur in the city and that our local representative's steadily changing report represented a correct view of rapid deterioration of morale, of mass flight and stampede.

"What is condemned without reservation by myself, by the officials of this Association and by every editor of the fine journals we serve is the absolute blackout of regular news from the stricken area. This order, given by General Womley Chute Banger, commanding officer of Guard units on duty in the region, is not only unfree, and so un-American, but unprecedented and dangerous. No similar abuse of 'martial law' comes to mind. The right to know is a public and constitutional right and the need to know the worst is part of the right. For when 'the worst' is known, imagination will not create still more terrible notions and react to such false nightmares."

Brownsville, Texas, August 5, 1976. UIPA. This is a city in mourning and a city trying to endure the unbearable: mass shame. It is a city in shock and a city in dread. The bees are dead to the last buzzing invader. Offices, schools and banks are closed. Only the parlors of undertakers and morticians, hospitals and refugee centers are busy. Only a few vehicles and slow-strolling, stunned pedestrians pass on the streets.

Tuesday, the day of ignominy, was clear, hot and calm. Now the dry winds are turning sheets of newspaper in dusty whorls and raising small spirals of the whitish, powdery insecticide that was crop-dusted on the city. It stopped the insects that had sent thousands of people into hysterical flight but the frenzy went on. The vast amounts used are now a cause of concern as the compound is new and its long-range effects on man are not yet known. Nothing else of a suitable sort was available in the emergency.

Up to this time only four deaths attributed to stinging by the "deadly" bees have been recorded. Seven other victims are still hospitalized but reported out of danger.

The official toll of those who perished owing to suffocation, trampling, car crashes, fires and other panic-related incidents has passed the thousand mark in the last hour. The injured now number more than five thousand. Bodies and injured survivors are still being found and brought to aid centers from outlying areas. Fires continue burning in the suburbs.

Already the agonized questions are being asked, "Why?" "How could it have happened?" The only correct answer is as clear as simple:

In a city of more than seventy thousand and an area of some one hundred thousand, a large fraction of these citizens were jittery owing to causes familiar to everyone. These people had been prepared and perhaps overprepared for the faint chance they'd encounter the most venomous mutant strain of the renowned "Brazilian" honeybees. When the swarms actually began to appear with dawn last Tuesday, panic gripped the minds of some early observers and they spread it like an instant plague. The real peril was trivial as the figures make clear. But the price of panic is always awesome.

Brownsville is paying the price in full.

And yet there may be some compensation. This reporter met a bearded, leather-cheeked Texan, an old cowpoke, who made the day's wisest observation. His name is Jim Deever. His boots are spur-hacked and his hands bridle-curled. His eyes are shuttered by range squint but gimlet-bright. Jim

Deever was born in Brownsville and his words fittingly conclude this tale:

"Maybe other folks in the rest of the nation'll learn how shaky we all have got. They should, and the fact ought to chill every son of a gun to the bone. If Texans can blow up over a bee swarm, we're all, all us Americans, nearer the ragged edge than seemed possible till lately."

7. A Document

CLASSIFIED

THE WHITE HOUSE

Office of the Scientific Adviser to the President

PRESIDENT'S EYES ONLY

SUBJECT: *Two Events under Study Code Names: Hot Water; Pickle*

FROM: J. D. Ovoth, Assistant Director

TO: The President

DATE: October 9, 1977

OTHER: Category: Top secret classification and *To Be Burned when Read.*

This data has been requested by the President for immediate study. Repeat, presidential and immediate-designation order.

Aides will not open, not hold up, as with same yesterday when aides prevented delivery, in person, by me.

Signed, JONAS D. OVOTH Asst. Dir.

MR. PRESIDENT: Herewith as required my "lay language" presentation of "Hot Water" (The Great Valley Report, Cattle-

Kill, etc.) and "Pickle" (The Harlem Trouble). Both problems are very technical in cause. My translation here is, in my
view, oversimple and scientifically near to culpable. Also, the
advisories on policy are not mine and were made over my objection. You have my resignation, "Yellow" File B, Drawer
12, if this attitude is an impertinence. Ovoth.

THE GREAT VALLEY REPORT:

This report referred to the affliction and death of some
750 cattle and horses habitually watered and allowed to wade
in Chenokee Creek. This small stream flows from its source in
NE Cattaraugus County through Great Valley and into Little
Jay River, which then empties into the Allegheny River and
thence to the reservoir. Chenokee Creek passes within a mile
of the General Recovery Corporation's facility, an installation
licensed to process spent reactor fuel cans. These are long
containers in which enriched uranium and/or plutonium still
exists but in amounts reduced by use below the effective fuel
levels. Though atomic, the fuel has "decayed" below reactor-
use value, the unspent residue and reactor-created plutonium
are exceedingly valuable. Recovery is a complicated matter
and involves separation from immense amounts of various
highly radioactive elements. While every precaution is taken
to store part of this "hot waste" in tanks until its level of
radiation permits its disposal in the creek, errors can occur.
Also huge quantities of long-lived, very hot waste materials
(long-lasting radioactivity in many elements) result and this
waste must be transported, in ten-ton, lead-covered special
containers, each with an independent cooling system, as this
material is also boiling hot, *thermally*, and must be kept cool
while in transit *and* after reaching storage tank farms where
tanks must be cooled by complex devices *for centuries to come.*
Accidents in transfer of this very dangerous trucked cargo are
not impossible. Low-level material routinely let into waterways
(Chenokee Creek) is carried off "harmlessly," in AEC term.

However, two unforeseeable accidents in the past winter caused an unusually high level of hot material to reach Chenokee Creek. One was the unpredictable heaving of earthen dams by frost in the record-breaking cold spell for the area of February last, 15th–19th. At that time the ground was covered by snow to a depth of 17 inches (average) and the fissures in the retaining "pits" (large, covered ponds) were not detected till the March thaws.

The thaws were gradual so that a considerable amount of "hot" material entered the creek. Immediately afterward, a lengthy drought occurred. The result was that an unusually large amount of radioactive matter first entered the creek in slow but steady amounts with runoff and then, as the drought was followed by rapid subsiding of the creek flow, much of this material settled in the downstream bed of the creek.

Weather Bureau records show no such combination of steady runoff followed rapidly by drop-down of the creek in question so it was not economically rational to take measures in advance for a situation with no precedent. Also, the assumption was, during the thaw period, that the earth-retaining walls were, as engineers had supposed, not leaking. This means that the leaks went unnoticed in the period of high water, when monitoring the rapid flow is not done, as it is assumed the radiation levels will be very dilute owing to the volume and flow of the stream.

A second and far less pardonable or predictable blunder of an individual added to the radioactive content of the waterway at this time. Owing to a shutdown of General Recovery's Minnesota plant for repairs, the Great Valley facility was nearly overwhelmed with incoming material. To keep pace with necessity some independent, local truck owner-drivers were hired for haulage (to the tank farms) of the very hot wastes. A driver of one such truck left the plant for Colorado but, having failed to understand his briefing, he became alarmed by the energetic sounds of the cooling machinery and those emitted by the lead-sheathed tank.

He turned into a woods two miles beyond the plant property and, using a tractor he fetched from his nearby home, off-loaded the cargo. He made no report and took up other work. The tank was not missed for three days until it failed to be delivered to Denver. Meanwhile, without proper driver attention, the cooling machine failed. All six containing walls, ceramic, ceramic-metal, stainless steel and lead, were broached and a tremendous quantity of very radioactive waste then poured out. It collected in a swampy sink which drained with the thaw into a small tributary of Chenokee Creek, thus adding to the other, undetected, hot leakage.

Fortunately, after this foolish and unthinkably dangerous act occurred, the low swamp contained 99% of the hot materials. The area has been covertly closed to public approach and to inquiry. The material is being recollected, a difficult task. There will doubtless be some delayed human effects (burns, cancer, etc.) owing to wind and weather carrying escaping hot gases and fine particular matter to nearby farms, villages. These will be "explained" when and as they develop.

The members of the Atomic Energy Commission have secretly reviewed the foregoing. Their (and this Office's) official recommendations will follow. The General Recovery Corporation is held by the Commission majority to be blameless. The proper technicians and appropriate inspectors from AEC had thoroughly checked and recently re-viewed the warning systems with an okay for all monitors, systems, personnel and so forth.

Effects of the unfortunate high levels of radiation in the sedimentary stretches of the creek did not come to notice until late April when a "hoof-and-mouth disease" scare brought to the attention of a county agent the fact that

THE END OF THE DREAM

cattle, horses and swine belonging to certain farmers were
developing hoof slough, hair loss on legs and mouth ulcers.
The area was quarantined and neither meat nor milk nor
other animal foodstuff was permitted for use or export although it was soon learned that the hoof-and-mouth fright
was groundless.

That something similar was locally epidemic, however, became increasingly evident as not only hoofs, limbs, hair on
limbs and mouths showed slough signs but tongues and stom-
achs exhibited an equally pathological syndrome, swellings,
ulceration, skin slough, ulcer and so on. Unfortunately, these
symptoms were studied for some time as surely of bacterial
or viral origin. It was not until early May that a radiobiologist
visiting the state veterinary labs in Rochester suggested the
tissues under examination looked like radiation burns.

Meantime, some human users of the creek—for drinking
and laundering water supplies, wading and fishing, and the
like—fell ill and a number have died as others now ill are sure
to do. Once the nature of the damage was certainly determined a swift check by General Recovery Corporation was
made and the entire phenomenon was then clear. A vast but
carefully disguised survey of the downstream river system was
initiated and (classified) preliminary reports are disquieting.
The waters of Chenokee Creek, the Little Jay River and the
Allegheny Reservoir are heavily contaminated with radioactive isotopes, "hot" elements, including plutonium, which is a
deadly poison as well as radioactive, cesium, strontium, etc.

Studies of the reservoir indicate it is heavily contaminated,
though it is so far thought that it may continue to be used,
owing to the dilution of that water by added waters from
other sources than the radioactive river.

To date, the policy has been to halt all use of contaminated waters and all entry of animals or persons into those
waters *above the reservoir*. The reason given is "an uniden-

tified bacterium or virus." In view of the certainty of large-scale panic if the true situation (radioactive and toxic plutonium content) were known, this long-planned "substitute hazard" has been given as the "real" cause for the widespread prohibition.

Unfortunately, not all citizens in the region are satisfied by the official announcement. Apparently several persons have evaded the guards along the waterway and have made amateurish but damaging radiation counts. Some of them have been arrested and held (on various counts, such as trespassing, malicious intent to cause civil disturbance, etc.). Such published claims as appeared have been refuted as "utterly in error," "irresponsible," "wild-eyed" and "crackpot." The guards have been increased to a degree where it is hoped further troubles of the above sort will be impossible.

Meanwhile, a total of 139 miles of waterways are of varying degrees of hazard. Some eleven hundred square miles of farming and village territory is in the blockaded region.

No effective countermeasures are possible.

The over-all hazards cannot be expected to diminish to safe radiation levels until (and unless) heavy runoff in the next spring carries away sufficient detritus to effect relief.

In that case, however, the hot runoff may make the reservoir unusable and for a currently indeterminable period.

RECOMMENDATIONS:

It is the conviction of my associates and of the majority of the AEC—and they are supported in their views by several top executives of power corporations and reactor installations, some of whom, I understand, are personal friends of yours, Mr. President—that the facts of this serious and continuing situation be suppressed *permanently*. A presidential broadcast is urged to shore up this policy. However, in my view the simple fact is that *the national reactor program is in trouble.*

115

The Administration is facing disastrous consequences if present ruses are penetrated. Immediate and full candor would prevent a new "credibility gap."

THE HARLEM MATTER:

The Harlem River is, actually, a tidal cut at the northern end of Manhattan connecting the waters of Long Island Sound and the East River with the Hudson River.

The Harlem River has for many years been "off limits" for swimming, bathing, etc. It is heavily polluted and has been for decades, by sewage, garbage, industrial effluents and the like. However, it is impossible to prevent swimmers, teenage boys and younger children especially, from swimming in the river. The already overwhelmed New York Police force cannot provide adequate manpower to police the "river" and halt forays into this turgid, foul-smelling but cool and tempting sewer.

At its northern entry into the Hudson near Spuyten Duyvil ("Spitting Devil") a vast turbulence is a characteristic phenomenon, and though the swift and unpredictable current has caused many drownings, the fact is taken as a challenge by many illegal swimmers. This wide and circling current has had the unanticipated effect of concentrating hot isotopes in the area, with the result that several scores of the so-called "Harlem Boys" have been made exceedingly ill and twelve, so far, have died, owing to a "mysterious" and complex affliction not yet attributed to what will soon, certainly, be found the real cause: radiation burns and sickness with some mortality.

This, again, is caused in an odd manner, not unlike that of the Great Valley area, reported above.

Briefly, the power reactors originally installed on the Hudson (Indian Point), and doubled in size in the late 1960s with other reactors now operational upriver, permit low-level radioactive wastes to enter the Hudson via coolant outflow and by low-level waste effluent. This regular and standard practice is relatively safe and causes as a rule no volume or radioactive buildup of an officially "unacceptable" amount. "Thermal pollution," the massive plant effluent of water coolant, at a temperature higher than the river carrying it away, does raise the downstream net temperature of such rivers with various changes in and/or harm to the fish and other life forms in these rivers, but is officially still classified as a "non-hazard."

The Hudson, however, is tidal. The vast coolant flow entering the Hudson does not, therefore, run at a constant rate and in near total volume into the Atlantic. Tides back it up. As a consequence, part of the radioactive fraction in the coolant falls with sediment to the bottom of the river. Here it accumulates.

If the sedimentation rate were uniform for the entire river below the entry point of the faintly "hot" water, many, many years would still pass before any resultant radiation problem would be even imaginable. However, owing to downstream current and to tidal backing, to the irregular formation of bottom muck and to the variable and not predictable circling currents in the river, the waste accumulation is *not* evenly deposited.

Largely owing to the special and freakish currents off Spuyten Duyvil, it has recently been shown that fairly extensive areas at the surface of the water, and including the Harlem River "mouth," can and do become dangerously radioactive as deeper "hot spots" are churned up by the peculiar, local turbulence. Their occasional but random and unpredictable radiation levels become, not infrequently, sufficient to make even a half hour of bodily exposure harmful. Any unlucky second and third exposure to such "hot boils" will cause severe exposure with radio burns, sickness, even death.

The power interests, again, are using their influence to try to keep the matter quiet. So far it involves, largely, a small number of slum kids, mostly Negro and Puerto Rican. That accounts for the fact that the story has received no public attention. Thus far radiation burn cases and fatalities have been confined to three hospitals. All persons aware of the actual cause of the illness and death have been sworn to silence, and have been fed by AEC representatives with an ingenious cover story to ensure secrecy.

The official recommendation here is that the policy of silence continue. It is suggested that if you, Mr. President, agree to make an all-networks broadcast about the situation in the New York and Pennsylvania area, code name "Hot Water," you might also refer to this second matter, "Pickle." By telling the AEC cover story it is thought you would divert suspicion, if any, of the radioactive cause of "Hot Water."

Having offered the majority-sustained advice, and having to the best of my ability presented in lay terms the basic facts of both very complex situations, and having offered my resignation, always open to your decision in any event, I wish to repeat my personal counsel as a scientist, an American citizen and a dutiful, conscientious servant of your Administration.

The American public is under severe and constant stress owing to known disasters and odd ecological reports. With the rapid increase of nuclear reactors under the rush program presumably demanded by electric power demands, there is bound to be an increase in planning, design, construction and operating faults. To date, the many and increasing numbers of minor nuclear accidents have been effectively belittled or even hushed up. The two now under consideration involve a far larger number of victims and a much wider area than any past mishaps. Others of far greater magnitude are probable, not open to concealment by whatever "cover yarns" or policing may be used.

Sooner or later these nuclear hazards will be known.

In such an event the Administration will be open to a fitting accusation as unreliable, even dishonest. This would insure political death. A detailed and true admission of both events would be welcomed by an already atom-alarmed public and also would doubtless serve to save lives of otherwise *still endangered* people in the contaminated areas.

8. Editorial Addendum: the Results

What happened? Did the President follow the majority counsel? His aides arranged for a half hour on the networks two evenings later so he could have time to study the problem. But the decision was taken from the Chief Executive's hands before air time. A group of leading nuclear physicists had been quietly organized some months earlier to keep a watch for just such radioactive accidents as these two, with a view to reporting them if any were kept secret. The day after the Ovoth memo reached the White House for a second time these scientists released to all media the major facts of *both* the Great Valley and the Harlem spills.

The story created a national uproar, of course. Every nuclear reactor was compelled to shut down for restudy. Unfortunately, the mood of mass outrage did not last. Brownouts, blackouts and electric rationing reversed the "safety above all" response, and in a few weeks the reactors were started up with a government-industry pledge that "the study would continue and the safety measures would be taken while the plants were operational," an actual impossibility.

That sort of reversal in behavior typified a dominant form of reaction by the people at risk—one of countless self-destructive acts which seem incomprehensible now. It must be remembered, however, that not one adult in a thousand in America or any other modern nation had the knowledge and the intellectual capacity to assess those disasters and their causes in a realistic manner. The people could not even tell whom to believe. They weren't able to *know for sure* that their demands were mistaken. They had been told as much and in scores of categories, from 1970 onward. But a housewife denied current for her washer-drier and forced to do her laundry by hand was ready to accept the sleaziest promise that her electricity could be safely restored, even when the experts said the opposite, because the politicians and power company spokesmen offered her lies. And a broker, a banker, a clergyman or a city mayor would be as readily persuaded that existing facilities, sewer and treatment plants, say, would suffice for some years, when the epidemic passed over and when they found taxes would be raised heavily if future epidemics were to be forestalled by new installations.

Thus the air became fouler, the dust it bore loaded with more dire particles, the water on the land grew more putrid and poisoned like the waters beneath it, and the sea drank in an ever less assimilable load of lethal garbage while the dry land accumulated an ever heavier burden of biocidal agents. The people in great majorities prevailed and the industries serving them stimulated their senseless choices as did their elected leaders, in the main. A technological society cannot persist as a democracy unless the people in their majority understand both technology and ecology well enough to know what they are doing.

9. *Three Perplexing Occurrences*

Mrs. Edith Greetlan looked in the hall mirror and saw, without her broken glasses, and the more dimly owing to the mirror's failing function, that her hair would do. She never went down to the mailbox without that assurance. It was brown hair and abundant, long, and to the old woman important because she thought of it as her "best feature." Perhaps it was, though it was duller than she imagined, dirty, and smelled like the dirty hair of an old person. Still, she'd managed to coil and heap it in a form not truly the one of youth and middle age but near enough; it is difficult to do such things when arthritis makes it painful to raise one's good arm head-high. But the turret hairdo didn't cant and wouldn't if she kept standing as straight as possible.

"Ready for our walk, Tumsie?"

A medium-sized mongrel, Tumsie was such a pooch as old ladies in small towns on welfare can obtain from the pound at no cost. A brownish, blackish, gray-streaked long-short-haired animal, a once friendly puppy, a long-time resigned adult and now a sad but not unclever senior citizen, Tumsie would have stuck to his mistress through thick and thin if there'd been any thick.

"Maybe," Edith said with what she felt was brightness, "we'll get more than the regular check. Maybe we'll hear from Verna. She usually writes to her poor old mother every month, doesn't she? And remind me. I must find the Scotch tape and fix those specs. Otherwise, how'll I read Verna's letter?"

On the porch in the bright morning Edith looked up Locust Street and down, shading her eyes with a cranky hand, and noting with pleasure the tall hollyhocks growing near the old fence.

"Look at those beauties! Pink and white and red and them raspberry-splotched ones must of been a mix from last year. Mighty pretty, eh, Tumsie?"

Tumsie grinned, panted faintly as if to get a lead on the warm morning and its sure, present demand for panting. So Tumsie apparently thought. He thought, in fact, that he had things pretty well arranged, now that the Conover family with all those kids had moved into widow Leesen's place, two doors down Locust, sloppy people with lots of garbage and loose lids on the cans, so even an old, medium-sized dog could get to the contents. And that was important for Tumsie since Mrs. Greetlan was given, lately, to thinking she'd fed him today when it had been yesterday. The Conovers were disposable-dinner folks and partial to the new Master Mix-frozen Foods which were said to contain all the rare elements and vitamins human beings required as well as the necessary proteins, starches and fats.

"Defrost, heat, serve, eat and chuck the leftovers, tray and all, in the garbage," every package said. Tumsie had had nearly a month of Conover supplement and, though Mrs. Greetlan hadn't noticed, he was getting fat, or bloated, or both, and was doing much more panting for much less cause than ever before.

Tumsie waited while the hollyhock inspection went on and then followed as the widow tettered down the five wooden front steps, using the handrail on the left because the right-hand one had fallen into the ferns. Once on the front walk, Edith moved steadily from the wild hedge of privet and weeds, where the fence had fallen and pickets still protruded, to the rusting, once galvanized mailbox.

She creaked it open and saw one envelope, Verna's. Not another. No welfare check.

"Lordy, lordy," she muttered. "Must be the mail is worse'n ever." She turned to Tumsie. "Plenty of leftovers to tide us through tonight, dear."

Still hopeful, she opened Verna's letter, but there was nothing in that either. It said, though she couldn't read it then:

"Sorry, Mom, about this one. I'm broke. Leo has been on a toot for ten days. I can't locate him but I'm scared to call the cops. I wish I could send the usual bill but—there it is."

122

Crying tears that felt dry, the widow moved slowly back up the walk.

She realized the sun was hot.

It took time to get up on the veranda and there Tumsie stopped.

"Want to stay out and make your numbers?" she asked.

The dog panted an affirmative, so Edith went in and sat down in the one comfortable front-room chair. It was cool and quiet there.

Tumsie's plan was delayed when he spotted a man coming by on foot. He sauntered to the place where no gate was and looked at him with a murky doubt, too hot to bark, too old to back up any barking. The man had a cigar in his mouth and as he drew near he struck a match on his pants to relight it. A motorcycle passed, bellowing, with boy and girl locked together.

The man, a renegade priest yet soured on life, didn't wave out the match because he spotted Tumsie. A dog-hater, he tossed the match at the mongrel, not with any expectation of effect, just to be mean. And at that moment Tumsie's recent feeling of flatulence became a promise of potential easement. He broke wind, the match fell behind him and he blew up.

The debauched ex-priest stared a second and then ran, till he was well up Locust.

Edith, of course, heard the odd sound, not a bang, more a wet ploop! She wondered and, later, when she thought Tumsie would be ready, and when she felt sufficiently rested to be able, she went out, wearing mended bifocals, and called. Then she saw the bloody mess on the walk where the gate had been, and all around. She remembered the motorcycle and was sure some kid, demon and fiend, had tossed a cherry bomb. Or a bigger firecracker of some sort. Tumsie must have grabbed it.

She got a shovel and buried what she could of Tumsie in the ferns where the ground was fairly soft. Then she went back to the front room and the chair and sat down. All alone now.

Time passed and she didn't feel hungry or sleepy.

Then she went to sleep.

In the night, something gave inside her skull. For several seconds of half-awareness she knew that a "ploop!" had happened to her.

They found her eight days later when the new Baptist minister reluctantly tried to call. Before he even rapped on the door he caught the odor that eddied through the place where there had been screening and where there was only a frame now. He went right in then. He found his "worst fear" was correct—and so the reluctant call turned out to be a really exciting adventure for Reverend Moselett.

The second episode concerned Father Trentchel, pastor emeritus of the Elk Hill Episcopal church, St. Anson's, a self-important man who, like Tumsie, had recently been aware of abdominal discomfort—gas, he called it. He did not associate these unpleasant symptoms with the diet that Emily, his daughter and housekeeper, had recently been giving him. For at the supermarket Emily had discovered the new Master Mixfrozen Foods, so cheap, so tasty, so easy. It was a pity Father Trentchel didn't put two and two together, for one day he eased his flatulence by breaking wind as he was standing with his back to a blazing fire and, again like Tumsie, he blew up. When Emily, alarmed by the noise, ran into the room, his entrails were running down the walls.

As any sophisticated person could guess, the peculiar death of a dog and a rector led to no official interest. But the exploding of a sow brought in the experts. The sow was a beauty. Her owner had a name as a pig breeder. He was also a penurious man, so when he found that the local Mighty-Mart would sell him over-aged products for a small price he fed this particular animal on the goods, mostly Master Mix-frozen Foods, which had a comparatively short life even in deep freezers, and tended to brown around the edges. His meanness was shortsighted, for on his way back from the Idaho Center Counties Fair, where Nellie had won the blue ribbon, he went too close to a fair booth where two luau lights were burning just as Nellie, like Tumsie and Father Trentchel before her, broke wind.

Nellie's flying head smashed her owner's skull. Both deaths were instant. Three people were injured by whizzing porker parts, and a man from Boise had a fatal heart attack as he raced to see what had exploded—and then saw, more or less.

Two veterinaries on the scene investigated Nellie's residue, for pigs were important in the region and a blue-ribbon winner was valuable. And here, at last, the laws of chance brought some results. The dead breeder's other hogs were taken temporarily by neighbors and relatives. Three sows went to a cousin, whose son, Ripler Cleeby, a chemistry major at Idaho State, was at home at the time with a broken leg. The young man heard all about the exploding porker, of course, since it was regional wonder number one for weeks. He also noted the bloated condition of the sows given temporary care by his dad.

Young Ripler, bored and restless, found something to do when he decided that whatever caused the bulge in the boarding hogs must also have caused the strange explosion. Clandestinely, he managed to syphon off from a doped sow a glass jug of the gas and found, with a first small-sample test, that it did indeed explode when ignited. From that discovery, tracking down the cause provided the youth with exciting weeks while his leg mended.

He found and verified the fact that Master Mixfrozen Foods, when allowed to defrost and stand for some considerable time, produced by a complex fermentation process and other chemical reactions a constant intestinal bubbling, and that the bubbles largely consisted of free oxygen and methane, in about equal parts. Some free hydrogen was also a by-product of the foodstuff when processed in the mammalian intestine. In short, the stale product, when consumed, brewed a very explosive mixture.

Under pledge of secrecy, Ripler confided in the local vet, who, when he found that the situation was just what the younger man claimed, in his turn swore Ripler to secrecy and got off a letter to the president of Master Mixfrozen Foods. With the letter he sent a copy of their long, chemical equations. Three days passed before the president phoned. . . .

Master Mixfrozen Foods took advertising space in the press as well as TV network commercials to announce the withdrawal of its frozen dinners and their immediate removal from retail shelves. The reason—that is, the one given so clearly, conscientiously and with such apologetic fanfare—was that one person in every five thousand "reacted" (to a federally approved flavoring material in the dinners) with a light rash and a low-grade, one-day fever. MMF wasn't going to risk even that tiny incidence of minor discomfort, not that reliable, economical, tasty, popular company, old MMF, no sireee! A new line would be available everywhere as soon as company experts, dieticians, food testers and other scientists had changed the formula, and the new product would be even tastier, even more nourishing and only one or two cents more expensive while remaining the best bargain of its kind. When the new product was ready a second advertising campaign told the world, and the demand for it was three times the original figure.

Thus the truth was never widely known, even inside the

corporation. And the fact that Ripler Cleeby and a wily country vet later divided a million dollars was believed to be owing to a drug they'd worked out together, patented and sold to a large manufacturer of animal medicaments.

This relation of the truth in *The Manhattanite*'s "Annals of Ecology" will not cause any unease. Both the gentlemen who so gently blackmailed the food company have passed away. And it was by pure happenstance that the author of this trilogy came upon the first two accounts, that of the ill-fated Tumsie and the sudden, sad expansion of Father Trent-chel. Master Mixfrozen Foods have not been marketed since their main factories were destroyed two years ago in the Wilmington disaster. The corporate records were kept, however, in a warehouse in Philadelphia and these records were carefully examined by clerks at the behest of stockholders after the loss of the plant. In a "confidential" file maintained under lock and key by the then president, two yellowed local newspaper clippings were found. They reported the widow's demise and the delayed finding of her body, along with a note about the witnessing of her dog's odd death from swallowing gunpowder anonymously reported by a letter to the editor. A second clipping from a suburban gossip weekly described Father Trentchel's end owing to "fall lightning" that came down his chimney and exploded, as such rare form of lightning often does.

The clerk showed the clippings to several persons and ultimately this writer heard of them. After lengthy investigation he was able to piece together the foregoing. While it may not seem to fit into the "Annals of Ecology," it nevertheless is germane in the sense that other, not dissimilar accidents, on vast scales, have marked the widespread consumption of insufficiently tested additives in the modern foodstuff of man and beast. Instances of long-delayed and widespread illness, and even mass death, from such causes have often made headlines which will be recalled by all readers.

The American public, nowadays, continues to consume, and to feed pets and livestock, victuals containing hundreds upon hundreds of exotic materials, none present in natural foods, and all added for exclusively commercial ends, so we are still, in spite of the many federal claims of "tightening up" food and drug scrutiny, liable to some unexpected, private, family or mass surprise such as exploding, under certain circumstances. Here, then, a still timely word to the wise, of which there are none, for who has his puddings chemically analyzed and who can say what yesterday's biscuits will bring on, twenty years hence?

A. J. LIMKIN

10. Mrs. Meller's Farm

Tommyhawk Creek in Nebraska flows into Snake Creek, which empties into the Niobrara River, a tributary of the Missouri. Tommyhawk Creek is 9.3 miles in length and courses through a bleak and rocky land, ruined by ancient glaciers for any important human use. Part of this hinterland is thinly wooded but trees do not do particularly well there, and part of it is covered with grasses, weeds, shrubs and vine. There are hollows, ice-dug, where postglacial soil has been collected and then deposited by the seasonal winds and by rain and as the result of erosion. In some of them the prairie grass that once supported bison herds grows abundantly. Tommyhawk Creek winds through such places, and in a few it forms small ponds that are known to ducks and used in their migratory flights.

A few homesteaders of the early nineteenth century occupied this poor region and ruins of many of their domiciles can be seen. Most of the second and third generations went elsewhere, and in 1950 there were only three families still on the Tommyhawk. By 1979, widow Meller was the sole person left on the creek, where she lived by herself in a dilapidated, paintless but sturdy house her grandfather had built. The nearest neighbor was more than two miles away. Mrs. Meller did not mind. She'd been born and raised in the house, and during her married life had returned with her husband for summer vacations. Bryant Meller was an amateur geologist of sufficient competence to have made several small contributions to technical journals. He had also done considerable hunting and taught that art to his wife, one he practiced as an economy measure, for food, not as a sport.

Ulla Johnston Meller enjoyed solitude now that she had retired from her profession of teacher. She did not mind being snowbound in winter and she did not suffer from the intense hot spells of summer. At the age of sixty-seven in 1979 she felt self-sufficient, placid, thankful to the Lord for having the outdoors and the lifetime security of a small pension plus the annuity her husband had accumulated for her. She appreciated a kind of freedom and tranquillity which had almost disappeared as an American characteristic long since.

She knew every square rod of the surrounding land in a ten-mile radius. She was interested in wild flowers and in the local fauna. Almost unconsciously, she had absorbed much of her late husband's geological lore. She was sharp and observant if solitary, and so, slightly "peculiar" to the minds of those who knew her and had known her all her life.

She was a tall and rather gaunt woman with a long neck and a smallish head which she carried at a raised angle, as if her attention were usually on some object above eye level. She had a heavy frame and yet small-boned features, brilliant gray eyes, wide apart above prominent cheekbones, and a leathery complexion. She might have seemed an "American Gothic" type on first glance but a second would dismiss that thought. Her movements were squirrel-quick and as sure. Her natural expression was pleasant, and her eyes very intelligent. Her voice was soft and cultured, her laugh infrequent, but musical. She was, in a rare degree, the ideal woman, even the ideal *person* to make her strange discovery in the spring of 1979. Perhaps no individual within a hundred miles would have noticed, as she did, the anomaly. And nobody else, having realized after a few days that it was just that, an oddity—nobody in that part of Nebraska—would have continued to observe the unusual if then unspectacular finding, and also take notes of the precise developments that occurred in the months ahead.

She had taken a walk along Tommyhawk Creek in mid-May with no more purpose than to revisit wild flowers beginning to bloom and to enjoy the green-scented balm of the warm morning.

Coming to a small pond into and from which Tommyhawk Creek ran, a pond of about an acre and the nearest of three to her house (which was six miles upstream from the brook's juncture with Snake Creek), Ulla stopped when she saw that a greenish-brown "slime" had bloomed in the upper end of the still pond water. She, of course, knew it was not slime but alga, a single-celled green plant. That day she merely noticed the growth, a balloon-shaped bushel of something she had never seen before.

Three days later when she discovered her Jersey cow, Reneta, had wandered, Ulla sought the animal in the likeliest place—at the pondside where it would be tearing up green, young shoots. As she caught the animal's halter she saw, with some surprise, that half the pond was now green-gold owing to the proliferation of the alga. She was aware that under ideal conditions many such primitive plants multiplied rapidly. She knew that the upper three miles of the creek drained several abandoned farms where houses had burned or tumbled down and nude chimneys stood, places where barns had collapsed or burned, too, so that rich manure piles were slowly eroded and rain-rivulet-carried into the creek. The ponds supported considerable fish populations, and she occasionally caught a few fish for her table. Even so, she felt this swift bloom was a bit excessive.

Not many days later she began her notes.

On May 21 the one-acre pond was solid with green "slime" which was not slimy to the touch but felt like fine wet netting. The stuff bulked above the surface more than a foot, and there it had turned golden brown. This portion was, plainly, dead and the green below alone was alive.

By June 5 the stuff had been carried into the two ponds downstream and all three small lakes were choked apparently to their bottoms with the growth. Several times recently she had donned her late husband's waders and, with a pitchfork, walked out into the mass and shoveled it about. She had found that a good many minnows and a few fish of eating size had been trapped in the fast-multiplying stuff and died there. The rest must have fled.

Experimenting with a sample in her rain barrel, she found the dead material floated without any lift from below. And in two more days her first pond and the two downstream, with most of the open, running water between them, were filled with dead or living algal cells. She was, then, fairly sure that the phenomenon was at least rare.

She realized that if this species could grow at such a rate there could get to be unguessable miles of choked brooks and ponds before the distant first frost. It would spoil fishing wherever it grew so densely. It would compel those few people downstream who watered stock to keep scraping open drinking places. And if it ever got as far as Beligman, a town on the Niobrara River which took its "city" water from that source, it surely would mess up things at the plant there.

The evening after she came to that conclusion, Ulla sat down and thought carefully about what action she should— or maybe shouldn't—take.

Her late husband had known many geologists and she had become acquainted with several of them. They would certainly know whom to give the information to: an algologist, if such a rare specialist could be found on the faculty of any university. Thinking of an "algologist" upset her a bit. Ulla hated to be made a fool of and what she thought was a novelty in the plant world could easily be something familiar.

She decided to wait a little longer.

Perhaps that was unfortunate. Possibly, even probably, it would not have mattered. Patrolling the creek and ponds now, she couldn't see any water but just two miles of solid golden-brown dead cells piled in trillions above the green living plants. This condition moved downstream to a long reach of the creek that was quite deep and fairly wide so that the flow in it was imperceptible in summer. It therefore was comparable to one of the ponds.

Here, soon, a change occurred. In a few days Ulla noted and clearly described that difference in her record book:

"As the green or living network of this plant enters the slow and deep area, its crust of a foot or two of dead plants riding above water level, it begins to turn pale, and soon the green or living material dies."

Later notes describe that process further: "Everything in the slow, deep channel is dead. And what still fills the stream and ponds above seems to be turning pale (the green stuff) too. Very glad I didn't call for experts. Looks as if the whole, gigantic 'bloom' is ending."

A month later she wrote, "Can't find a single patch of

green (living) material anywhere. All of it dead, golden brown and floating high, but nothing has passed beyond the channel, as a series of boulders block up that stretch by forming a barrier across the channel's end. That is what made the deep-water place. Only in high water does the creek pour over this natural dam, though it trickles beneath it always. So the show is over! It's over, except for the fact that, in and above the natural dam, there's a bank-to-bank, thick mountain of the dead stuff. So far, it hasn't rotted. It doesn't smell badly, just like woodsy soil or peat.

"Under my magnifying glass I can see that each cell, when dead, has formed a hard coating around itself, one easily felt when you rub a bit between the fingers. The dead plants are like minute, spherical, high-floating nuts, with hard shells, and inside them is a little fluid and the rest air, or maybe gas. When the fall rains come this will, I hope, be carried away—as it still chokes the stream and pond from well above the water to near the bottom, thick and slippery and tacky, sticking together pretty strongly."

In August a two-day series of thunderstorms and near cloudbursts greatly raised the creek and, Ulla observed, a fair amount of this odd debris broke away and went over the natural dam, downstream, in chunks and clots that increasingly broke up in fast-running stretches of the brook. The "fall rains" that year were abundant, and by the time ice started to form on the ponds as well as on the long, slow-current stretch, most of the dead material had been washed downstream. After the ice became thick, Ulla observed that the fish which had left the area were returning.

She could not have been expected to carry her inquiry or even her guesses any further. She had no means to identify the alga as a mutant. She assumed it had used up whatever it was fertilized by, and had also completed its cycle. Neither she nor even her geologist-hobbiest husband had discovered, in the "long, slow stretch of deep channel," a mineral spring that flowed in from underwater. She could not be expected to realize that the chemical change in the channel water, together with nutrient exhaustion, had stopped the progress of the strange plant above that point.

Much less could she, or any layman, have imagined that the living plants which perished in the mineral-altered area had left in the bottom sediments billions of spores, and that many of these were new mutant forms which would and could produce plants able to survive the minerals fatal to the parent stock.

The year 1980 was rung in during a blizzard.

[Editor's note: Although this section, Part II, has been confined to events in the seventies, a brief exception seems appropriate here.]

The winter of 1979–80 was marked by heavy snows in this part of Nebraska. When the thaws came, they were torrential, with the result that several times the average annual load of fertile material entered Tommyhawk Creek above Ulla's place. In May the bloom began again. Also a bloom of the double mutant occurred in and below the channel with the mineral spring.

Once Ulla discovered the alga had passed the natural dam and was multiplying for a mile downstream she decided she must take action.

Feeling foolish, she nevertheless composed a letter to one of the professors of geology she'd met, Professor Wayne Collet, a very nice man at Nebraska State. Ten days later her letter was answered by the arrival at her farm of a small, middle-aged, red-haired, slope-shouldered man who introduced himself as Dr. Elgin Peterkin, of Kansas State, sniffing, every three or four words.

"I happened to be doing a visiting lecture tour at Nebraska

and Collet showed me your letter. I'm an algologist, and I found your word interesting but not, say, *astounding*. Just—interesting. Perhaps you'd lead me—"

Ulla did.

Dr. Peterkin had various jars and bottles in his car trunk and, after he had scouted a half mile of green-gold clogged creek and ponds, he filled these containers with samples. In that process he seemed to resent Ulla's presence. He kept muttering disjointed bits about other "similar blooms," leading her to assume that her strange finding wasn't all that unusual. He mentioned the "Sabre Lake explosion" for one, said the alga was a "close relative of the stoneworts" and so on, dampening Ulla's confidence in her boldness—though she had thought that, on his first view of the mess, he had been excited but not wanting that to show. She did not like him, really.

He refused an invitation to lunch rather brusquely and, before driving off with his samples, made it clear that this "local phenomenon," his words, had set him on a "wild goose chase." He also suggested that she keep the situation quiet as the bloom was "self-limiting" and any tale she spread around would only cause needless worry and end up making her the butt of ridicule and the agent of starting annoying, unsound rumors.

It was not then known to Ulla that the scientist, a mediocrity, had twice humiliated himself by erroneous conclusions he had caused to appear in learned journals. That double blunder had cost him a full professorship and violently damaged a very tender ego. This strange and, the man knew, unprecedented finding filled him with the desire to report it first and so gain the credit. He deliberately miscued the widow in order to gain time in which to study this novel alga and then announce the discovery as his own.

In that, he succeeded.

A very late and record-breaking frost a few days after his visit set back the algal bloom before it reached Snake Creek. In early August the widow found that the scum was growing again but it was a cold summer and a September frost, not unusual in the region, once more killed back the fast-multiplying "stonewort" relative.

Meanwhile, Peterkin, back at Kansas State U., grew the alga in jars, then barrels, and then, at the end of June, furtively tossed a green handful into a farm pond he had driven around the near countryside to locate. It duly became clotted and puffed up with the plant and its growth rate staggered the algologist. At that point he mailed his already prepared paper to the *Journal of Algological Biology* with photographs and notes of other botanists and biologists confirming what the monograph stated. This document was published in the fall quarterly issue. By then the farm pond bloom had been winter-killed after its ruin of the farmer's fish-culture pond. The deposit of cold-resistant spores in the choked pond were carried next spring over the earthen dam, under a highway, to a brook and thence into the Cinnamon Run, which paralleled the road.

In the following summer widow Meller read a report in the Cedar Rapids *News-Enterprise* of a green-scum plague that was spreading in a considerable area of Kansas. That it was *her* mutant alga she didn't immediately guess. It was not until mid-August, when the green, living plant avalanche with its golden-brown topping clogged fifty miles of the Niobrara below Sears Falls, that the widow realized the Kansas "water plague" was indirectly owing to her concern in the matter. By then, the "Green Slime War" was national news, and as a result Ulla grimly fought a war of her own. Conscience told her she could have acted a year before she did, and that she could have alerted more scientists than that pinheaded Peterkin—now claiming entire credit for the alga's discovery and lending his name to it besides, *Peterkinsis*. But sheer stubbornness fought against Ulla's conscience. She'd done what seemed most sensible the whole time and the best thing to do now was forget it and try to ignore the news stories and TV pictures.

The origin of the distant and much-altered stonewort relative, *Peterkinsis*, was demonstrated by a brilliant young biologist, D. D. Wilson. His imaginative and resourceful efforts to that end elicited a tale which, even then, was becoming a ritual. For the horrendous green pest was virtually handmade by man. That synthesis began after the great public brouhaha in 1970 over the creation, stockpiling, storage and transport of chemicals and other materials designed for "germ" or "biological" and poison-gas warfare.

Nixon ordered a halt to all such diabolical effort excepting what was required for defense against those weapons. To create in the laboratory a defense, whether against bacteria, viruses or poison gases, it is first necessary to obtain, breed or fabricate the living or inorganic "weapon." So the Nixon fiat did not stop the ongoing experiments with such lethal agencies. But there was so much continuing outcry, by "environmentalists," against similar war agents, the "defoliants" used in Vietnam to strip jungles of leaves and thus render the foe naked, that a certain part of the continuing research into exotic weapons (and possible counters) was transferred to other federal bureaus and the work was mingled with other projects as disguise.

For the motive of concealment the Department of Agriculture erected a very extensive research facility in the remote, little-populated southwest corner of Cherry County, Nebraska. Ten square miles of wasteland were triple fenced with guarded openings only for a new road and rail spur. To this posted quadrangle were brought a large number of scientists, aides, engineers and others, all of them having been cleared by the FBI and sworn to secrecy.

The fact that a dozen discoveries of benefit to man came from this "plant and insect research center" is beside the present point. What is of moment is the work of Johann Pollenni Schuckebber, a world-famous algologist. His project was so secret that only his superiors in Washington knew its purpose. That was to develop a strain of algae which would do, if seeded in enemy waters, just what Ulla's actually did do.

Starting with five hundred species of algae, Dr. Schuckebber created mutant strains in thousands, using chemicals of the many varieties then known to induce gene changes, as well as a cobalt source, and other less ordinary means. He developed several strains, species, perhaps, with hard, enduring cell membranes. But none of his long lines of altered plants had all the properties he sought, and his work ceased with his death in 1976 from a heart attack at his benches.

No one was found to replace him, which terminated the project. The Nebraska center was crowded for space, and the research director was relieved to get Schuckebber's many large rooms. These were cleared and the thousands of glass containers of algae mutants were disposed of.

Inside the fenced and guarded compound, as well as beyond its boundaries, there were many small "soda lakes," as alkaline ponds were locally called. These had served Dr. Schuckebber perfectly for the disposal of his myriads of mutant colonies that were unpromising. The caustic waters had speedily killed the plants. So the director simply ordered that the useless strains on hand be dumped in the same manner, along with the unwanted residue of the chemicals which the old man had used to cause mutations.

What did not occur to the superintendent in charge of the crew clearing out the laboratories and plant-culture chambers was, simply, that one of the several ponds near the buildings differed. A clear and rather deep-looking pool, set in a hollow, it was not alkaline but fresh. Owing to that slight error of judgment, the work of Dr. Schuckebber went on posthumously and untended. When, out of it, came a "slime" that covered the pond and took over the nutrients of other forms so they perished, the fact was called to the attention of the director, who immediately had it sprayed with three different biocides. Afterward the bloom died and sank since it was still almost wholly in its green phase.

D. D. Wilson was able, however, to recover from the banks of that pond several hundreds of the waterproof, hard, floatable, dead form of the organism. The sprays used at the director's orders had effectively exterminated the alga. They were not, however, sprays that could be applied to waters people drank, or swam in, or even dunked a hand in.

Wilson's reasoning about the transport of the species to Tommyhawk Creek was logical even if not susceptible of proof. The bloom at the secret research center occurred at a time when many species of birds were migrating north, including many kinds of waterfowl. Occasionally, some few such birds would drop down and spend awhile drinking from and feeding in the only fresh-water pond within several miles. So it was entirely probable that one such bird had picked up on its legs or feathers a bit of the "slime" and that, on a next descent in some upper pool of the Tommyhawk, the live matter had been washed off, thus initiating the great surge that came later.

Wilson accounted for the time gap by proving that the final mutant form of the plague had occurred upstream from Ulla's farm. He found the ancestral form from which it emerged as the very sort the old biologist doubtless had hoped to develop. By the time Wilson announced his triumph of research and deduction, however, people in general had little interest in how the breed came into being owing to their concern about the way it spread.

It did them little good—none, really—to know this menace, like many others, had been brought on man by himself.

11. A *Letter, a Document, a Memo, a Transcription*

LAMSON-WORLD PHARMACEUTICALS
LAMSON-WORLD TOWERS
DEARBORN PLAZA
CHICAGO, ILL.

July 2, 1979

Office of the President

Miles S. Smythe, Director
Foundation for Human Conservancy
Smythe Building
Fifth Avenue at 57th St.
New York, N.Y. 10022

Dear Miles:

Bill MacCall will hand you this letter as I don't know what would happen to me if it were found out in several places that I sent you the enclosed.

As you know, I've spent much of the past fifteen months working on the President's Special Commission on Water and Waste Futures. Enclosed is a copy of the synopsis of the final report which we are going to turn over to the Big Boy next week. A quite different report will be made public and Congress will get a third version, with some exceptions who'll see this one.

I tried to write a minority report and wasn't permitted to. I'm expected at a big and very quiet conclave of my business peers to discuss this enclosed brilliant plan and I shall try to take some recordings, covertly, sending you the gist of anything that might interest you.

I know I can trust your discretion. I have betrayed my top-level colleagues and plan to go on doing so. But this filthy and sneaky scheme turned my stomach. I don't know how to be loyal to treacherous bastards—traitors, really, if this project could be put over, and, it might!

As ever,
ROBERT L. LAMSON

TOP SECRET
PRESIDENTIAL EYES ONLY
BY PRESIDENTIAL REQUEST CODE NAME *Cataract Whitewater*
TO BE BURNED WHEN READ

SYNOPSIS
Herewith. Full report if requested.

NOTE
Final from Com. W W F

Copy Number One. Copies extant, XXX 23. No date, no signatures, one abstention, unanimous.

Urgent.

Confirmation for Meeting as Suggested, Requested.

1. In spite of federal, state, city and private funds employed for the improvement of the polluted condition of all but a very few minor rivers, lakes and watersheds in the nation, the levels of pollution are rising universally and in degrees everywhere far greater than the control efforts.

2. By 1985 or 1986 it will not be possible for some eighteen major urban regions to continue to draw on current sources

for municipal water supplies. Different aspects of water use in different areas affect this situation. However, the basic and most common factor is this:

By the date noted the chlorine levels for purifying river and lake waters for drinking and other uses will have reached that point where additional chlorine will make the water not merely unpalatable but undrinkable, that is, medically and physically harmful. No economically feasible means to purify polluted water after that point is reached has been found or is likely to be, in the visible future.

In effect, by 1986 or *earlier*, an estimated 135,000,000 Americans will have to be provided with water from other sources or by some currently not envisaged method of treating the extant sources.

3. The Canadian watershed could furnish very pure water to middle USA if agreements were made and boring and other facilities were commenced in the very near future and urgently rushed to completion before the deadline.

4. Desalination by nuclear power is already effectively supplying potable water to coastal populations. Inland communities cannot be so supplied at a competitive cost.

5. In view of this situation, it is suggested that current federal, state and other policies be changed. Funds now being expended on or appropriated or budgeted for anti-pollution and water recovery might better be diverted to the enterprises suggested here, the massive diversion of Canadian waters with the additional development of facilities for conveying such added supplies into USA to areas now endangered.

6. Since the drainage basins of USA will be polluted to the point of non-usability in the short period here stated, it is suggested that the public be gradually acclimatized to the idea of using the natural drainage systems entirely for waste and effluent removal. While such use would gradually destroy

certain riparian values, many of those could be reconstituted when adequate fresh water from other sources was available.

7. A vital point here concerns industry as well as big-city, urban and other threatened persons. Were these various entities able to terminate current and demanded procedures for the purpose of water-source protection, sewage treatment, the costly disposal of toxic and other industrial wastes and affluents, the result would be a major tax cut and a major lowering of manufacturing costs of the Gross National Product.

8. It is the informed opinion of many of the most knowledgeable scientists in these fields that fully vented industrial waste would lessen or even destroy raw-sewage pollution in most areas. Where it did not, cheap chemical treatment would serve to inhibit bacterial growth and the like.

In effect, if the river systems of USA were to be made mass-effluent conveyers of all wastes and if other fresh-water sources were developed, channeled and expanded, a net saving to the nation would follow on a huge scale.

9. This change-over would, of course, be accompanied by many local and perhaps large-scale objections and other difficulties. These should be foreseen and planned for, prior to their occurrence.

OFFICE OF THE PRESIDENT:
MEMO
FROM: Him
TO: Miles
RE: . . . .

Miles!

The damned gadget I carried at this meeting made a spotty recording so I have had the tape transcribed, taken out a lot of repetitive stuff, and send you the gist, verbatim or as near to it as the recording plus my recall makes possible.

A few of the boys hadn't gotten inklings of what the secret confab was all about, and I thought nobody was going to make any important counterclaim till the wee hours when, as I note, the opposition really got busy. Not much of a dent made by them, tho. Most of us tycoons think always and only in terms of money and cannot think usefully by any other value system.

Your favorite antagonist, General Ranklin Snare Gode of the Army Engineer Corps, was present in mufti while reported in the press to be touring Brazil. *Everybody* at Saratoga had a cover story, except those who are regulars, baths or ponies.

Hope you can do something about this very secret but well-advanced piece of non-think *cum* lust by big industry. Hope you can also keep my part between us two. These colleagues are as serious as unprincipled.

I'm not any more keen to be the corpse in some "accident" than the next big shot.

Burtley B. Kelley chaired the President's Commission on Waste and Water Futures where I've been a nettle, as you know from my first letter. He got up this meeting with White House knowledge, again as I think I wrote. Everybody knows he's board chairman of the world's second biggest oil combine, D.D.M.E. and Solar. But he's also the quiet but main stockholder in the East-West Conglomerate, news to me! And that's about it. Best to all—Bob.

Here's Burtley Kelley's windup of a damned effective speech and presentation.

". . . and though I have seen a good deal of consternation on some of your faces, men, I think, to whom this concept is

144

unfamiliar, I have also realized that even those whom it first disturbed rapidly began to see its urban and industrial advantages. I'd like comments."

WHITE. *Big Steel.* "Something of the sort has been whispered around in my bailiwick. Not quite in the bold and extensive terms you set out, Burt. But I had a hunch about the aim of this gathering. So I made some rough estimates. My own company, allowed unrestricted use of river facilities for waste disposal, would save forty millions in new hardware. On our next four-year program. It would cut roughly eighty million a year from operating costs. And that is only for us. It would save the industry as a whole well above an annual billion. So, Burt, in my view, you have something."

BILLINGS. *Coal.* "I hardly need say what it would mean to us. The God damned states, federal authorities and Congress pass new laws regulating us every week, seems like. If you strip-mine here, you have to cover and beautify, for Christ's sake, the *tailings!* Yonder, acids have to be kept out of creeks and where do you dump *them?* So you haul millions of tons of wastes, that means for a hundred miles, from some mine heads. But how you going to sell the public on any such program? Not these days! Your industry threatens a duck, today, a sea gull, a damned violet—and you're dead!"

RANSON. *Copper, Silver, etc.* "Burt mentioned that our aggregate wastes would sterilize germs. Put all *our* mine, reduction-plant and smelter effluents into waterways and I can name five or six major rivers that wouldn't have a live germ for hundreds of miles."

WHITE. "Same for steel."

BLAKE. *Grain: Growers, Storage, Transport.* "It sounds fine to us for just us. Suppose it's done? Imagine every river and most major brooks and creeks loaded with industrial effluents added, raw, plus the sewage, untreated, of maybe two thirds of the population. Maybe more. All of us, I should think, can envisage the rivers at that point. No fish. No aquatic life at all. Brown. Slow-flowing. Not stinking if we can assume that end could be dealt with. But—chemical-smelling, say. Long stretches practically forbidden even for boating—too dangerous to fall into. All right. My question is, what happens if the nation does go for the scheme and then, once the money is spent, people reject the result? What then? We've got a national mess we made and we'll be expected to unmake. And how about side effects? I mean, suppose the grain belt rivers—and this is *my* territory—get to carry a load of industrial junk that'll evaporate, fog up the air, ruin crops along riverbanks for 'x' miles?"

COOPER. *Bulk Chemicals* (to the group). "Jeff Blake's assuming there won't be any prior studies of such potential hazards. He isn't assuming that any such potentials would be special, and subject to treatment. He doesn't realize that, in general, acids and alkalis will cancel out. Or think, by golly, of the fact that nearly every single acre-foot of such moving water will be oil-scummed, if not from industrial effluence, then from city wastes. Storm sewers. Such scums will tend to hold down evaporation of the—well, the messes—beneath. In fact, I'd nearly guarantee that this total-use idea would result in oil cover for so much of the water involved that we'd have almost no such problems as Jake has dreamed up."

(An hour later.)

WILLIS. *Electric Power.* "I haven't entered the utilities case because it is obvious. Several sides to it. I've been doodling some figures. One item. Some of the rivers will be caustic, or acid, chemically abrasive, anyway, to a degree that'll erode turbines and so on. Hydroelectric plants will suffer more—and

146

we're already changing the alloys in some water-exposed machinery, at considerable cost.

Second item. Where this scheme concerns us, I assume we could dump in hotter water any place? What, though, about coastal water? Where all this would end up?"

BULLEN. *Heavy Machinery and Land-moving Equipment.* "Good question. But—wouldn't the coastal seas be so charged with junk that added heat wouldn't matter? And won't the as-is situation wind up wrecking those salt-water deltas, estuaries, the like, in ten years?"

WILLIS. "Dr. Bullen's right. When you look ahead you see that river-mouth ocean areas will be ruined anyhow, no matter what's done. That is, if the ten-year waste-disposal projection is correct."

GENERAL GODE. "It's correct, all right."

WILLIS. "Can you expand on that, General?"

GODE (after a pause). "Well-l-l-l, not officially. Off the record, amongst this distinguished company, I might say that—well-l-l-l—the White House has our figures that set the 1985–86 river-collapse point. Nobody on the inside would admit such a study has been made. They'd deny it. Politics. The public isn't ready to face this fact—by a long shot."

DOMININI. *Banking.* "Have the Engineers made any survey of the Canadian potentials?"

GODE. "Of course. This project has been suggested since the sixties. Maybe the fifties. Over-all and specific studies, if any exist, would, of course, be top secret." (Pause.) "If, however, you will agree to keeping the matter confidential— your eyes and ears only—gentlemen—"

(Murmurs of agreement.)

"I can give you some quite fascinating data—"

General Gode then hung up a large relief map of North America. State and national borders had been traced on it.

For half an hour he outlined the "theoretical potentials and engineering requirements" involved in damming north-flowing rivers in Canada to reverse their flow, pump, where flow reversal would cost more or be impossible, and then send, by enormous conduits and tunnels, that vast water supply into USA. The Red River would help. Immense pumping would be needed. But General Gode showed how and where it would flow inland to cities, industry and for irrigation. His audience gave him rapt attention. Even such men, accustomed to vast operations, were awed by this proposal.

When he finished there was a long silence.

Somebody, finally, voice unidentified, asked, almost in a whisper, "How much, General?"

"Over ten years, a hundred billions."

"*Jesus!*" (Etc. Voices unidentified.)

KELLEY. "It's now past one o'clock. I think we should take a break. If you agree, I'll buzz and we'll have a bar brought in. Coffee. Anything in the way of food you gentlemen would like."

Discussion resumed in some forty-five minutes.

For about an hour, Miles, it was the most bloodthirsty money talk I ever heard. Finally, and to my surprise, Sturdevant Alomon of the business machine Alomons got the floor. Here's how he started talking, loud, fast and mad:

"I want to be heard here and now! Otherwise, I am leaving! I've listened nearly all night to you bastards discussing something that would really sweeten the pot for yourselves and your stockholders. Something you say would bring a great economic boom, and so on. The whole thing's shit, gentlemen, and you know it, or should. Probably Canada would let us take their surplus water, at a price. I am sure the Engineers could move it to any points desired—at about

148

three times the cost given here. Okay, gentlemen. But listen to *this!* You cannot use the river systems for sewers as you think because that would ruin any ground water still usable. And you can't let the garbage from your industries travel to the sea. The seas are in trouble as you know and maybe that already means mankind is in trouble. If our government didn't stop your sick scheme, all the others on earth would."

Sturdey was plenty sore and plenty vehement, Miles.

Rebuttals were weak. Mainly, they said the coastal waters were already so bad, and doomed to get so much worse, that, in ten years, nothing anybody added would matter.

Then came the Niobrara thing, which had been touched on a few times, before. People in your Foundation, maybe you, yourself, know more about this than I do—did, rather. A number of new items came up in this night session, new to me, anyhow. They stopped the Kansas spread of the green slime by diverting some minor rivers into land areas they then flooded. Treated every infested river, creek or spring, even those suspect of *developing* slime, with a lot of deadly junk and won the battle, there—though I didn't realize how much and what miles of waterways were now poisoned. I had no idea how many tens of thousands of people had to get out. Or that the treated water left what it covered dangerous even to walk on and for years. Did you?

I knew the Kansas battle was supposed to be won. And I knew they'd only managed delays, on the Niobrara, in the first years of the scrap with the gook up there. But I believed what the President said in his latest TV, "Candid to the People"—that they were going to stop the alga in Lewis and Clark Lake, by a dam and screens, chemicals, what not, short of Vermillion, South Dakota, by ditching and pumping the sludgy waters to the Nebraska Sands for final extermination. But did *you* know it turns out that the plan isn't going to

149

work? So they're going to use three "defoliants," stuff that kills everything green, in massive doses on the entire infested area. *Secretly*. That is, they'll say publicly they're using some new and harmless chemicals and then put on the killers. That'll theoretically wipe out the last of the pest, the last damned green one-celled horror. *But*—what else it'll do, the three defoliants, as they continue downriver, when the dam's opened, God knows.

As you can imagine, this whole tale merely reinforced the program of the evening. If the alga got into the entire area— the Mississippi—why, that would doom those rivers and their tributaries, if also infested. So there'd be nothing to get hurt by their intended project. If, though, the defoliants worked and the pest was halted, but the rivers were full of that deadly trio of plant killers—why, their planned effluents wouldn't matter either. They couldn't lose, either way. That did give the rivers-for-dumps majority quite a lift.

Six of us, Dwaite, Pauling, Rayne, Smith, Cassinti, and I, went to bat against the proposal on the grounds already noted by various speakers, and on the standard grounds. I won't say we had zero effect. But the two basic arguments they came back to, every time, were not easily opposed:

1. The rivers are going to be lost *no matter what*.

2. In eight to ten years USA has got to have every drop of pure water it can get from every source for distribution in what then will be roughly two thirds of the nation's area facing water famine.

The second one can't logically be refuted.

Trying to combat the first with that bunch, their majority, wasn't easy. They're not fools. And they brought up all sorts of expert opinion. They're pretty sharp on public attitudes, too, since they all have departments for the sociological and psychological study of the folks, so as to predict what they'll buy in the future if urged by advertising. And all their charts show there's a deep, growing and not too conscious depression in the American people right now. They feel the environmental recovery, or salvage, will be a flop—and rightly. More and more, too, the average citizen expects technology to save the world, if it's saved.

But none of the tycoons, barons, czars and powerhouses in that meeting—if I can immodestly accept myself—has a broad enough and also deep enough knowledge of the over-all picture, the sciences involved and especially the biologies, to *think for himself* with any value. A man in pharmaceuticals, like me, has to have a mass of biology and chemistry in his head. Nobody else there needed such a background. Petroleum chemistry, metallurgy, yes. Physics and engineering, quite a bit of savvy. Nothing much on ecology.

The meeting broke up before dawn. Nothing settled, really—that is, not *openly*. But, plainly, the Kelley-General Gode position had majority support.

If it's all going to materialize, I cannot stop thinking, My God! My God! There won't be any rivers any more!

We couldn't budge the big majority with our insistence that the rivers had to be saved, cleaned up, not devastated, in the eight to ten years ahead. The past and present ratios of efforts and outlays to achievement simply show, to such men, that we're losing, in spite of all we've spent and done. We cannot afford much more—so the price tag on a real cleanup isn't acceptable.

Are we going to lose, Miles?

You're the only guy with the organization to block this nightmare "project."

I'm so damned angry that if need be, and you say so, I'll crack the whole classified thing and tell the media what I've told you, confidentially.

However, since six of us went away at least unconvinced,

maybe you could act from a "leak" and not say who leaked—
which would protect me, perhaps or even probably.

EDITORIAL NOTE: What Miles did was to call on the President,
state that he had added up some meaningful items and was
guessing the scheme they implied. The President had to
acknowledge that "some such" a plan was among the "dozens"
being "winnowed for a solution" of the waste-waters problem,
now, admittedly, desperate. Miles then stated he had enough
about the program he pretended he had deduced to make a
public statement, condemning it. The President didn't try
to prevent that, and Miles realized why not. He would be
sending up a "trial balloon" which would serve the supporters
of the plan pretty neatly. They'd get a free reading of public
reaction without being involved—because Miles, as the President well knew, would not name names or point to the White
House, specifically, or the Army Engineers, save generally.
Miles had honor. But he tried.

The Foundation bought the first hour available on the
networks, and Miles went on the air over NBC, CBS and
ABC, nationwide.

He is a very impressive speaker and his face is great on TV.

He wrote his own speech and it was ingenious.

First, he pointed out the failing effort to catch up with
pollution in the waters of USA. Next, he showed the water
dearth that would lead to, in eight to ten years. Then he
asked what could be done.

And *then* he said the Foundation had come up with
a dramatic and fascinating plan—after which, he set forth
the project he wanted to throw a block at. But he made his
own organization the alleged originator of the whole thing.

He had ninety million or more people on their chair edges,
by that point.

So he told them why the Foundation proposal, brilliant as it sounded, would not work.

Recovering the rivers, Miles said, by a many times greater effort than all those past, present and planned, was the only way to save the show, even save America. His solution was documented with Foundation facts and figures so even morons in the viewing multitude could see his plan.

The broadcast was a three-day wonder.

Then the other side started hacking at it. The tax cost would be so great that the national living standard would be cut by at least twenty-five per cent. Construction industries would be slowed or stopped for the long period while the materials they used would be going into the "Smythe scheme of river and lake recovery." With the purified waterways and lakes, the cost of the GNP would perhaps *double* because every industry would either have to clean its wastes completely or else transport them a thousand miles and often more, to the desert deposits then gaining in use. Moreover, Americans would inevitably be "set back to the 1950s for power" and "rationing would be general and last for decades," while "available electric current would cost triple present prices."

By Christmas, the majority still wanted clean rivers but it wanted, far more, no such misery for attaining that end. The Foundation tried hard to refute such exaggerations. But the truth was, they were only that: blowups of what clean rivers *would* demand of *America*.

Nothing, in that countercampaign of industry, was said about the Canadian water purchase scheme or the total use of rivers for sewers. That was the clever part of the act.

Miles realized soon enough that his efforts had been blunted, even demolished. The American public, nearly en masse, wasn't about to go for river recovery at that cost. So the general public was psychologically ready to accept the schemes that Miles had ripped apart on that expensive broadcast.

What actually happened, however, was different, occurred in a few years and related to neither program.

12. *An Incident*

The Cleveland Straight Speaker
Ohio's Greatest Newspaper
Monday, August 6, 1979

RIVER EXPLODES!
WORLD'S WORST DISASTER
EXTRA

Cleveland, O. August 6, 1979. At 10:10 this morning Cleveland was devastated by an explosion so cataclysmic it was attributed to an atomic bomb. A ring of fire as much as two miles across now rages on the perimeter of an area of total ruin and thousands of smaller fires elsewhere in Greater Cleveland are still burning. More than one hundred thousand people are dead or missing and the number of the injured cannot as yet even be estimated. Beyond the area of total destruction in the city core is a ring of fire, and farther out building walls are still collapsing and flames are still spreading, both taking their toll. Cleveland Memorial Shoreway, from the West 25th Street Exit to its juncture with Interstate Routes 71 and 77, and the stretch of the combined throughways partly bounds an area where everything is, simply, gone—everything those routes enclose and much beyond.

The disaster was not due to an "atom bomb" as has been generally assumed up to now. The presumption was reasonable. No known agent of blast except the sort used on Hiroshima and Nagasaki at the end of World War II could have caused such massive and far-ranging devastation.

What is now known to be the cause, beyond any further speculation, is this: *The Cuyahoga River blew up!* Approximately a mile and a half of the Cuyahoga, a long-time "fire hazard," became explosive and, like liquid nitroglycerine, the explosive content of the river for that distance detonated this morning with the effect a nuclear weapon would have. In a statement made a short time ago, Governor Wittley declared:

"Panic and terror due to radioactive fears must stop. Such fears are groundless. Martial law has been declared. The President has (Turn to page 4)

The Cleveland Straight Speaker
Ohio's Greatest Newspaper

WHAT CAUSED THE CATASTROPHE?

by Elmo Bateson
Science Editor

Cleveland, O., August 7, 1979. As this great city still writhes in the thrall of history's most awesome industrial accident, with hundreds still dying in a continuing holocaust, the world is already asking, *How could so appalling an accident occur?*

As the *Straight Speaker's* Science Editor, I have been chosen to set forth what is known about the cause of the titanic blast that ripped the heart out of this great city and now threatens it with firestorm.

The cataclysm occurred yesterday, Monday, at 10:10 A.M. Central Daylight Time. Approximately one and three tenths miles of the Cuyahoga River, upstream, from a point well above its mouth in Lake Erie, simply blew up. Virtually all buildings within three quarters of a mile were destroyed. In the next half mile damage was generally severe. Fire instantly erupted where devastation was total and in much of the severely shattered area beyond. This titanic and spreading conflagration has not yet been brought under control.

Further details of the destruction, the fires, casualties, and related latest information will be found on Page One in adjacent columns. My assignment is to explain what is known about the cause, and to add such theories as I have managed to gather from the few scientists of appropriate disciplines I have been able to locate.

The Cuyahoga River is a minor waterway that loops through northern Ohio, touches Akron and meanders lakeward at Cleveland. The lower miles of the Akron-tainted stream pass through Cleveland's vast industrial complex and hundreds of industries, including iron, steel, coal, other heavy metallurgical types, huge chemical works and plants that are smaller but often "major" for their products. The Cuyahoga has been used for industrial (and other) disposal ever since the first water mill was set up on its banks, long before the city was incorporated in 1836.

For more than a decade the Cuyahoga has been officially classified as a "fire hazard." It was the first river in America to be given that novel but disgraceful designation. In the years between 1970 and 1976 industry and government, acting under public pressure, spent scores of millions in an attempt to clean up these waters. Several major plants were closed for varying periods while devices were installed to reduce their contaminating effluents. However, when legal efforts threatened to shut down certain smaller plants it proved that they were doing work essential for national defense, some of it so "hush-hush" that the products were never publicly stated.

These plants were heavy polluters of the Cuyahoga and their effluents were of many exotic, highly corrosive, toxic or in other ways hazardous sorts—unless speedily diluted. When it was known that these factories could not be halted, enforcement of the recent and harsh anti-pollution laws languished. If the Defense Department wouldn't or couldn't stop fouling the Cuyahoga why should anybody stop? Plants and factories grew in numbers and in size, too, as new mills and complexes replaced old ones.

In addition, some raw sewage entered the river when storm sewers in Cleveland flooded treatment plants. It was also and recently found that an enormous load of untreated human wastes was entering the Cuyahoga from the several new "boom time" developments south of the city, where suburban growth was so extensive and rapid that adequate sewage disposal facilities simply were not built.

Finally, with the development of the Lieson-Carter film, a desperately needed means was found for "sealing" the river. The patented sealant, one of the silicones, with a silica gel component, was released on a segment of the river in May of last year and has been augmented as required, by automatic devices. The results were "excellent," to the popular way of thinking. Mile upon mile of what had been a brownish-black, stinking, turgid movement of something having a thin-syrup consistency became a non-watercourse with a glittering, opaque surface, from the upstream farmlands where it was polluted only by Akron, by some sewage and by agricultural runoff, to its mouth. There, a surface barrier and "skimmer" system recovered 99.4% of the Lieson-Carter "glaze" for shipment back and for reuse.

That film or coat, some ten inches in thickness, in effect turned the river-sewer into a tunnel. Occasionally, to be sure, a great bubble or surge would erupt through the film. On other occasions chemical reactions beneath it created a "fountain effect," spurting large volumes of chemical mixes on top of considerable stretches of the film. Some of the escaped "bubbles" have ignited, apparently spontaneously, causing brilliant but short-lived flares. And some of the material in the geysers has been noxious in different ways: highly caustic, flammable, putrid-smelling and nauseating, as well as productive of fumes which, in one case, were lethal and took seventeen lives before they could be managed.

This was the general aspect of the Cuyahoga River last Monday morning. Perhaps a quarter million souls were in the range of possible death. Not one had the slightest warning.

In addition to the main demolition and fire, heavy objects, parts of steel buildings, whole machines weighing many tons, trucks, bulldozers and cars were hurled outward for distances up to five miles or more, and lesser but still lethal missiles caused death, injury and damage to homes and other structures and also set several fires at distances out to nine or ten miles.

The blast was actually "atomic" in its force. This force has been calculated by readings from gauges at three sites where such equipment was being used experimentally to test various pressures in gases. All three of these measurements agree the blast at "ground zero" had a force of twenty-one kilotons, plus or minus two. The explosion registered on countless seismographs and is now given a value of 6.7 on the Richter scale, that is, the power of a moderately severe earthquake.

Since the explosion was relatively free to drive upward and outward, that downward force, measured as a quake, is astonishing.

What caused the explosion? The "general" answer is by now surely clear. Following are some more specific, if inadequate, expert thoughts.

158

Dr. Vandane Truesdale of Cleveland State Tech told your Science Editor: "In my opinion, an unknown catalyst in that unforgivable chemical brew suddenly separated the water molecules into their components—two parts of hydrogen, one part of oxygen—thus creating a massive quantity of tremendously explosive gas in a matter of seconds."

Dr. Bagley Sickle, Chief Chemist of Temper-Wickerson Hale Products: "My rather preliminary thoughts and hasty calculations suggest that the Cuyahoga, being a chemical factory of myriad potential products, laid down, over a long period, layer on layer of one of the trinitrotoluols, say, or perhaps nitroglycerine. This explosive accumulated till it pierced the Lieson-Carter film somewhere. Then a carelessly tossed match, anything of the sort, would set it all off."

Professor Raoul Weaver, of Cleveland State Tech, a chemist, added this interesting fact:

"I drove over to the Cuyahoga at a little past eight on Monday morning. I often do on the way to the new campus, the one near Woodmere. An act that gives me morbid pleasure. This time, I noticed a new phenomenon which I truly relished. I parked and walked to the bank beside the Cone-Riverson Refining and Sintering Plant Number One, on East Dill Alley. There was a fissure in the film near that point, below the new bridge, and out of it boiled a mass of froth. A plant guard who was standing on the bank behind the stone wall, at that point, said the night watchman reported the 'whole river had been bubbling and gurgling and hissing for hours.' That sound was still clearly audible, a shushing noise that came from under the glaze, save where the stuff had broken out. Elsewhere, in both directions the film was heaving and bulging as if waves churned beneath it. This process was occurring as far as I could see.

"I drove on to the campus, well aware that this unspeakably abused stream was acting in some new fashion. I was amused and hopeful. It did not occur to me that it might be fomenting a terrible explosive. I did think that, if the foaming continued, something grim enough to wake up the polluters might occur.

"It may seem anti-social," Dr. Weaver continued, "but I hoped this new activity would be sufficiently dramatic to get some action. As a scientist, I have given expert testimony for many local, state and federal bodies on a wide assortment of industry-environment subjects. I, like my colleagues, have usually lost our end of the argument. We had the true data— all they had was a big yen for profit, plus political influence. We have been proven correct whenever we could and did make firm statements. With what thanks? Some of us lost jobs, and in academe, where the loss is death. Some, like me, simply didn't get the chair or the deanship we had earned. Most all of us have been ridiculed as well as vilified in the press and on TV. The public doesn't know which side to trust but it prefers the side that promises more jobs, higher wages, cheaper products.

"So I told nobody the Cuyahoga was turning into some sort of high-density suds. Suppose I had told everyone I met that morning before ten o'clock? What salvation for Cleveland would have come about? None. A few inspectors would have been routed out of bed to poke around. The low men on the Health Department totem pole, young chemists, would have taken samples from beneath the film—to analyze in the morning, or next week. I did not, could not know the stuff would blow the heart out of the city. And I will add this, which I doubt you'll print. The present holocaust in Cleveland might and should make all America wake up to the fact that it's on a powder keg. But my guess is that our tragedy won't teach much to the other folks."

Dr. George Cotton, Chief Chemist of the Red Badge Company's riverside complex offered the following suggestion:

"Many outfits on or near the Cuyahoga made a practice of storing their more corrosive, toxic and otherwise dangerous wastes over the work week and dumping them on Sunday. This is simply because Sunday was the day when most of the plants weren't in operation, and so weren't running their effluents into the river. This meant, at least theoretically, these exotic materials would be diluted faster in the less sluggish water and would get into the lake sooner. It is therefore at least possible that some unusual combination of

(Turn to page 36)

. . . And so, to the Unique, Never-before-witnessed spectacle of a river bursting into flames, one fateful decade ended and another began. . . .

III
The Eighties

1. *Documentary*

NOTE: The following is taken from a TV documentary. The interviewer was Donald Cason of IBC-3-D-TV. A "narrator" is unidentified. The filming was done on Thursday, June 30, 1983, two days after the event it records. First shown was a series of shots of the Argie Beeley Fish and Fun Camp and the woodland charm along Little Dwain River on which it is located.

The camp, surrounded by pines, consists of twelve motel-like cottages and a main building housing the office, dining room and "bait 'n' tackle" shop. The accommodations are modest but clean and attractive. These scenes include vistas of the Little Dwain River, a clear and generally fast-running tributary of the Kentucky. Its many wide and quite deep pools make it a paradise for trout fishermen. Owing to Beeley's energy and competence, two creeks entering the Little Dwain have been dammed to make lakes of fair size which yield bass, bluegills and bullheads. It is upland mountain country, Daniel Boone country, in truth, and a village named "Booneville" is nearby.

Argie Beeley has lost a leg in the Vietnam war. But he is agile in using an artificial limb, though when fishing or guiding in a boat, he "goes it one-legged" by choice. His wife,

Drolan, was the "prettiest senior" in her high school class, a dark-haired, dark-eyed and now alluringly plump mother of five children, the oldest, eleven, the two youngest, five and six, just deceased.

COMMENTATOR: It happened for the first time in this rolling, wooden region of Kentucky, southeast of Lexington and, so, near the blue grass country. It happened to these happy, ordinary, innocent, hard-working American folks. Argie Beeley is a war veteran who lost a leg fighting for his country. Drolan, his wife, was a beauty queen and, as you see, still is. They had five children—until last Tuesday.

Starting from scratch, Argie Beeley developed this fishing camp. It began as a rickety dock with a few rental boats and a shack where he sold snacks and bait. It became the handsome spread we're looking at, worth at least one hundred thousand dollars, and it was all the Beeleys had—or needed. It's been open year round, now, because hunters fill the Beeley cabins when angling is suspended. And it's a living, a very comfortable living. Rather, it *was*. No one's going to make a living here now, however. Something went wrong.

(Here the scene shifted to a shot of Cason standing outside the main building of the camp with Argie Beeley, a rather thin-faced man with sun-squinted eyes and a harsh voice, but a man who talked easily and seemed to have a natural philosophy that made him warm to people and, so, liked.)

CASON: When did you learn about the new power plant upstream?

BEELEY: Five years ago; least that.

CARSON: A nuclear reactor?

BEELEY: Yes, sir.

CASON: Were you told it would affect the river?

BEELEY: Wasn't told anythin'. Hadda ask.

163

CASON: And then?

BEELEY: They said they weren't even sure they'd ever touch the Little Dwain. Planned to cool the powerhouse with water from Licking River. Lot of hoo-hoo about that but they went ahead. Never bothered us none.

CASON: Other factories were built nearby, right? And used the Licking or Kentucky for cooling?

BEELEY: Sure. But nobody told us they mostly could all hook into the Little Dwain if they had to. Kinda set up on the q.t. They built reservoirs for times when the water's low so it never occurred to me they'd use our stream. Without even a warnin'—

(Mrs. Beeley appeared in camera and the three walked toward the river, away from the fishing camp.)

CASON: The older children were in school?

MRS. BEELEY (she is trying not to weep): Yes. The two tykes wasn't. Ronnie had a cold and stayed home. They pushed out on the river in a rowboat—just playing—both tykes born water rats—they've lived with rowboats and skiffs —they kin—could—swim, o' course. If I hadn't kept my Ronnie outa school . . .

CASON: When did you know—

MRS. BEELEY: I heard—heard—the—screams—

BEELEY: Let me, Mother. (Angrily.) Shame to torment her so!

CASON: I'm very sorry. But your story is important. It should help prevent this sort of thing and save others.

BEELEY: Mebbe. Hope so. Anyhow—I was behind the main house, and Mother came for me—

CASON: Yes?

BEELEY: I run around and down t' th' docks. I could hear 'em but not see 'em. Whole river was boilin' and steam thicker'n fog ever was.

CASON: The river was boiling? Literally?

164

BEELEY: I mean, boiling. I know, now, they had a situation at the reactor where they couldn't help using the Little Dwain. And some other plants had to, on that account. But, Lord Gawd! who'd think a river could be set to *boiling*, mile after mile!

(The trio walked out on a pier and the TV camera showed the river, and the dock area. The river, about a hundred feet across at that point, deep and slow-flowing, was steaming faintly.

CASON: So the two youngsters were out on the water when the change came. The surge—the emergency?

BEELEY: That's it. They couldn't see to row back. Come on 'em too fast. We couldn't go out to 'em. Not even stay on the pier. They was screaming—bein' steamed to death, o'course. Cooked alive. Took ten minutes, maybe more, before they even began t' quieten down.

COMMENTATOR (as Beeley choked up and the scene faded): It has been predicted, almost jokingly, for years. But now it has happened. The sudden cooling requirements of industry have actually made one river boil. We can say that it was a small river where few persons lived. Only two lives were lost. Little kids steamed to death like puddings. And only one business was ruined. Because there aren't any more trout in the Little Dwain River and there never will be any. Why? From now on the power plant and some other factories upstream will draw on the Little Dwain steadily, keeping it warm. Of course, an unanticipated, emergency demand for power by the east coast grid forced the Boone Reactor Plant to run up its load to capacity. And then a little jam in one atomic pile required a lot of cold water right off. A small accident. But when that water left the plant it was boiling hot and partly superheated steam. They had planned that grab of cool flow from the Little Dwain as "insurance." But they took more than expected for the jam. And they got the trouble fixed, even started up the pile without much trouble. The only damage was to the Beeley family.

(There followed shots of other rivers to match the Commentator's final words.)

COMMENTATOR:

All over America, rivers are getting warmer. Thermal "surges" of the kind we just saw are not common—yet. But fish kills are common. Here's one in an Ohio river—a solid mile of dead bass, bluegills, pickerel, pike, catfish and so on. In this reeking mass, everything from miles upriver lies dead. The power people tried to call this sort of horror scene "acceptable." Not any more!

Here's Villadonna, Illinois, where the water supply from the Francis branch of the Kayo became heated to the point where the cold-water faucets in every home ran too hot to drink. There just wasn't any cold or cool water for the town until wells were drilled. Approximately a third of our lakes are warming up, also.

This concludes the third installment of IBC featured documentaries, a new program called, "Think About It." If you live near a river, pond, lake or a brook, even, remember the Beeley family and—*think about it!*

2. *The Saturday Slaughter*

Miles sat halfway down from the mayor, that Friday. There were twenty-one men and two women at the conference table. The mayor had insisted the meeting be kept secret. There had been protests, by Miles and others, but to no effect.

Miles and some of the others present, a minority, listened to Mayor Tabley's opening statement with guarded hope at first:

166

"As all of you know, the five boroughs of New York are in the fourth day of a weather condition, an inversion layer, which is widespread in the East but has been peculiarly intense, if that's the word, here. Up to this noon only voluntary efforts have been requested in pollution abatement; obviously, if the present situation continues for much longer, more drastic measures must be considered.

"I would recommend the application of Condition Red measures at once, were it not for two factors. Others can perhaps explain them better than I. This is a crisis that cannot be met by normal response. That is why we have a special envoy here. Let me introduce Lieutenant General Thompson, who comes to us from the Defense Department."

The general, like the mayor, did not stand to speak. Desk microphones were arranged at each place. In the red-draped new City Hall's private dining room, at the black table, faces turned. There were two uniformed police at each of its tall, black double doors at the room's end, and dozens of plainclothesmen in the halls and lobbies, beyond, in case some reporter or other smart representative of the media had cleverly tagged the mayor on his way from Gracie Park or learned through a hotel minion bribed to call in about covert arrivals of VIPs. Such security made Miles doubly wary. The general was large and commanding. His hair was sparse and brown-addled-with-gray. He had small brown eyes and thick fingers, a battered, small nose and fat cheeks. He opened a dispatch case with two keys, making of the act a threat. He produced papers stamped in red capitals, SECRET. Miles had known him, slightly, and mostly from rancorous public debates.

General Thompson cleared his throat. He looked like a man with a growling bass voice. His thin tenor surprised the few who had never heard it. But the voice was not wholly a handicap. It penetrated, stung, whipped, rather than bludgeoned.

"Ladies and gentlemen," he began, "I have been authorized by the Chiefs of Staff to give you the gist of these secret
reports. Such an order and act is, of course, unprecedented.
The military data I shall capsulize are to be regarded as absolutely confidential, top secret. Not to be leaked, not to be
mentioned even to one's intimates, one's husbands, wives. I
hope I am clear?"

He waited as if administering an oath. People mumbled
assent, acceptance. The general riffled his papers and spoke
as if with great reluctance. "The Arabian United Nations
police action, the so-called Desert War, was followed by an
economic slowdown of disastrous magnitude in this nation.
The recrudescence of Communist pressure and outlawry in
South Asia is far more hazardous than we at the Pentagon,
pardon, the new Decagon, have been permitted to say publicly. The State Department and the White House feel that
to reveal the many and shocking facts of enemy intrusion
and subversion would lead to such national rage as to make
a next war certain. This new threat has been growing since
the Middle East Agreement of 1985. The federal effort to
prepare for any further action of the Korean, Vietnam or
Arabian type began postwar and was a major factor in the
nation's swift recovery.

"This rearmament and resupply activity has reached a scale
far greater than is publicly known." Someone muttered an
ironic, "No!" The general stared. "I prefer no interruptions.
Now. In and around Greater New York fourteen hundred
and seven major industrial plants are contributing to this
absolutely vital and very hush-hush effort. Some seven hundred of these factories have been listed by your pollution people as serious threats in an inversion crisis. We of the military, however, think less than a quarter of the number are
properly defined as significant contaminant producers. It is a

matter that should have been arbitrated with the military at high levels."

"I object!" Dr. Bill Clemment, pale, haggard, his eyes bloodshot, had spoken with force.

The general stared at him. "Objection noted. And tabled for later—consideration." He made the word menacing. The Pollution Control Commissioner met his eye, shrugged and buried his thin face in long-fingered hands, stained by cigarettes which he smoked almost constantly.

Mayor Tabley scowled. He had been in office only ten months after his landslide victory in an election that had wiped out the previous, liberal administration. Tabley was a businessman and his platform had been simple. *The do-gooders must go ahead before the "good" they do destroys New York.* The retired head of a supercorporation, Tabley was beginning to find out that the chronic and ever growing "problems" of New York could never be solved by managerial skills or, perhaps, by any other combination of skills. "Problems" had been his campaign term for what in fact were a series of city calamities, always greater, more alarming, odder and less expectable than had been anticipated.

Now, however, the tight face of the mayor and the glare in his pale eyes was directed at the general. "Briefly, General," he said in a strained tone. He did so to remind the group that he, not Thompson, was boss.

"Very well." The general's fleshy face turned red. "In that case, *Mister* Mayor, I shall skip giving the details I felt were necessary to show the why of our conclusion. If you wish them later, very well." He looked around the room. "Ladies and gentlemen. In view of the actual, confidential and secret scope of industrial effort in this period of crisis—and I refer to the threat of war, not to a merely smoky city—it is imperative that all defense-involved plants continue on round-the-clock shifts. Am I clear?" He smiled nastily as he looked with disdain from face to face.

There was a lengthy silence. Miles broke it. "You have the authority?"

The general remained red and angry. "Not here and now. It would, however, be forthcoming, I am sure, if you local people tried to put in effect any scheme that would interfere with defense production."

"A stoppage," Miles continued, quietly and with a faintly amused look, "of a couple of days, say, would wreck your entire military buildup? Your margins are *that* meager?"

"I said, Smythe, we would not have the work shut down."

"If you can bully us to comply."

The general's wrath was great and largely because he had been sent for precisely that purpose: to bully the city officials, civilian experts and local leaders present into holding off Condition Red control measures. He rose and said rather shrilly, "I shall, with the mayor's consent, call my superiors on this matter."

He went out.

Several of those present grinned or winked at Miles.

"Mr. Mayor!" That was Reginald Lacey, the elegant, Harvard-educated merchant. Miles was often confounded by Lacey: in his tailored, blue-gray and draped suit, with its carnation, he seemed a complete fop, not dissipated or debauched—just limp, languid, concerned with his own elegance and style. Yet he was one of the most ruthless men in America, which, Miles reflected, wasn't saying very much in view of the numbers of such men.

The mayor had relaxed noticeably. "Yes, Reggie. Go ahead."

Reggie nodded, smiled vaguely, fitted a small cigar into a golden holder, lighted it with a gold briquet, said, "Ahhh—" and stopped. Restarted. "Let me put it this way." He stopped

170

again and gracefully inspected his cigar, held at arm's length.
"The merchants of New York had their first hope of an excellent year in a long time. Today there remain but—ahh—
fifteen—yes, I think—fifteen days, business days, for Christmas shopping. I hardly need add that November was—a disaster, for us. Christmas business, in fact, is off, for Manhattan, and in other boroughs too, thirty-eight per centum. If, in
the few shopping days remaining, any event, any Act of God,
of weather, if—ahhh—*anything* should lead to a further diminishing of the shopping crowds, I can guarantee you that
thousands—yes, thousands—of business enterprises will be ruined. Manhattan, other boroughs, will see a catastrophic collapse, a new depression, a tax receipts drop of unthinkable
consequences, a—total calamity. So—while we endangered
merchants do regret that if this present and truly repellent
—ahh—meteorological phenomenon—continues—and causes
distress, yes, even some slightly advanced dates of death—
amongst already doomed elderly persons—the effort to delay
their—ahh—passing, and to allay the general—discomforts—
would not amount to a hundredth of one per cent of what
would be lost by any—ahh—quixotic—act."

Miles saw Bill Clemment shudder.

The mayor was smiling. "Thanks, Reggie. Very vital aspect
of the whole. And, I might add, understated, if anything. For
—a—thirty-eight?—thirty-eight per cent loss in business at
this time is based, I believe, on last year's totals?" Lacey
nodded gracefully, bowed, in fact. Tabley bowed back crisply
and faced the group. "However, as the recovery has been on
a splendid upswing, the business expectations for this year's
Christmas sales were some fifteen to twenty per cent higher.
Hence, Reggie's figure, applied to actual expectations and resultant inventories, would actually mean for this year, unless
the remaining days permit a shift, something near a fifty per
cent drop in over-all sales. Which would, of course, trigger the

unthinkable disaster we cannot permit to happen. The shop-
pers are ready to throng—thronging, now, in spite of the—
smog. They are more affluent than in any past year. Given
the chance, in the remaining days for shopping, this crucial,
yes, terrifying financial situation may dissipate, as we trust,
and pray, the inversion will. Dr. Weisman, I see you've just
been brought a message. Perhaps it's good news?"

The meteorologist and head of the Weather Bureau was a
small, nervous man with large eyes, and pale, almost pink
hair in a thin and total disarray. He nodded toward the mayor
absently and returned his attention to a yellow sheet of elec-
tro-facsimile type which a police officer had brought in so
quietly few of the strained group had noticed. Weisman finished reading and stood up. He was little more than five feet
tall and mike-shy; all weather data broadcasting was done by
young assistants at the Bureau. The chief looked, now, almost as if he were not sure where he was, whom he addressed,
or what he was expected to say. Then his deep and assured
voice came, unamplified and no need for that:

"Mr. Mayor, members of this emergency committee—or
whatever it is called. This is the latest bulletin. In general,
the fronts are still motionless. A slight deepening of the low
trough west of us has occurred but will probably not alter
the picture much, or soon. If the deepening increases swiftly
there may be a start of circulation and slight improvement
in this area by midday tomorrow. On the other hand, meas-
uring stations set at some forty points on Manhattan, and
more than three hundred in the surrounding areas, show an
average rise in the index of eleven points, since ten this
morning. A small lift of the inversion layer immediately
above us, and of the second, above that—we have a rare
double inversion—has caused a constant eddy of air from
northern and middle New Jersey to drift at low levels into the
New York area, especially Manhattan. If this process should

continue, we will get the polluted air from Jersey industry. In that case, I can only say, God help New York!"

He looked at his yellow sheet. "Let me add a bit. Pollution is not properly shown in the index we use. The public index we are *told* to use. Sulphur and sulphuric acid compounds are always high here. Other toxic gases, fine-droplet compounds, poisonous, particulate matter and fly ash is always present in higher proportions, relatively, in New York than other cities, but these counts aren't given. Most alarming of all the toxic data is the rapid rise in the nitrogen oxide levels in congested streets—meaning all streets, in Manhattan, anyhow. So the data we give the public are a snow job."

The mayor was frightened. His face became flinty to hide his state but his tapping pencil sounded like an insect with a fast rattling call and that tremor gave away his face-freeze. He finally said, "Damn it! With all the money—years—on weather research—you lads still can't be sure of—a damn thing! Including all this talk about toxins. Even medicine doesn't *know* they are dangerous."

"We've been ninety per cent accurate on twenty-four-hour forecasts this year, eighty-two per cent on long-range and that's some progress! We pretty well told you about November, in October. The heavy rains. Fogs. Ice storms. And we've been telling you politicians about the nitrous oxide menace for years. Shall I run over that again?" Dr. Weisman was calm.

"Please." Miles cut in. He knew that most of those present had no scientific background for what should now be a wholly scientific discussion.

"Simple. We got exhaust devices on every car, years ago. Then the Desert War came. Car production was halted for war production. The exhaust devices began to wear as they and cars aged. Now, with cars pouring out of Detroit, the new

173

systems are excellent. But less than ten per cent of the automotive vehicles in use are new models. The prewar vehicles, even if they still have exhaust devices, are less than ten per cent efficient, on the average. However, their emission of nitrogen oxides has increased over its originally considerable rate to a very high incidence.

"Finally, the city of New York had expected to spend three billion in air pollution control over the past six years. Nothing was spent. And new plans are still on paper, only."

Reginald Lacey interrupted. "Weisman, old chap! Give us your most dire—ahh—extrapolation—if the present increments continue for a day? Even, two days?"

The weather man grunted. "Impossible. I'm a scientist, not a fortuneteller. You've read and seen TV broadcasts of the pollution disasters in Europe. Japan. The lesser one in USA. London, last year, had five days and sixty-seven thousand deaths. We could make that look trifling."

The heads of various departments had their turns at speaking. Health. Hospitals. Streets and Highways. All, politicians or political appointees.

All, well aware that if the city was shut down, and if, then, business collapsed owing in any part to their actions, their politically dependent careers would be ruined.

Other items came up.

Someone questioned the advisability of going ahead with the "Free Bus Program" scheduled for Saturday. It happened to be an enterprise Miles hadn't learned of, and he listened to George Willis of the Mercantile Transportation Authority describe the operation—with a feeling of stupefaction.

"Beginning early tomorrow and continuing through the pre-Christmas shopping days, we have some two thousand buses available for travel to Manhattan's shopping area from the suburbs. Each shopper who shows he has made purchases of twenty-five dollars or more will be returned to his town free of charge."

Somebody whistled softly. What an extra two thousand buses would do to midtown traffic was hard to envisage.

In the silence that followed, the mayor turned to Miles. "I think, Miles, we should hear from you, perhaps. Though we all know what you will say." He chuckled, not convincingly.

What followed was one of the few occasions on which Miles publicly lost his grip on his gathering rage. He knew, when the general returned from calling his superiors, looking smug, that there was no hope of sensible action. The fourteen hundred plants with "defense" work would go on operating. The merchants and the politicians would insist on taking whatever the risk might be. Miles had held his peace thus far with the intention of making an appeal to reason, quietly but earnestly. For these people were, surely, fundamentally responsible, not madmen.

Perhaps it was the "free bussing" news that cost him his control. Perhaps he'd never had as much self-command as he'd believed, for he had realized that if the defense plants continued to operate it would be impossible to halt others. Possibly the mayor's patronizing tone was the ultimate straw. His mind quit, whatever the final cause.

Miles stood, towering, tremendous, formidable, unable for a long moment to say a word. Then he said just one: "Murderers!" and stalked out. Nobody ran after him. No one dared.

He strode down crowded streets to the place where his limousine waited. He said, "Home," to his chauffeur, who had kept the motor running to supply power to the air conditioner. When he reached his penthouse Miles went into his "study-den" and locked the doors.

He ate no lunch.

He refused dinner.
He could not be reached by phone.

That left me in charge at the Foundation.

I sat in my luxurious office and took the reports as they came in. And I saw the people whom I needed to see, as well as those who wanted to see me. I had lunch on a tray from the executives' kitchen. Around two, Nora called and told me about Miles. "He's almost out of his mind," she said. "He wouldn't even answer *me!*"

So I knew, perfectly well, what had happened at that secret conclave. I also knew, from the Foundation's special monitoring systems, just how bad the contamination was, and the data grew more sinister every hour with the regular bulletins. I could scarcely believe what Miles's condition surely meant: that the authorities had refused to act. Manhattan's air wasn't really air, by late afternoon. Thousands of elderly persons, many people of all ages with heart and respiratory troubles, were being taken to hospitals, but not "rushed," as ambulances vainly tried to siren a way through traffic that did not give space because it could not. Weak children and many of the old were dying. It had happened before on a similar scale; but my mind was on what could happen the next day.

We did our best.

To every daily paper within two hundred miles and to every 3D-TV station reaching that same area, as well as every radio station, we sent out our advice and the supportive figures. Those releases accused nobody. They merely said that it was self-evident that the people in authority did not sufficiently understand the nature of the accumulating contaminants and their near-certain greater concentration on Saturday. Our data followed and made our advice plain enough. *That was, Stay out of New York, and Manhattan especially, tomorrow.*

I tried, with zero success, to buy some time on a network

or even on a major local radio station to give the facts, that evening. No one had a half hour at any price. Management doubtless knew that a spokesman for the Foundation for Human Conservancy was not going to urge the masses to come shopping in midtown on Saturday.

Miles did not show up at his office the next morning and I had not expected him to. When his anger and the despair that follows it reach this point, it might be days before he returns to his desk—looking almost normal, hardly contrite but perhaps a little sheepish.

Nora drove me to the Foundation in the new car with the new conditioning unit which cut down most of the haze that hung and swirled in the outside world, a compressed fume blanket, into which a cold sun dimly shone, at times carving great diagonal blocks of shimmer in the murk. People were weeping and sneezing and most held handkerchiefs to their faces but even so they suffered, and they hurried to get indoors where they worked or proposed to shop. The morning news, phoned to me at breakfast, was worse than even our very worried scientists had feared. Almost every bit of densely polluted air from around Greater New York was being pulled into the Manhattan-Brooklyn-Bronx area by a slow whirlpool-like eddy.

After seeing the ten o'clock reports I ordered everybody to start for home. By midafternoon I could no longer even see the traffic, stalled eighty floors down, in Fifth Avenue. I checked the executive suites to be sure they were all empty, spoke to the night superintendent about keeping watch-men indoors, and then took an automatic elevator down to the street level where there had been an all-day braying of horns in the usually motionless, briefly inching traffic.

I am not ashamed of my subsequent behavior.

From Fifty-seventh Street south to the excavation where a new library was to rise on the site of the old, the sight was usually fantastic. Colored lights bathed the façades of every towering structure on the avenue and their walls fluoresced, owing to chemical treatment which had that purpose. The concealed and high-powered light-sources bathed the canyon in every rainbow hue and the colors moved, weaving and parting, like an extra-vivid play of northern lights. Above this rainbow-walled scene came the New Music, the "Fifth Avenue Beat," clear, ringing, almost drowning motor sounds and the babble of people who inched along in two solid masses that spilled from walks on both sides of the gaudy valley into and among cars—private cars, trucks and an ice pack of buses of every description from which and into which people poured.

None of that, of course, occupied my attention particularly; what I concentrated on as I forcibly held my position at the side of our building against the pressure of the human river was the air over the street. For a half dozen blocks the chromatic dazzle was sharp, but it dimmed beyond that point and vanished in murk beyond. I could not see that gaudy and glaring panoply as far as I always had, to Forty-second Street. It was for once dulled out by smog, blue-brown, eddying, swirling, appalling.

The air was chilly and it was almost dark. Clouds could not be seen but they hung low, I knew. One's first breath of this air was painful and every ensuing inhalation added misery. People passing in their thousands were coughing, choking, eyes and noses streaming, handkerchiefs held to filter out some portion of the pollutants.

I had almost decided to return to the office when the blow fell.

At first, from where I was pressed against the wall, the onslaught was not definable as to cause. Above the music and the engine pulse, louder than either and overriding the human sounds of a myriad conversations, curses, warnings to watch out for cars and abjurations to hurry, came a strange susurration, a sort of whispered scream as if a chorus of hoarse banshees had cried aloud some blocks to the south.

It was a shocking sound and people began to stop to listen. In seconds, it became a roar.

For the first instants I had thought it the result of a massive accident in that avid multitude. But the sound swept toward us—as it did in the opposite direction—and I clambered up on a brass fire hydrant nearby to add to my considerable height for a better view.

What I saw was almost incredible. The crowd on my side of the street at a distance of four blocks and beyond had become dwarfed. It took a moment to understand that incredible phenomenon. It was as if everybody had suddenly become two feet tall. And this strange endwarfing was spreading. The standing masses were serially shortening—and then it was plain.

They had fallen.

They were falling like wheat cut by an invisible reaper, one that was approaching. They were, I knew, dead.

Then I saw the next effect. People on the crammed walks near enough to the approaching and, to them, incomprehensible scythe started trying to run away from the fallen toward the tightly compressed masses, in my direction. To know what was happening, as I did, was to be certain that a lethal concentration of nitrogen oxides, NO and NO_2, mainly, would reach the area where I stood on that hydrant in a minute, or perhaps less. And the nitrogen oxides, at this kind of concentration, kill suddenly and without warning.

In a few seconds the pressure from those trying without hope to flee would roll against the people around me. Already they were looking back with panicky eyes and then turning to rush into the lobby of the Smythe Building. The offices on the ground floor were closed, brokerages, all of them. The lobby was vast but not air-conditioned. Waiting with the inrushing crowd for an elevator and escape to safety was a bad risk as, coming down from the hydrant into the tightly packed and now terrified mob, I could see that nobody, at my distance from the banks of elevators, would live long enough to get a turn.

The voice from the south was now terrible, a roar and scream of fear and desperation tearing from thousands of throats. There was no way to direct this ever denser multitude that would not simply augment stampede. I plowed through the jam at the building entry and on, crossing Fifty-seventh Street in a mass so dense I sometimes could not feel the pavement with my feet. It was almost as horrible going over Fifty-eighth but at the next corner the people, running at top speed, were fanning out as they leaped over walks and walls and plunged into the park, I with the rest.

Central Park offered the only region nearby where the roads were few, the people present, until the fringes of the mob joined them, were very few, and the air, presumably, would be less contaminated owing to those circumstances. I continued to run as fast as I could till I had reached a mid-point in the park about opposite Seventieth Street. There, panting and hot, lungs scalding, eyes inflamed, I sat down on a bench and tried to recover my wind and my nerve.

Somewhat later, as surges of horror and floods of humanity swept into the park, I began to make my way to Park Avenue and the apartment. I did it cautiously and with a method I tried, on the way, to explain to such others as I was able. It was a simple technique.

Where, on any side street, no one moved, you turned back. Where, before crossing Madison Avenue, you saw fallen figures or forward-leaning figures in vehicles, you looked for a different place to make that passage. Park Avenue, though solid with traffic standing still, was not yet afflicted—and some sturdy police, aided by citizens, were getting motors killed.

I did not join those who tried to help them. But when I had reached the lobby of the apartment where Nora and I live I brought along a small parade of mothers and nursemaids pushing prams, children with schoolbooks, couples and single adults and three youngsters of preschool age I managed to grab and carry against their frightened protests. Our lobby is air-conditioned, and though it was crowded we shoved inside and some of us began to get the hysterical calmed and the crowd distributed on halls in higher floors.

It was what I did and all I did and I might have done more but I believe not.

We stayed in our apartment, Nora and I, looking down at the finally dead avenue.

But the inversion layers did not budge, and the blue-to-brown pall of death pushed turgidly and at random from the center-city concentration. Now, of course, every TV and radio station in the area was pouring forth advice. *Turn off your motor* was the principal command. But there were some avenues and many cross streets where motors ran till their gasoline was exhausted. Dead people cannot switch off the ignition.

As the hours passed a torrent of information began. A mob sighted the mayor getting into his car, pulled him out and literally stomped and tore his body to shreds. Looting, of course, rose to a scale beyond accounting, the looters, with their spoil, often dying in the stores where they'd smashed in. Fires caught and engines often failed to reach them as their crews died on the way.

Morning dawned murkily. Smoke rose here and there. People were still dying, on the streets, in their homes and in countless buildings, including many where old-fashioned air-conditioners failed finally to clean the air.

Nora watched our visible stretch of Park Avenue for more than two hours without seeing a soul move. The dead lay where they'd fallen. A car caught fire and burned out, fortunately not setting adjacent vehicles aflame.

A breeze sprang up toward late afternoon and we watched the veils of poison as they swirled, curled on one another and gradually thinned out. Martial law had been declared on Saturday evening, but only now were any numbers of National Guardsmen, in gas masks, entering the worst regions. After dark, tanks and bulldozers with blazing headlights began to batter lanes through the stalled vehicles. With paths cleared, masked Guardsmen began to collect the corpses which were carried off by city trucks.

These cadavers were laid out in Central Park and elsewhere for identification, a process that was never complete as so many of the dead were from out of town and, of them all, a great many had been robbed or trampled, had lost pocketbooks, and even their clothes. Relatives and friends who might have identified thousands refused to come into the city area and could hardly be blamed. A thaw followed the period and bodies began to putrefy, those waiting outdoors to be named as well as thousands in alleys, houses, in the vast slums, in apartments where ventilation failed and many had hidden beneath rugs, car blankets, beds, under cartons and in closets and even trunks and boxes.

The city smelled like a battlefield.

Mortality from other causes than the combined toxins were also fantastic. In the vast regions peripheral to the deadly smog, tens of thousands more died, cardiacs, the old, people with respiratory troubles, handicapped persons unable to get to less choking areas, infants and small children without number, and pets.

Looting continued in spite of the Guardsmen and police.

For the areas of death were all but intolerable to persons without protective masks, and these were insufficient for all save the essential personnel. Most of Manhattan and much of the Bronx as well as a vast stretch of Brooklyn soon became deserted by all but the soldiers, police and other city workers —and looters.

The death toll was estimated, finally, at just over one million two hundred thousand. An exact figure was out of the question.

But even that massive self-execution was not the end of the disaster, and perhaps not even its worst aspect.

Although I have here recorded my own experiences in the "Saturday Slaughter" I do not feel competent to give a clear and detached concept of the whole. However, Raymond L. Bainter, writing in the *North Atlantic* for December, a year later, skillfully presented certain circumstances that are relevant here, so that what will presently follow is taken from an article by him in that excellent magazine. It was called "The Suicide of a City."

Raymond LaFlange Bainter was one of those young men who proliferated in the late seventies and early eighties, a "brain" but also an athlete, talented, but usually within limits they failed to perceive. He graduated from the University of Miami (Florida) and went on to take an M.A. at the University of Wisconsin and a doctorate at the University of Colorado. Ray was writing a syndicated newspaper column while still a senior in Miami, and by the time he started on his Ph.D. at Colorado more than three hundred newspapers subscribed to his thrice-weekly "As Youth Sees It," and he had made several quite spectacular appearances as a panelist on network TV.

We at the Foundation for Human Conservancy became well acquainted with young Bainter in the period when he was still getting his degrees. He wrote about our work and he came to see us, meeting both Miles and myself several times. Like most of his generation, he fancied himself as a conservationist and an environmentalist, sometimes referring to himself in his column as "your unemotional ecologist." In the effort to save the environment his stand was certainly the most common among people of similar backgrounds and also people with his brand of education, at whatever levels.

He believed that technology could and would perfectly suffice to undo or reverse the admitted sabotage man had performed on his ecosphere. He went all out in favor of any and every device, machine, process and installation that was even claimed useful for pollution abatement. So he felt the Foundation position was extreme, even hysterical.

At twenty-one Bainter's writings were widely read into the Congressional Record by like-minded politicians, the great majority; and Bainter's arguments, set forth with what appeared to be sweet reason, total understanding and utter fairness, helped defeat several bills the Foundation backed. Young Ray shared the general feeling, for example, that Nature was present to provide humanity with resources, and that no land, desert, or forest, swamp or coastal wilderness should be permitted to "lie fallow." All wild lands should be open to "multiple use" if more than one use for such areas could be found or even invented.

Later, when various measures to protect wild lands from the erosion and ruin of public invasion were passed, Ray Bainter was almost willing to go that far in the matter of saving a few regions of such sorts. He went along with the idea that roads for cars should not be built through such shrinking, priceless masterpieces of nature, but he insisted on trails and cabins so that even the "preserved" or "closed" places would be open to back-packers, horse or mule parties, and snowmobiles in winter.

By 1970, to pluck a date at educated random, there were very few men living anywhere who had entered and dwelt for a time in a genuine "wilderness," one in which they were the first of their species to become known to the indigenous fauna, the first men of whom the "wild animals" had had any memory, parental teaching, any warning, or any instinctual pattern relating to the proper way of accepting, fleeing, living with or watching genus *Homo*.

So there was virtually no longer a way for mankind to find out what natural animal behavior was and would be, if not altered by human passage or presence. Similarly, the opportunities for ecologists to study cross sections of life forms that had not, also, been man-changed was small. But leaving a region untouched, unoccupied, untrespassed, in order to allow it to recover from "human shock," seemed a preposterous waste to nearly everybody.

The foregoing is set down by this editor not so much to define the intellectual attitude of Ray Bainter as to show the near impenetrable defenses which the Foundation encountered, the subtle sorts, not the overt kinds where sheer profit, greed, ignorance, fears, all sorts of other, "normal" human conditions made the bulk of mankind hostile to nature. Trying to tell a Western man, even one as highly "educated" and as brilliant as young Raymond Bainter, his *biological* location in the living world, and the endless fragile, balanced life systems on which he was dependent, was an all but hopeless task. If one began to succeed in such an effort the pupil usually became so downcast as to give up—feeling man had no survival chance whatever.

Raymond Bainter and his ilk simply could not accept the hypothesis that man was still so completely dependent on forms, systems, natural phenomena, delicate balances of vast-volume elements like air and water, that "science and technology" could not find a way to save him from those very many and often very possible menaces we had listed.

Yet in the end Bainter was one of the few men of that time who were "converted" and came firmly to believe that the reason why no human culture yet devised has achieved stable and indefinite viability is that—to put it in the crudest terms—the more sophisticated the technology devised by man, the faster it erodes the environment. Bainter's own account of that "conversion" appeared in a book which he published in 1980—two years before the New York calamity, and three before his essay in the *North Atlantic* of December 1983, from which I have selected certain relevant passages.

3. *An Article*

The North Atlantic, December, 1983

SUICIDE OF A CITY
NEW YORK'S "SATURDAY SLAUGHTER" AND AFTERWARD

by Raymond L. Bainter

Official figures for casualties in the Greater New York disaster of November 1982 stand at "about" one million two hundred thousand. But these do not include the numbers who died in the weeks and months after that Saturday-Sunday-Monday catastrophe. Perhaps twice as many would be about correct. And multitudes suffered harm from the polluted air or injuries owing to trampling, to fire, to assault by ravaging mobs, whose lives are shortened or handicapped permanently as still another result.

After the mayor was slain mobs went hunting for other city officials and some sixty of these, many having no connection with or responsibility for the disaster, were cruelly murdered. Wild gangs descended on the stricken area, and virtually every major store in the central shopping area of Manhattan was repeatedly raided.

The police lost 1157 dead in the first week. Their injured ran to some five thousand. Guard losses were approximately equal. The Guard and police between them killed 14,178 looters and an unknown number were wounded. Nevertheless, the richest portions of Greater New York were ransacked and hundreds of thousands of persons escaped with booty, often highly valuable.

The hoped-for "record Christmas sales" became, instead, such a great loss for so many that tens of thousands of firms are today financially ruined. The comparatively few able to set up business again have no present intention of doing so in Greater New York. Scores of thousands of well-off city-dwelling families have moved out and more will do so when able. New York City, itself, is not just bankrupt but so many billions in debt that none of the holders of its bonds or other paper expects any return.

It became a half-deserted city, a city of alarms and crime by day, murderous by night. Regular Army units can still be seen, everywhere, as the city is under federal management and law now. Wall Street is sluggishly active again, but the market will move soon to Chicago, or perhaps some less vulnerable city in mid-continent. Shipping is regaining its life on a reduced scale. A few great structures even in the worst ravaged area stand untouched, some bank and office buildings that proved resistant to every assault, also the towering Smythe Building which was built by Jason Smythe and later housed the central offices of the Foundation for Human Conservancy. Many of these edifices are in partial operation under heavy guard. Buses show the snouts of machines guns.

What is the future outlook for New York?

187

No one can surely say.

But what is certain is this:

It will not again become the great megalopolis it was, the world's fifth largest and the richest urban complex in the time of man. Nothing new is being constructed and little reconstruction is in progress. Half of its buildings are damaged. The roar of the collapse of some shoddy structure, or of a building weakened by mob acts or by dynamiting for fire belts, is a frequent sound in a city otherwise strangely quiet.

The financial failure of the great commercial center of America touched off the current and deepening national depression. The means of the death of New York sits like a leaden weight on the spirit of Americans. Most, alas, live in or near some huge or near-huge urban center, nowadays. And all these are asking themselves a question few dare speak aloud: *Could it happen to us?* There have been too many calamities.

The Cleveland catastrophe left that city stricken and it has not yet devised financially acceptable plans for reconstruction. New York had already suffered the disaster known as Black Valentine's Day; but its general recovery was fairly swift, after a considerable period of shock. For a time it appeared the Missouri-Mississippi River basin was doomed, as the mighty waterways and many tributaries were increasingly gorged with a terrifying indestructible, fast-multiplying alga, a mere one-celled plant which, it seemed, man could not conquer.

Other cities and many non-urban areas in this nation have suffered many sorts of agonies for which man was, in the end, the cause. Yet here, as before, reaction is not an admission of human fault but at most a silence and, commonly, a reflection of human responsibility. Even for the New York calamity of last December, blame is laid on a few politicians and their appointees, along with some merchants, as if these were not either elected by the people or else providing the people with what they desired. Yet not one in a hundred of those who castigate such specific individuals would have acted differently in the same positions.

The intellectual disavowal of common fault for events all men share blame for has become infamous. The three somewhat destructive quakes in California in the seventies occurred, in every case, near huge reservoirs, a known cause of earth movement owing to their placement of masses of water over a previously not loaded geological spot. Those three quakes have added stress on the great San Andreas Fault, already strained beyond the point where relief will be sure, eventually: tomorrow or in a hundred years, the experts say, the San Andreas will slip. But should the worst happen and the cities from San Francisco to San Diego be leveled, or tossed into the Pacific, men will call that an act of God. So it is, but one, if it happens, that man will have accentuated by his dams and reservoirs and one that will involve millions, perhaps, in death, because they live in that area, knowing well their implicit hazard and the risks they added.

Again, John Frakant, Secretary of the Department of Interior, backed by the Secretaries of Labor and of Welfare, has recently condemned China in congressional hearings on the ground that China's swift and almost incredibly massive industrialization has measurably and increasingly contributed to the pollution of much of the atmosphere reaching USA. Forced to industrialize by the least costly means, China has automatically used the most polluting methods. And now the American air as it circles ever eastward in the North Temperate Zone arrives in an industrially dirtied state. Again, men did it—Chinese men. But what is then carried across USA and the Atlantic bears our vastly great burden of contamination, yet we give no heed to its next recipients, the people of Britain, of Europe, of Russia.

189

Men did not have to use, to enter New York on that fatal Saturday, vehicles of ancient vintage with controls which have deteriorated. Men chose to do so as a "right." And the wave of crime which has continued to rise for decades, and is another menace to all Americans, is the doing of men, not an act of God. The many great oil spills, from undersea blowouts of wells, from breaks in huge pipelines and from accidents to the fleet of ships in which single vessels transport a million tons of "black gold," are always a human fault and not some unanticipated event which no drillers, designers, pilots or engineers could foresee. Each of these is the result, and a statistically absolute result, of the fact that men everywhere in the world demand petroleum for fuel, power, automotive vehicles and, in general, for the major energy base that permitted our "progress," as we go on calling it. Now the lapses in that single enterprise are killing the very seas.

Nobody has to live near the San Andreas Fault, and doing so is now causing an anxiety that bravado merely emphasizes. Men lived without petroleum too.

The harsh demands of the Desert War had to be met, I agree. We could not have allowed the breakdown of whole states and nations that led us to support the UN-sponsored effort to "oilice" the riven lands in North Africa and the Middle East. Support was vital and America answered the call finally and with ultimate success. The weapons and supplies for that conflict had to be made, with no regard to the effect on environment. The broad and bitter crisis was resolved and it may well lead to stability in that long-turbulent region.

But men made that war; not us, at first; and not the Israelis, till they were massively attacked; but the Arabs, sworn to push the little state of Israel off the earth. We fought, too, because Red support of the Arab nations had reached a point where those passionate, ill-informed multitudes would have not only erased Israel but also let the Soviets take over the desert oil empires. Take over the Mediterranean, too, probably, and move into Africa to arrange for its fall into Red hands, in time.

But was the American postwar leap into every possible fabrication of every possible item, whether useful, merely luxurious or even harmful, necessary? Did we have to jump into a deluge of consumer-goods-making at full steam when we knew that haste would leave no time or funds for a slower, more careful and less polluting industrial shift from munitions to cars—and all the rest? Is boom the one answer to depression, the end of man, boom?

A year after the debacle New York is becoming, with a certain few areas and streets and avenues excepted, a ruin. For decades, men have struggled to keep it viable and men have also expressed doubts that it could be governed. Its rule is military now. But it is not being "governed" because most of that great city is a void and a void cannot be managed or governed. In time, only islands of business, industry, other activities will remain and remain operational. In fifty years and with luck, those islands might begin to spread and touch and create a smaller but functioning city. But it is entirely possible, also, that Greater New York will simply decay, topple, turn into the first true American ruin, a giant heap of ultimate rubble for future archaeologists to pick at.

In their present mood, sullen, frightened, with guns and newer weapons, most urban and suburban dwellers still look to arms for personal safety rather than to what causes debacle. And their fears are motivated by recent findings. It was not just the Harlem blacks or the slum dwellers who took part in the ravishing of New York. Many "ordinary, law-abiding citizens" joined in—professors, doctors, lawyers, accountants, the cream of the urban crop, even some ministers. Our young people ask, rightly, why the law should be obeyed by them, when such others have turned thief.

The next issue of the *Northern Atlantic* will appear in January of a new year, 1984. Many readers of this summary and comment will recall George Orwell's book, entitled 1984. He predicted that by then the world would be split into two camps, both absolute dictatorships. The two would wage eternal but limited war, to maintain the totalitarian state. There would be no freedom of speech but only forced hewing to the ruling line. All individuals would be under constant, electronic surveillance. The Ministry of Love would be the enforcement bureau, using refined torture on any dissident or suspected antagonist of the state. The Ministry of Truth would be in charge of propaganda, of state-supporting lies, and it would rewrite history as the ruling group and the chief tyrant, Big Brother, wished history to say, not what it was.

There has long been fear, much justified, that America has been and is drifting into such a nightmare. But up to the year Orwell set for the world he foresaw, the many efforts to infringe on most freedoms in USA have been resisted, if proposed, and outlawed, if briefly on the books. Ours is still a democracy.

It is in the larger areas of menace that we have failed to grasp the perils and failed almost absolutely to devise remedies, let alone put them in action. The seas stand even more painfully than the air in our North Temperate Zone as proof of a defection that outweighs the advances we take such pride in.

The Gulf of Mexico is a dead sea. So is the Gulf Stream, now a river in the Atlantic that is barren, relatively, of life. The Baltic became dead long ago and the Caspian and Black

Seas followed. Our coasts, Atlantic and Pacific, no longer serve as the breeding ground of many fishes we once caught commercially or for sport. Who would stick a foot in Lake Erie, Ontario or Michigan and most of Huron, for fun, today? The lumbering and other industrial enterprise so recently launched in the Amazon basin, and so extensively, are "helping Latin America out of poverty" and they are poisoning the South Atlantic also.

Our long-time fear and hatred of Russia and its Reds, and of China, too, has been lessened owing to world-wide contaminations that recently drove us together to seek means to end the ultimate death of the ecosphere. But the means in being are, still, not a fraction of those required and agreed on. All parties in this debate blame one another and none is willing to appropriate the essential money. But the rapprochement was a great social gain, for it served, and serves increasingly, to bring all men together in a common attempt to survive. The dread of Communism that once paralyzed USA, even though few of the folks could say what Communism was, is not the old lever for whatever military, political or other group could be mustered to attack anything they called "Communist."

The two great but different political systems, theirs and ours, stand at odds still. But both systems have, almost without using the term, adopted many principles from one another.

So the long effort to be ready for nuclear war, which, if it had occurred, would have erased the North Temperate Zone, from the middle sixties on, is now known for what it then was and will remain: nothing any nation is going to start. There can never be a "most powerful nation" again, where arms are the measure.

But even with such stresses relieved, we Americans, no

more than any other nation, have not as yet come to grips with the issue of our perishing planet. Fly across the Atlantic or a stretch of the Pacific, and the oceans below will still seem blue and clear and clean. Cross by boat and you will find your ship often plows for hours through masses of floating debris, junk, some items identifiable such as plastic containers, most of the rubble oil-soaked and unrecognizable, flotsam that some human being or beings dumped there, or dumped where the rains and wind and waterways would carry it out there. Close to the oceanic surface on sunny days you will see in the clearest areas an opalescent coating, petroleum and its products, mainly, that has changed many characteristics of the oceans, from light-reflecting capacities to surface tension. Look a bit closer and you can discover, if you have the technical ability, that the former minute life forms on and near the sunshine of surface water are now rare, in most places, and absent in many.

Like the sky itself, which we know is never quite as blue as it used to be at its clearest and bluest, like the increased cloud cover our satellites and space vehicles report, like the ever greater stretches of land worn out by man in this century, our biosphere is contaminated, scummed over, dustier, more toxic and killing the tiny life forms that support the food chain. We and nearly all nations agree this grim danger must be halted and must be reversed. But we cannot agree on who pays what proportion for what measures that will have to be undertaken.

America was once a nation that courted challenge and boasted of its giant technical successes. Russia, too, England, Germany, Italy, and many more. But an anxious and subdued America isn't rising to this scale of challenge as it should. Its very way of life is shrunken and its concerns are local, largely commercial and acquisitive. What happened to New

York City is going to happen to the whole earth if we retain the present, ingrown, blame-rejecting state of mind.

What happened to New York, indeed, should serve as a final lesson, for all who still needed the instruction. And the lesson is elementary. It asserts that you (and I, of course) are the agents of that slaughter. And it states that whatever is to happen to man today, tomorrow and as long as man endures is the result of what you (and I) do, whether its net is to improve or poison us. The laws of nature are absolute, inviolable and, when disobeyed, unforgiving. If there should be a God, then He made those laws. He would be a fool to permit their violation, let alone condone the act and then shatter His principles in order to salvage a species that imagined it could thrive by lawlessness.

Raymond Bainter's article in the *North Atlantic* contained an overview that expressed the "aura" of the period. And what was true of USA was true elsewhere. The many disasters of the past dozen years had created a drive in civilized men to make their machines work, to create prosperity by an act of will, and that intent did not include massive expenditures for environmental benefits. All that filled the public brain was a ravening desire to convert to goods production on a scale surpassing prewar records.

Was everybody so blind? Didn't anybody foresee what was certain, that the time was at hand when Nature would strike back on a far vaster scale?

Of course many did!

Many had foreseen very clearly not just outlines of what lay ahead but the precise kinds of calamities that would be the fate of billions. Miles Smythe was one of them. But their voices were faint cries in the wilderness of greed and fear, as vested interests fought for an ever larger share of the ever diminishing profits, and the private citizen, uncomprehending and terrified, willfully shut his eyes to the doom to come.

4. *The Sexual Redemption*

Readers once revoltingly called "pre-teeners," a term only commerce could coin, will already have looked at the index of this tome—if tome it becomes and index it has—then turned right to this chapter.

At ten or twelve I would have.

No young person ever can find out enough about human sex.

There are reasons for that, though not as many now as there were.

In the past, a major adult effort was to prevent young people from learning anything at all about sex. Even in the seventies, the period where this text begins, there was no "sex education" in most public schools and great controversy about whether or not it should be added to the curriculum anywhere. Most parents of that era either passionately believed or, at least, publicly supported what was still the majority's ideal for sex behavior: a girl should enter marriage a virgin (never having fucked), and a boy, too, though virginity on marriage was not as firmly expected of him as of his bride; married couples should never have sexual relations with others; homosexuality was, to the majority, all but unspeakable (though it appeared more and more in movies and as a discussion item in mass media) and even incest was seen as more "understandable" (though deserving of the death penalty) than sex relations between two men. Similar relations of women were widely unknown to occur and, when known of, judged by millions as less evil than the male counterpart. Relations with animals were regarded with horror except in rural areas where they were ignored, if possible.

Common law sustained this basic Christian (Protestant-Catholic) posture. Sexual relations were allowed between married pairs, of at least the age of consent, when performed in one position, woman on her back, man atop, and people permitted this much sex could be "married" by the civil authorities, though some churches refused to accept civil ceremonies as genuine or adequate. This is *all* that the churches sanctioned and many states backed up that sum with laws carrying exceedingly harsh punishments. The limitations can be clearly seen to approach closely that point at which further strictures would interfere with population growth. Of course, at the time these needle-eye permissions were made dogma and became the basis of civil law, population "growth," or reproductive fecundity, was essential as only a large batch of babes could provide enough survival material to keep a nation or a congregation increasing at even a minor rate.

All sexual acts not allowed by the above mandate were, of course, ungood, sin and evil. But inasmuch as most other sins—thieving, murder, mugging, embezzling and the lot—are felt as such by normal people, and inasmuch as normal people tend to commit such sins (crimes) only under tremendous pressure, or with great temptation, and only when they hope they won't get caught, the church had a different problem when it undertook to grasp the total management of human sex behavior as a way to get hold of the soul entire. For sexual or erotic antics proscribed by the church (and federal and state laws) didn't quite seem, in all cases, to parallel the more clearly criminal acts.

Yet the effort to make them seem parallel was undertaken ferociously and with effect. Sins got crime names. Masturbation was self-abuse, self-defilement. Bedding a neighbor's wife was "stealing" the woman. Her spouse was robbed. And of course both gamesters were defiled. Every erotic act not condoned by the church degraded, defiled, polluted, contaminated and befouled the dirty bastards. All sex was made bestial and filthy except this narrow minimum and even it was *pretty* dirty, if essential, a fact some sects drove home by creating castes of men and women, priests, monks, nuns, et al., sworn to celibacy—which oath elevated them above the rest by several magnitudes of sanctity. This, of course, was to make the folks feel cheap, the folks who reached the age of consent, wed and screwed face to face, the gal on her back, as allowed, and with none of your foreplay or positional experiment—jail was ready to clamp you in, for that sort of thing, lewd, lascivious and unnatural crime.

The finest human way of life was sexless. Failing that, the least sex procreation demanded was the most a person should engage in and, even then, he and she knew they were dirty married weaklings and needed shriving for every orgasm, if any females managed them at all, or even for "doing it," no matter about fun. Indeed a woman had to assent when her husband demanded it, as she was his property.

The effort of the godly to prevent any flouting of the basic and God-given Least-Possible Code, by dirtying and criminalizing infractions, was probably the most intense, continuous and effective public relations campaign in the history of propaganda. It had to be to achieve the goal or even approach it.

It would be interesting to reproduce Jiggermeter's catalogue of terms for sexual behavior having derogatory intent and effect. It might be, for some, a way to show what human beings at the opening of the twentieth century were up against when they made any effort to think or feel about sex and sexuality in any but the ordained one way. Unfortunately, the list occupies three hundred and eighty-seven pages of fine print.

Consider this, however:

There were no words for sexual acts and organs that were socially allowable in correct company. Medicine, obliged to acknowledge sexual anatomy, stuck to Latin. Parents, either unfamiliar with Latin, or feeling it a bit embarrassing as too explicit, had thousands of euphemisms. A girl might learn her opening was her "place." Children did not micturate, urinate or even void, they "piddled," "tinkled" or "made wee-wee." A nice boy had no idea what to call his penis till he got to school or church. A romantic adult pair with a specific mutual desire would find its spell shattered if he or she were to suggest "cunnilingus," but what else could they say? Cunt-lapping? Muff-diving? Eating hair pie? Going down?

Let that suffice. By 1970, when some effort was afoot to give sexual "education" in public schools, there was still no vocabulary for the courses. That is like proposing to teach arithmetic without having a numbers system. What people failed to see, there, was that a proper vocabulary wouldn't be acceptable if designed. For sex is an emotion-loaded subject and education in it, to be sane, should not try to evade the charged reality by teaching the anatomy and operations involved as if the process were automobile mechanics. Education aimed at helping young people toward a sexual life of a normal and a contenting sort would have to use words for sex that had at least a pleasure connotation if not one of ecstasy. But any school program for sex education would have had to avoid any "pro" words and provide a very different connotation, *whatever* terms were used.

American society and, indeed, Western civilization was anti-sexual, brutally, bitterly, overtly, violently, legally, and with God's cruel heel stamping offenders. Nothing quite so a-natural or vicious had been managed culturally thitherto. But for a long time this power of the churches to administer sex by issuing minimal permits and by seeing that civil courts carried out its barbarous penalties for infractions did work because it did give the churches a grip on man and woman so fierce, basic and unyielding that it could face down Darwin for millions to the end.

Of course, other instinctual needs of man were limited by the church in so far as was possible or bearable. Pissing and shitting could not be prohibited or even restricted to special days. But they could be boothed and confined and made nasty if done before others. People had to eat, but here was a somewhat delayable drive so it could be church-throttled, or the opposite, to a degree, as by fasting and feasting. Little can be done to regulate breathing, but you can make breathing incense a periodic compulsion.

The entire process evolved slowly. It was wholly designed to concentrate power over masses in the hands of the ruling few. Vestiges of some old religions remain in which the temple used sex as a reward, providing for the righteous (and the heavily contributing men in the sect) a string of Vestal Virgins, priestesses, temple dancers and the like, for sport of the virtuous. Some temples still supply stone gods with large and convenient phalluses wherewith widows and perhaps other females with rights unguessable can and do "console" themselves.

But it soon proved that fear, terror, guilty conscience, a self-debasing assurance of sinning, along with the most fiendish punishments currently permissible by the tribe, not to mention others relating to the afterlife (heaven missed and hell assured), were vastly more effective techniques for mass subornment than mere rewards. Of course, a few interspersed rewards, heaven as a hope, or a promotion in the church peckery, could be added—in which case, the system was exactly that of brainwashing and as infallible.

However, a sexual tide rose against this situation as it existed in USA. The first surge was for suffrage and started before this century. In the twenties, the movement became broader. Women's sexual emancipation was a goal, free love an effort and aim, "companionate marriage" or "trial marriage" a suggestion, and many other projects for a less demon-throttled state of man and sexuality were given public airing. Unfortunately, with the end of the twenties in the crash and the Depression that followed, few persons had time, energy, spirit, money or even the gall to promulgate better sex living, since people were going hungry for food and to mention sexual appetite at all was, clearly, not apt.

The amount of progress made by those early rebels has never been given suitable credit. They changed a great deal of the unconscious bigotry of the masses. They undid some of the churchly investiture of sex with horse shit, pus, bacteria, the road to idiocy and ruin, so that, as the "sex revolution" in the late sixties got going, it had a better ground to seed. The rebels in the twenties were well aware that their crusade would be met by the armies of Christ. Those of the later period weren't all that pressed or endangered as the churches had lost a good deal of mileage and authority between 1929 and 1969.

Too many discoveries had been of sorts that showed the clerical dogmas were unsound, untenable, nothing for sensible people to fool with. Darwin and Freud put out at least one papal eye. Medicine began to show Christians needn't accept a "lot" of agony and early demise as tests of faith. Worse, for the church grip, good prophylactics were burgeoning and better ones sure to appear, but even in 1970 a girl with a few dollars and a little care could screw fraternities in series and not fear she'd get knocked up, as the church made folks say. Miracle drugs took care of VD, if people took care. These two bastions of church chastity fell: you'll get a bun in your oven, clap or syph, the terms the godly allowed us.

And so in this era people, led by students and those under thirty, launched a crusade for sex revolution, and older people joined in millions, to the best of their ability. Actually, this second sex revolt, thinking it was first, followed the going system of all the countless revolutions then in progress—drives against the establishment, the system, war, the Vietnam war, everything in America, pollution, education, educators, and other institutions, ideas or what not. The basic philosophy of these revolutionaries was simple, contagious and inane: whatever the over-thirties do, refuse to do; what they don't do, do it.

The over-thirties, members of the establishment and system, were, in 1970, not living in their totality by the standards set forth here as those basic to our national sex morality (and legal code) in the past of the nation. In fact, by the time the late-sixties student-sex rebels got really on the march, they attacked a lot of targets that were already torn to ribbons and flattened. Homosexuality was being discussed and openly, and it was under lessening demonic persecution than before. Cadres of perfectly nice American couples, in the system, establishment and church, had been increasingly practicing a thing called "wife swapping" and they now numbered many millions, though the census of the seventies didn't try to determine the exact figure.

Premarital sex was happening. Many examples had parental consent. All sorts of married couples were fucking in sixty postures, for the sake of variety. And about then, some one of those trivial Supreme Court handouts apparently opened the so-called floodgates of pornography. The Court had said, more or less, that an adult or group of agreeing adults can read what they please, look at any snapshots or paintings they select, including movies.

Erotica, called "pornography" (and nobody drew distinctions or seemed able to try—when the distinction was easy), swept Europe and homed on USA. Only Soviet Russia and Red China resisted, Russia being sexually much like the Christians and their church as described here. The Chinese may have been too busy carrying hods. Japan, interestingly, alone took the erotic deluge calmly.

Having obliquely required it of myself, I shall define the difference between erotica and pornography. Would that the Supreme Court had had the discernment—they might then have altered destiny!

Erotica is any treatment of sexual acts, and related acts or material, which gives rise in a beholder (who is not antisexual either consciously or subconsciously) a sense that what is presented shows how sex enhances his species in a special or in many ways. Beings who do that, he or she feels, are truly elegant, wonderful, and not just animals but the best of animals, for what these have added to this display that lesser creatures cannot achieve, or cannot in that degree. That quality of an erotic work need not give every beholder any intense reaction of that sort. But, minimally, it should have some elevating or enhancing effect however meager, but above the level of indifference.

Obviously, good taste is mandatory here. The quality of our erotic bodies and imaginations requires every quality in its artistic expression.

What is pornographic, then, is whatever concerns sex that is debased and debases the viewer, by vulgarity, by presenting sexual behavior as nasty, dirty, or brutal, sadistic, masochistic. To be sure, many contemporary people were most "aroused" by that very sort of pornographic display, violence, sadism, masochism, et al. Those were, all, sick—and the church made them that sick, as is evident from the above exposition of church practices.

We know and knew, truly, the difference between erotica, which is a glorious thing, and pornographia, which is anything less. But most Americans, most people in "Christian" nations, were so brainwashed in the dirtiness of sex and its wickedness (with the accompanying demand for punishment), that they could not accept the erotic, since it was beautiful, uplifting, a scene in praise of humanity and one that had no punitive result nor did it require brutality as the price of pleasure. Nor was it vulgar.

That much could be said about sexual entertainment.

But America fell beneath an avalanche of sexual movies and magazines, books and private pictures, public acts of sexual relations, private acts by entertainers, in all of which no such discernment was made. The great bulk of the material was, indeed, vulgar, debased, and much of it was sado-masochistic, a vast amount involved female homosexuality and, some, male action of the same sort. Very little was imaginative, the actors were in general unskilled, ordinary, without pride in their achievements and, if proud, then of the wrong aspects of their work.

In the midst of this, the young and their sex revolution were hard put to find anything they could rebel against, with force and novelty. They tried "unisex," that is, pretending no sexual differences existed, dressing alike, with long hair for both, and engaging in floor parties where males and females crawled about copulating or orally locking in with either sex at random. This effort usually involved drug-taking but so did many other revolutionary activities, such as rapping, trashing, identity search, seduction of others to the cause, boredom-flight, cramming, and, perhaps above all, "belonging"—to non-others of like non-mindedness.

Alienation was the regular alibi for much the rebel young

did—or refused to do—and it now seems surprising that so many youths deceived themselves, each other and a large fraction of the adult world by that pose. For all men are born alien, live as aliens and die alien. They all have some opportunity to find what they can of themselves and the world, reality as it is known in their time, and a meaning in life, if they try for that ferociously and unrelentingly; even, failing there, they all can abet the need they felt and failed to fulfill. They can and must, if honest, devote their lives to making the best chance possible for the next generation or some beyond, to try where they failed—but with the better chance they made for others. Myth? Self-sacrifice? Unrewarding? What else is there to do?

The mind of man is for that end. The more he uses it properly the more clearly he will ascertain that he will never find a final answer in his days. But he will also know that way is the fact which matters: if he tries he has a chance of finding some small, new step nearer to one of the final answers. To expect more is to identify the self as God, plus the universe and all time. To think the effort can be jettisoned and that a human being with a brain has used it properly, used it at all, by concluding the universe is absurd, senseless, without point or meaning, is to abdicate mind absolutely, it is to imagine one has become God and cosmos by saying what these are not (as if one knew that!) and by mere self-inflation to be judge of all time and space, by anti-thought and non-thought, becoming, then, a hollow skull before the fact, and preaching to skeletons who, alone, can be said to hear non-sound, if you get people that near to brained bone.

Not all but all the more popular forms of "existentialism" are examples of such metaphysical ways to refuse to learn or think, while giving out as final nothing-answers, to nothing-hearers, an intellectual impossibility as it is a physical impossibility, too. One makes no headway against alienation by starting with the counter-cartesian premise, I am absent.

But such diffuse forms of non-thought pervaded the seventies. Young people became students, so called, of astrology Tarot, with other superstitious copouts; they took up superficially mystical philosophies of the East and the Orient—and called all our proven knowledge, science, irrelevant, and said reason was a trick of the establishment.

With such people engaged in a sex revolution, anything could be expected—except improvement of our understanding of human sexuality. Almost everything occurred. There was a surge of "Women's Lib" based, it first seemed, on the real, vast and unbearable injustice of humanity to women. But this decent effort soon turned into a simpler war against males on all counts, thus debasing both sexes.

Nobody knew, in 1970 or 1980 or 2000, what the ideal for human sexual behavior might be, was meant to be, or, say, what "morals" would match our biology and our meaning as a species of a somewhat novel and very experimental sort.

Nobody really had any clear and demonstrable idea of how to rear children, as sexual beings, or adolescents, so no one could possibly imagine what would be right and what mistaken for adult sexual behavior. No one knew what was normal, its limits if any, and if any, why!

The idea that this ought to be inquired into till the correct answers came in hardly entered a modern head in a million. Instead of trying to learn who we are, sexually, America and the world simply withdrew from any effort to give our sexual behavior any guidance, restraint or purpose, supervision or even an aesthetic; in sum, the hands of man were washed of the problem.

For those readers of the future who might enjoy a long and detailed chapter on sex in USA from 1975 to 2000, I feel the facts would disappoint. It ought to be sufficient to note the highlights, or low, if you prefer, of what followed.

With "pornographia" a "gold mine" for movies, by 1970, the next "gold mine" was obvious: home movies, cassettes, or, later and better, cable TV.

The corporations soon got the message. Cable TV and 3D-TV could be transmitted on home-selected channels; what the viewers wanted to view could be provided as selected. The next and, again, obvious program shift involved "live" sex. Nothing ever made a swifter hit: live sex acts, via cable, became a multibillion-dollar business in a year. And, by the later eighties, another inevitable shift was occurring, also predictable by history.

The fifty-odd millions wired for cable X-raters tired of the ordinary casts of sex shows even though they had favorites of both sexes, as well as favorite "combinations." But soon they asked for "real" people, personalities of the non-erotic TV companies, celebrities of the stage, notables outside show biz—and, of course, they gradually got their wishes.

The result of a successful appearance on a sex show became fame of a truly fanatical sort. When a popular lecturer on science, a personable man whose genuine claim to fame as an astrophysicist rose from several new concepts of his origin, and also produced a Nobel prize, one night, masked, and introduced only as a great scientist who would take on both his secretaries, very artistically and positively brought two (masked) but elegantly designed lasses to multiple orgasm, he became the most famed man of science ever, by whisking off all three masks at the finale, and, while helping dress the girls, telling the viewers who he was, news to most of them but not all by any means. He was thrown out of several scholarly societies for the act—but also made a top man at Du Pont with a salary of $500,000 for the first year, escalated beyond.

207

THE END OF THE DREAM

Then a hard-pressed candidate for the Senate in a Wisconsin race, a Democrat to be sure, with a wife who had not long before been "Miss Lakes and the Cheese Princess," after great soul-struggling, went before network cameras set around their bedroom. He gently brought in his wife, not masked and recognized by millions, and made love to her with élan, passion and considerable show of athletic prowess. Shocked politicians held their breath till the election count. The man who so thoroughly enjoyed his ecstatic wife on TV, apparent loser by polls of a few days earlier, took all the votes of his party and ninety-five per cent of those expected to go to his opponent.

This made presidential hopefuls nervous.

They were saved by Congress, which ruled their sort off the air in such ploys.

After a little rioting, high schools began to construct erotic rooms for students with parental permits and, soon, some of these rooms were provided with viewing galleries. Societies that had been furtively forming in the sixties to practice their belief that boys and girls of eight or more should have sexual lives as a right, with complete freedom as to partners— moms, pops, siblings, other adults, other kids—began to get air attention. Watching a nice-looking and (masked, unnamed) daddy have his first intercourse with his cute, nine-year-old Olivia was new—and big.

What ruined that TV geyser of gold, after it had become the fourth business enterprise in the land, was the Gardner-Gibson Love-O-Mat. A technological combination of various old and a few new scientific findings made the Love-O-Mat an instant marvel, a public passion, for all its high cost in the early years.

In effect, the Love-O-Mat patron entered a perfumed, dusky bed-centered chamber with a dim dome crowded with

many unguessable bits of equipment. There the patron, his
fee paid, undressed, with opposite-sex aid if wished, a live
being, who also inquired what the client would like, in the
form of a "love affair," without anything but casual enthu-
siasm for any choice and the same degree for all.

Then came an even more alluring part. From dozens of
albums—if need be—the male, in this example, was asked to
pick the lass he wished as co-celebrant in that special erotic
rite. At no time did these albums lack choices among the
most lofty picture and TV stars; Broadway actresses
abounded, too, and a staggering number of merely well-
known, well-dressed swingers of the jet routes, often married
and not even between divorces or even planning divorce.

The weekly demand for these women had become a higher
symbol and more sought by many than "best-dressed win-
ners," "most elegant," "best hostess," etc. Fees for this
role soon reached six figures, but playing the roles required
months of very hard drill, rehearsal and acting, with and
without partners, depending on the fantasy being computer-
ized. For it amounted to that.

Once a damsel or matron had registered on tape every
erotic act she was willing to perform, and had performed it
in all the variations writers and directors felt would suit the
oddball element enough for a profit, a woman might feel
her fee earned. But since no poor performances were used,
though paid for, the ladies who were Love-O-Mat choices
gathered fans in myriads, great men, nobility, but not all
welcome at close range. The studios took care of such problems.

The gentleman client when stripped took his place, prone,
on a plastic-sheeted table. He was carefully and completely
sprayed with a pleasant-scented, silver-hued, elastic material
that dried but did not stiffen. He turned over and was re-

sprayed. No part of him expected to function, or even liable to, unexpectedly, was left uncoated. As he dried, music of his choice began to play softly. The plastic sheet was whisked away. The table became part of whatever sort of bed (or other love-support) he had selected. Lights died down and then, slowly, the lady of his choice appeared, dressed, nude, or however semi-accoutered he had noted on the list tendered to his real maid-aide. The damsel would have three dimensions and be very solid-appearing, too. When she took his hand, exchanged a first kiss, or merely talked, as she touched him here and there, she felt real, warm, alive, herself. She was scented as he wished—or as she did, if he asked it that way. Her voice was hers. He could feel her breath. For now the Gardner radiation-responsed phenomenon was in operation.

She was a creature of light but also one around whom and within whom several million Gardner radiation-propagation units were activating the sprayed skin of her lover, inducing exactly the same sense the action by a real female would produce. When she lay across him, he felt her weight, where it would press on him, in the right places and degrees.

What led to his reactive motions was also monitored and a light-swift feedback made adjustments of both to match. Her kisses were as deft or wild, as ranging or limited to thrust, as his responses to them indicated his wants. And when they had spent whatever time he had wanted, or paid for, in mutual excitation, the road to orgasm was as real, living, as actual relations, and often far more uninhibited and joyous. For here, he had no inhibitions and here, too, the lady, perhaps a great screen star he'd never seen in the flesh, was completely subject to his desires.

My first experience with this long-established device was done on a dare and I discovered, not with complete surprise, my wife was electronically available. It occurred to me to ask if it was possible to see other chosen persons with partners. It was, for a fee. I found Nora had been recorded with another man and decided not. The other man is a friend. I understood the situation—Dr. Jason Smythe had, by then, made considerable progress with his initial thesis that if incest were not taboo, but optional, no oedipal or electra complexes would arise. His supporters were now producing evidence to show he was at least often right.

But a thought followed. Jason's second wife, Pat, and her daughter Zillah, had always made it much too clear to me, after I met the family, that either one would adore to have me sleep with her any time I stayed with Miles, which was often. I had resisted even when Nora was away—just to have something of my own, I think, at their palatial residences, even if it was only a reluctant, negative and often ball-burning and sole "own" possession.

Zil was in an album. So I had Zil. Three ways, three times. It seemed a decent way to deal with a still red-blonde sex engine who still beckoned.

It amazed me. It felt real, looked real, sounded real and *was* real—except it was reality projected by a machine that materialized dreams. I went out ready to tell Nora and even to insist she try one of the ladies' suites. But I postponed that confession because it dawned on me that, through our teens, while I never fell an inch away from my fall for Nora, she'd often watched me shake free of Zillah, but, for sure, with visible reluctance. She might not think I'd make up for that long self-discipline and sometimes undesired fidelity. And I wouldn't want Nora to think I was cheating, testing the evaded fire—even this way.

Such, then, was the Love-O-Mat, widely regarded as America's top scientific marvel. The machines spread world-wide save for the USSR. The Politbureau's final refusal to import them was the lit match that blew the powder keg. Without that puritan vote there might never have been the next People's Revolution that tore the USSR to wisps and shreds, to acreages that showed the earth's curve, where only weeds stood in former grain fields, and anything on a horizon would be a ruin with long-unfound and buried dead.

What the Love-O-Mat did to the American public, God knows. The birth rate shrank, collapsed, frightened all sorts of people who thought America needed another hundred million or so, but the babies actually born were, beyond doubt, wanted, a new thing. And maybe the Love-O-Mats provided joy where there was not much left outside their scented doors. Perhaps to possess any movie star or other public libido-goddess you desired, any way you wanted her, or, maybe, to love someone old, for the novelty, or one of the grade school kids, really did provide sex with a fresh, new, young and natural sensation. I don't know. That much of our original curse may stick in me because I still feel I'd all but die of shame as my adult organ entered that of a girl of eight, however sure I was she'd adore it, would not feel any distress, was, in fact, giving love to get it from a big cock like her uncle's, dad's, grandfather's but not mine. I cannot change in all ways.

Finally it should be said that the Love-O-Mats changed sexual mores, conversation, the American mood. People agreed they didn't debauch them or increase sex crime—on the contrary. Sex, and a very dandy form, seeming real as reality in every way, save for instants spent on button-adjusting, would have had a far more varied and deep and perhaps somehow harmful final effect, had it been available long enough.

Some discussion of the devices occurred at a recent meeting of Faraway Committee for Sexual Studies. One of those present, a teacher, a cute, bright holder of an M.A. and a Ph.D., a Phi Beta Kappa key-wearer, who is no more formidable than girls as chic and taunting who lack high school diplomas, summed the matter up:

"Maybe when our sexuality is acknowledged from birth, and when no restraint is placed on its expression, save if that is mean, or for vengeance, jealously incited, or just impersonal lust, when we grow up with a long list of lovers in adolescence and then settle on one, we'll be more generous than we'd imagined, fifty years back.

"In fact, the idea of sex performed as generousness never got any time, in my youth. We constructed it to be selfish, possessive, if nothing else, and we sure spoiled a lot of love, not to say most marriages, by that tomb structure. A man admires a generous wife, always did. But what about a wife who carries the virtue into sexual acts, occasionally? And yet, why is this *not* a virtue as great as any other the Christians named?"

We see a lot of such hints of hope, here, these days.

Faraway is pretty lovely, of course, as Nature made it, and man changed only a little that he had to. It's a loving town, in a way unknown in other cultures, especially those last, greatest, most civilized "triumphs," with the shortest fuses such arrogance sets, and the biggest bang when they go.

5. *The First World Cataclysm*

PERSONAL NOTE TO MILES AND ALSO BOARD READERS, FROM THE EDITOR:

Seen from this time and place, it is difficult to remember, as the first world cataclysm approached, how hard many men and women tried to prevent the future that became fact. For all who did not even live through the interval, a correct concept of people and their behavior at the time will be near to impossible to form without special help. If *we* are asking *ourselves* how *we* "let" it happen, what will future readers of this work ask? What will they imagine? Unless the project envisioned here (or some other with the same end) is successful future generations will assume that "everybody" living between 1950 and 2010 was too utterly different to relate to, in any way. We will appear to have belonged to a different species.

The present and future generations will know that science is knowledge, nothing else, and that the work of scientists is to advance knowledge and/or teach what is on hand and how to add more. They are clearly aware that technology is not science but applied *parts* of science, and that technicians, engineers, gadget-inventors and so on are not scientists at all. Further, *we* stress education in the whole of science, not just one field. So future people must be led back to the public state of mind in, say, 1975.

The difference between science and applied science had not then been made, even for "highly educated" persons. Technology *was* "science" to the masses and their elected or appointed authorities. They couldn't "think scientifically" because the word itself set them thinking about artifacts, gadgets, miracle drugs, space ships or nuclear power plants, which the masses didn't understand *even* technically. Where opinion on technological matters was needed, they consulted technicians, not scientists, whom they wouldn't have understood, probably, and whom they considered woolly-minded, impractical, dreamer-professor types. The mere suggestion that scientists were the only truly "worldly" people around would have made them laugh merrily.

214

But even scientists were not educated, as a rule, in all major sciences. Such an individual would have been called, in those days, a "generalist"—as a term of derogation. For it was widely believed that any "generalist" was possessed of a mere smattering of knowledge of superficial sorts, since it was believed that there was far too much, in the whole of science, for any one man to learn well. To the specialist, that "learning well" meant learning in minute detail. Even he did not conceive that the major *lines* of the main *branches* of science could be learned well, and kept up with as they advanced— well *enough*, and more, for general understanding and, so, accurate "extrapolation," as they called foresight.

Scientists themselves rarely tried or bothered to learn much outside their "field." A physicist would be considered very "wide-ranging" if he had a working understanding of the main branches of that one discipline: astrophysics, nuclear physics, solid state physics, cryology, radiation propagation physics, engineering, laser physics and a broad understanding of chemistry, inorganic, at least. Such a specialist seldom had time, the urge, a reason or, even and often, any chance to add, from a freshman course in biology, the steps and main lines in the hundred or more vital branches of *that* science, or "life science." Where could any such person, if he existed, add years of enormously intense inquiry into (and experience in) the psychologies? Or inorganic chemistry?

And every passing year meant a "generalist" would have to put new towers of data on top of old, as well as look into fresh fields, some with names but a year old! Finally, human beings, scientists like the rest, with few exceptions, disliked to be found wrong or ignorant—a situation which up to then all men felt as humiliating. Few welcomed a correction that repaired an idea in error or supplied a lesson in a field in which he was not informed.

Unbounded curiosity lets the imagination learn without limit, indeed, makes the process *fun*. It was not so thought of in 1970 or 1980 or even 1990. Educators now are most urgently trying to teach that being corrected, put right, being relieved of some firm belief that is proven false, is a joyful experience, a source of elation. But then it was regarded as an injury to the ego, shameful and shaming, an insult even, and, personally as well as socially, a wound.

The material I have offered in the following part of the survey is to show that condition as near universal in the old days. When a group brought up some topic of importance, a member who was ignorant of it would not say, "I don't know" if he could avoid that "confession," for it would be seen as humiliating. I shall not include the predictions of the scientists who saw where the world was going, for, though startling when they were made, they are more nearly ancient history now than prophecy. But a comment by one of these scientists was especially astute:

"A guy in Iceland will catch a cod with an odd spot on its gills and then another and then write the Icelandic Forest and Fishing Agency that something's going wrong with cod. That'll be the first news of what will turn out to be the death warrant of a few hundred million people. But the agency will file the letter and do nothing. Then some professor will publish a monograph on *A New Fungus Affecting Five Species of Teleost Fishes*. Nothing will happen there either, till the myriads start to die and then it will be recalled that old Doc Bernard A. Bergman made the discovery. The mold will then be called *Bergmani* but nobody will ever remember Hans Johnssen spotted it first."

The "rice blast" had such a start—and such an end, too, though the middle story differs. From here, then, I turn to the first of the great world cataclysms and to how it initially came to notice. I now enter a photocopy of a letter that reached the Foundation for Human Conservancy shortly after its date of sending.

WILL GULLIVER

Head man, Human Saving Foundation, Mr. Standish,
Smithe Skyscraper on Avenue Five.
City of New York,
July 11th, 1985.

Dear Mr. President:

My name is James Rolle and I live in Louisiana near a town called East Jefferson Parish, name same, Route 1, Box 126. I have not much schooling. I and my brothers have some tenant land and raise some cotton and rice and the usual yams and collard greens and chickens and hogs. Not far from here is a United States Government Plant Experimental Station and has been, for some years. These people have test plots of many farm things. There's some land nobody's farmed for years, near their place, and I found that it puts up, every summer, a pretty decent stand of rice, various types seeded from stuff the federal folks are planting. For a couple of years me and the wife, Ella-Maytell, with some of our nine kids, been hand-gathering this here rice as it gets ripe and thresh it out with flails. Not a big deal. Maybe we get two bushel of mixed-up kinds of rice or so, otherwise gone to waste. But we're poor and nobody ever threw us off that weedy land and who owns it I have no infor. This summer, tho, when it was time for the heads to be ripe, most sorts, anyhow, we set a day off and took baskets and went to cut the rice to lug to the cabin. It was all dead. Every kind that the wind seeded from that federal place. Not a grain in the whole lot was anywhere near eatin' size or hardness, jest teeny and now turned soft, as the plants was, also. I was

217

worried. I seen, last few days, the plots of rice them federal science folks have made is beginning to die the same way. I ask a superintendent, a nigger but college-educated, what's the trouble. He isn't a Tom type but he tells me they're gonna find out, but haven't so far. Says it must be a wilt, a mold, or something of the kind but I sure I seen every wilt and rice-pest they is, nothing like this. If this trouble spreads there'll be a lot of poor farmers this season, even big ones, too. I thought maybe you was the right place to inform. Rice is a thing folks eat a lot. Hope this letter isn't a bother. Best wishes to your company for savin' folks, we need help.

Sincerely,
JAMES ROLLE

That letter was sent on by somebody in the mail department to somebody in our Division for the Study of Plant Diseases. There, it lay around for a time but was finally answered by a Tolbert Thackery, who, I assume, was one of the thousands of students serving as volunteers in dozens of Foundation activities during summer vacations. I haven't checked him and perhaps should. Most of these undergraduates or graduate students were training in special fields and found their time with us very useful. The Foundation, by then, was anything but popular with the masses. Professors and teachers tended, however, to admire it and urge students to volunteer, even when that urging had to be covert.

Young Thackery, if I'm right about him, answered the Rolle letter the day it hit his desk. That was a week after its arrival, no more. Here's a carbon of Thackery:

Dear Mr. Rolle:

You sent your letter to the right place. The Foundation for Human Conservancy is very interested in what you wrote. If any further rice crops, including those at the experimental station, are showing further signs of dying or blighting like those you described, we would like to know. For if what you reported is more than a local and limited blight, or the like, some freak event which occurred in the very small area you have under observation, surely the Agriculture people are doing something and, in any case, we at this Foundation would like to send an observer. Many thanks for your kind letter to us, for your keen observation and your quick action. I enclosed a stamped, self-addressed air mail envelope to save you any cost in your reply.

Yours sincerely,
Tolbert Thackery,
Dept. of Plant Diseases

There was no reply from James Rolle.

But, ten days later, Thackery did get an envelope, smudgy, smeared, sent by regular mail and containing two clippings from the issues of *East Jefferson Weekly Journal and Cajun Courier.*

One was from an obituary column and briefly noted the burial of James Rolle, farmer, after his death in a "hunting accident" on land where he was poaching. The tone of that notice might as well have said, "a shiftless, no-account, thieving nigger."

The other clipping from a front-page story with a two-column heading reported that the reason for the "recently erected canvas fencing around the Experimental Station and for the quarantine of all employees at the Station" was a sudden appearance of an unidentified "blight." The station manager had ordered the protective measures to insure that the blight would not get beyond the confines of that plant grounds. It added that the disease was being studied intensively and a counter to it or cure for it was to be expected very soon.

That pair of clippings was carried to the worried Mr. Thackery's superiors and they dispatched a team of specialists to the area. There were three in the team, two plant pathologists and a mycologist whose specialty was fungus on edible crops. They found all roads to the Federal Station were closed and guarded by armed men. When, returning to their motel that afternoon, they tried to question local people, they got evasive answers. The editor of the weekly, reached by phone at his home, said, once the caller identified himself, "We're saying nothing because there's nothing to say, Doctor. Federal orders. If there is any such a blight, it's halted and under control. Meantime, more rumors would only panic people." He hung up.

The next morning, as the Foundation team prepared to make a survey by rented car of the vicinity, they were taken under "protective custody" by "marshals" and put on a plane for New York. The armed "custodians" did not have identifying insignia.

This cavalier, near-incredible act was not without precedent in past decades. As Miles was in Alaska and I had gone to Belgium on two other disaster situations, the acting head let the Louisiana matter stand till one of us returned. The first happened to be Miles and by then the story was out. In the airport, in Chicago, Miles picked up a paper with a banner headline:

GULF COAST RICE DOOMED
Texas Crop Endangered
Half-Billion-Dollar Export Cereal
Prey to Unknown Blight

Headlines, yes. But American headlines.
American headlines for a week or thereabouts.

Then the headlines began to speak of the West Indies, of the Philippines, Japan and, less definitively, of China.

In the following fifty pages, Miles, I have entered every diverse account I could find, to give the variety of the effect on nations, on masses, on individuals, and to fill in the whole horror. I have entered records of the (eventual) fifty billion the USA appropriated to lease bottoms to convey food to that stricken world which depended on rice to exist.

I have given some pages, translated into lay terms, to show how the entire fraternity of "advanced" or "technological" nations became just that, a *fraternity*, devoting every bit of the spare energy, the surplus foods, they could to save the rice-dependent billions. It was estimated in mid-1986 that one third of the world's biologists and at least twenty per cent of all other relevant scientists were fully or partly engaged in the effort to halt what became known as the Rice Blast or Black Blight.

I have entered eyewitness accounts of cannibalism in a dozen regions and described the "human meat markets" that rose openly in more than fifty nations. And I have also presented, somewhat against my will, those shocking examples that became fairly numerous and quite vocal, of people who opposed "wasting treasure on trying to save the yellow race," people who often resurrected the Hearst term, "Yellow Peril," for our stricken fellow men. Included with such grisly assertions are a few by certain demographers and kindred experts who were crass enough to point out that the Black Blight, soon world-wide, was solving the population explosion problem. I also have entered parts of a discussion by worried scientists on the possibility that the Black Blight might, in some not inconceivable mutant form, attack other grains, wheat, oats, barley, corn and so on.

I included a tape recording made by a federal team that overflew the areas of death late that summer. Most of the cities in rice-dependent regions were on fire or had burned, a predictable fate when the inhabitants were either dead or had abandoned their homes. Forest fires were equally commonplace and I have the USSR figures, gathered in 1989 and more accurate than our own, of the timber lost in those conflagrations, roughly a third of the world's virgin trees of commercial value.

I included the fact that many rice-eaters died because they would eat no substitute grains. That cause of death, starvation, however, was minor for a time in many populous areas. For soon enough human flesh became the usual food of those billions. When it ran out, which was a year to three years from the beginning, the cannibalistic survivors died too.

I have graphic accounts of the initial efforts by all nonaffected nations to allow stricken people to immigrate. And I have proud accounts of the ships that sailed to the dying world of rice-eaters to gather a cargo of the hungry and bring them to Europe, the USSR and USA.

I documented the next rather swift change in that initially generous and humane endeavor. For as such immigrant hordes arrived, ill with countless diseases not even endemic in most of the "civilized" lands, their bones showing through their flesh, unable to speak any language of their saviors, spreading their diseases, too weak and too untrained to work, the public tide of resentment rose and the immigration program was halted.

Japan's brilliant and long-lasting effort to feed its people, as civilized as any, finally failed when the Japanese had nothing left to trade or barter, but after some twenty million of them, chosen for their technical skills, had been accepted in other lands—with families at first, later alone. But by that point the willingness, in America, or any other similarly able nation, to accept more starving aliens had vanished. I have a very beautiful account of a man who thought he was the last to be alive on Honshu, not correctly, but near enough: his fire-suicide poem.

My collection of scientific efforts to save man from this mighty foe is highly laudable of many. Scientists in thousands perished when stranded in some suddenly abandoned area where they had gone to do research. The effort to find the agent of this Black Blight was magnificent. For, of course, to find a remedy, the cause had first to be discovered.

It was observed that the black horror spread faster than any previously known blight, rot, smut, wilt or the like. Indeed, it seemed almost to flare up spontaneously in regions remote from any then infested. It killed every form of rice used for crops, every experimental mutant or hybrid, and all plants with a fairly close relationship to rice, including a variety of grasses and "weeds." But it attacked no other farinaceous species, or the world would have died nearly to the last man.

It had soon become scientifically certain, or as near certain as science ever admits, that the cause was not a fungus, insect, bacterium, virus or the like. No single scale, mite or other organism, however tiny, was found in a sufficiently wide sample of the dead or dying rice. Meanwhile, of course, there were the expectable exchanges of blame between nations. The USA was charged, and with some validity, as the agent of the horror—which was guessed by the Soviets to be some sort of escaped "military disease or gas." "Imperialist America" had developed it and let it escape—that or, with greater subtlety, some other sort of chemical recombination of some such secretly devised weapon meant for war.

Such charges gained credence owing to the fact that the Black Blight first appeared in USA. It was even said that the massive American effort at relief (which was not to endure very long) was evidence of bad conscience. There might even have been wars among the leading nations over these and other, wilder charges. There is evidence that China had actually targeted its nuclear missiles on major cities in USA—and only failed to launch them, apparently, because famine and then death struck down the military and scientific men able to do the launching before the word to fire was passed down from Peking.

The delay in finding the cause of this plague was owing largely to the early certainty that it would resemble other rots, smuts, wilts and blights in some manner. By the time (February 1988) the Lerner-Samuels-Zworkin group announced, in *Science Today*, their finding of a small molecular chain on the stems of some least-afflicted plants they had chosen to work with, even the plantings in scientifically housed structures equipped with every known filtering and disinfecting device were showing signs of death. Thus the last supplies of healthy or merely afflicted plants were scarce; and the people in charge of research were beginning to feel that rice might vanish from the earth forever.

That molecular chain, soon known as the "LSZ radical," had also been identified by various chemists in the waters of all oceans and it occurred in rainfall, world-wide, evidently. But the chemists did not then know a world blight was coming. They merely listed the complex stuff as "widely distributed, origin not known, observable effects: nil." From the LSZ note, however, it became possible for the same team to show that the molecular chain spent only a short time, hours, on rice plant leaves, then it vanished. Under the surface, they found no such radical. The molecular chain itself, meantime, was found to be self-made in sea waters at a wide range of temperatures owing to the energy of sunlight, which enabled several common pollutants to recombine and form the novel compound.

The Lerner group with the collaboration of a number of specialists from MIT, finally showed how this supposedly innocuous chain molecule was able to dissolve the cell wall minutely—the "outside" of the rice plant—at any point, and, after more combining with leaf material, enter the plant through the "hole" it created. It then added three parts of three molecular structures in the plant to create a longer but tightly wrapped and very inconspicuous new substance closely resembling various carbohydrates that appear in plants during photosynthesis and are known, technically, as "sugars." Its close resemblance to those natural sugars doubtless accounted for its long oversight. But the new substance, once in its final form, powerfully interfered with the plant's mechanisms, its enzyme chemistry, doing so in a matter of minutes, or an hour at most, after which it disintegrated into, this time, molecular chains again normal to the tissues of victim or host on death with initial decomposition.

In short, this was the first event of that magnitude among the many predicted for at least three decades by scientists. Man was pouring hundreds of thousands of chemical matters into the oceans, none there naturally, and of these (not studied or even known, really) there would be recombinations. The seas were like a chemical warehouse factory, with a million compounds in stock that were stirred together, outcome unknowable.

I ended this part with several accounts of mobs looting cities, granaries, any place where food might be kept or stored. The whole takes some seventy pages.

My abstract, here, is for advice, from you, Miles, from the Board, from any persons you deem able to help with my problems.

In the part beyond the eighties and up to my final chapter, a long one, itself, on the ultimate cataclysm, and in addition to twenty-seven shorter entries, I have covered the other "great cataclysms," as I and most others call them, at the length indicated by the foregoing outline of the Rice Deaths.

These are, and I hope all agree:

1. The battles within cities.

2. The radioactive excess findings, world-wide mortalities, etc., and the resolution of that somber situation.

Those two occurred in the nineties.

3. Also starting in the nineties is the world-wide epidemic of homicidal mania. I have nothing in the Foundation Records to indicate the cause of that dreadful epidemic was ever found. If anybody at the New Congress has data I would like to add it to the book. It finally seemed to burn itself out but there must be *some* explanation, whether found by now or not.

4. My already noted and personally written account of the last, greatest cataclysm runs to another long as well as separate effort: my *Part VII*, sent with this.

What I seek counsel on, then is the following:

1. Granting that the telesponder time permits the sending of the work, to this point, plus that final section, what is the general opinion of *this much*? More cogently, what is the probable reaction to the part that will not reach Paris for a week, and perhaps much longer, if what I hear of the world communications load is true? The World Federation material surely has priority over all else!

2. Assuming it is decided all the material I will now send is roughly okay, what about the part yet to come? Can we put out so huge a book in one volume? Is it readable for moderately literate (high school by old standards) people?

3. Little has been recorded so far of successful efforts at *staving off* disaster. They were many and the Foundation's share could fill a book. I haven't tried to portray it—too much like patting our own backs. Besides, the efforts to halt pollution, etc., even when successful, were almost invariably temporary. Commercial interests waited till their opponents

died, or got into something else, were bought off or were persuaded against prior conviction, etc. Then the projects to save environments were stopped.

4. How much of the actual inhumanity, cruelty, violence, the selfish and murderous behavior of our generation can be set forth without scarring later readers; without, perhaps, giving them a sense that man, themselves included, must still be the omni-predator he became? It worries me to present history as a tale of human degradation, ignorance and hate, of disinterest, apathy and absence of compassion. Am I wrong there?

I am adding, before the final essay, one further incident of the eighties, again with questions. It appears as an account of the "vibes." Should the horror prevailing in that event be given this full an exhibit? What I offer is true. But I get sickened by these things. There's so little compensatory nobility, so little simple compassion in these events.

Questions, then, about many things, the last entry before my final chapter, with other questions and uncertainties. Take the vibes. Did you know the first surviving witness to their onshore movement was a somewhat retarded Fort Lauderdale kid, a small-boat mate and dock boy? Here's his verbatim narrative on tape, recorded soon after his rescue by a Dr. Samuel Sniggins, a psychiatrist in Pensacola, who got on to the existence of this eyewitness, God knows how.

6. An Eyewitness of World Cataclysm Two

SNIGGINS: Your name is Oliver Washington Williams? You're nineteen?

(Mumble of assent.)

You lived in Lauderdale with an uncle and had a job as a mate or else a dock clean-up boy—*man*. (Assent.) You were in a skiff with an outboard when the vibes appeared, on June 17? (Assent.) The skiff was one of your uncle's but in bad shape. You had aboard a five-gallon can of kerosene? And you let the boat drift about on the marina waters while you cleaned off tar? (Assent.) But you were wearing rubber boots in that hot weather? Why?

WILLIAMS: Kerosene and gas is why. That dratted boat was a sieve. I had it a week in water to swell the seams. Then this cleaning job came up. I got rags, gloves, put on boots and shoved off.

SNIGGINS: Why—

WILLIAMS: To get far enough from shore so my dratted uncle wouldn't hoot at me to work faster, and such.

SNIGGINS: Why the boots, I mean?

WILLIAMS: So I'm having to stand in a skiff where the water keeps rising and I gotta bail, now and then. On top of the water is kerosene, and more coming, and maybe some gas.

SNIGGINS: You wore boots to keep from contact with the kerosene and gasoline?

WILLIAMS: Ever try standing in kerosene, gas, for a few hours? It scalds you, about.

SNIGGINS: Oh. I see. Well, in your own words, what happened?

WILLIAMS: For an hour or so, nothing. I drift over toward Elysian Fields Island. Rich folks. You know? (Grunt of assent.) Sea wall and riprap. Oh? Riprap is loose rocks piled up to hold a shore line. They got that, and a double cement sea wall, too. Lot of trash and garbage on the riprap. Birds at it. Rats.

228

SNIGGINS: Rats? On *that* island?

WILLIAMS: Rats wherever there's folks. Rich or poor. There'd been a real wet blow, not much wind for a hurricane, but it sure did litter the canals and bay and marina and all with trash. Them big houses—the people own 'em are up north. Caretakers and such, private cops, all there is around, this time of year. And some maids and so on are pretty lazy about putting out garbage cans regular. The water's right there—so they—

SNIGGINS: Yes. Well, you are in your skiff, working—or just staring around—and there are those estates, with a few people about, and gulls, rats, on the bank. Then?

WILLIAMS: Then the vibes come in.

SNIGGINS: Let's have it *fully.* What you *saw, felt, did, everything!* You're an eyewitness to what was the first invasion of the creatures. Only one, maybe. So you saw *what?*

WILLIAMS: Well—a sort of swell in the bay water, coming at the boat. Then under it. You know, Lauderdale water isn't gin-clear. A great shadow, lightish, goes under my boat and past it for, maybe, like a hundred feet. Something pokes up a million times near the boat but it has this oil slick all around. Fish, minnows, I thought. Then that wave moves on to the riprap. And the vibes start squirming out by the million. Look like macaroni—

SNIGGINS: We all know what they look like!

WILLIAMS: So okay. But I never seen none before! It's a new varmint to me. Inch and a half. Two inches. Like worms, all white, more a maggot color. The birds take off and then the first rat screams.

SNIGGINS: Screams? A rat?

WILLIAMS: Okay. Squeals. But loud. Then another. Then I see a couple and they got these worms on 'em and they are a-hollering. Squealing. I come in closer, use a oar for a stob pole, to see better.

SNIGGINS: Foolhardy!

WILLIAMS: Look. I ain't no fool. Not too bright, sure. Four years in grade six and quit. Okay. But I never seen nothing like worms coming out of the sea and hanging onto rats, okay? Do I even think *I* could be in trouble? Not then, I don't. Okay? So I see these worms—like a rug of 'em, moving, and I see one nail a rat. First to get that rat, see? Well, the rat doesn't know it's got a worm on it, then. Like ticks. You feel nothing and come home and got a dozen bastards on you! Same thing with leeches. Wade in, feel nothing, step out and you're a-dangling.

SNIGGINS: I'm a scientist, young man. I understand the mechanisms or chemical processes by which biting species can anesthetize the site. Bats, for example, some. Proceed.

WILLIAMS: So you know all the answers. So how come they call 'em "vibes"? They got no vibrations I could feel.

SNIGGINS: Typical student error. One of the university's Marine Laboratory summer students gets shown a dead something that the peasant who found it believed to be *Negeedulatia Cornuta horribilis*—the correct name. The girl brightly said it was a *vibraculum*, absurd on the face of it. Showing off. What she probably saw, in any case, was a *bryozoan*. But the ignorant boatman started telling everybody they were "vibes"—all he remembered from the lady's triple blunder— and it spread—so, continue, please.

WILLIAMS: Yeah. Sure. Thanks for nothing. If you don't mind, I'll go on saying "vibes." Can't rightly remember that

Nitwitted corny terriblest name, nohow. Okay? Okay. Where was I?

SNIGGINS: The rats. The rat with a single attached specimen.

WILLIAMS: Oh. Yeah. That. Well, I seen what he did. But that's not when I caught on. It was later. You want it all? Okay. So, like I said, there's this one rat, a big old-timer, and one of them white worms, leeches, them vibes, has got it on the leg. Like where a man's thigh is. And for a while the rat goes right on eating. Chicken gut, it was, I think. Then, I'd say, it sees the worm and takes a look and grabs it in its teeth to yank it off, see? Pro'ly not even thinkin' it was alive. And that's when it screams, I mean, squeals.

SNIGGINS: Instantly? The instant it bit the thing?

WILLIAMS: I ain't holding a stop watch but I'd say, from seeing the same thing over and over, that as soon as the vibe feels teeth, it does something that hurts whoever bit it, and anybody that grabs at it, too, he gets hurt awful. The first rat did what everybody would. Here's a thing don't bother you when let alone but if you try pinchin' it to pull it off, Jasus! Stings like twenty scorpions—and you ever been hit by a scorpion?

SNIGGINS: Yes, my boy, that I have! And not these mildly venomous species you have in Florida. Some real killers, nearly. Go on.

WILLIAMS: Well, now, did I say, I'm poling in pretty close to see what the hell is going on. I'd of thought they was maybe ten rats on that curved strip of riprap—hundred feet—two—something like that, what I can see of the stretch. But as them vibes start flowing ashore, like a white rug dragged over the riprap, up the wall and onto the lawn—*big* rug—maybe nearly as wide as what I can see of the wall from

231

where I pushed in the boat—the vibes must of scared up about a hunnert rats. You know what they say. Rats is real smart. You see one around the place, they say, an' it means you got eleven living there. Like that. For every rat I spotted there was ten more, anyhow, camouflaged like, or behind rocks, gorgin' on the garbage that got stranded by the tide, or dumped from the nearest house, behind the tree, place belonged to an up-North banker named Robert L. Kipper.

(At this point SNIGGINS took up the tale and described the area young Williams discussed. It was one of the newest and most luxurious developments in the Fort Lauderdale area—comprising five islands, all artificial. Intricate canals and waterways set the islands apart and made private channels for several estates in the usual Florida style that gives thousands of homes, mostly expensive places, a "waterfront." Just beyond the marina and behind a concealing stand of mangroves was a slum, where Williams lived and where, too, many of the people who did summer care jobs in this and other luxury areas had shacks. Perhaps nine hundred persons, the majority children, then occupied the hidden slum or nearby areas that hot, clear, early summer day, black and white and all shades between. Before returning to Oliver Williams' account, it should be kept in mind that his was, at this period, the only record of a "vibe" descent as seen by a close observer. The invading organism was a brand-new genus and species to science. Not a marine worm, mollusc, borer or oceanic leech, not a close relative of any known form of life that quickly suggested its evolutionary relationship, *Negeedulatia Cornuta horribilis* appeared as suddenly and in as vast numbers as this account suggests. It later proved to have one close relative, *N. C. boreas*.)

WILLIAMS (having paused lengthily, produced a crumbled cigarette and used Dr. Sniggins' desk lighter, blew smoke,

and—his nerves evidently steadied by that—went ahead):
So here's them rats, bitin', screaming and a-rolling in the
wet rocks, rough as they are, slimy with green guck, too. And
some rats rushing into the water, swimming around with the
plain idea that'll maybe get the vibes to let loose of them.
Right around the boat! *Everywhere.* And then, I see, some
rats are starting to lie quiet. So I watch an old fellow with
vibes hanging on him, like, say, ten, as I see he's weakening.
In a minute he falls down, kicks awhile, and he's stone dead.
Then, vibes cover him. That's what's now going on with all
of 'em.

SNIGGINS: Let's get this in order. First, a single—vibe—at-
taches itself to a rat. The rat feels nothing until it sees and
tries to bite off the thing—

WILLIAMS: —or pull it off with a paw—

SNIGGINS: Exactly. Any effort to pull away a specimen that
has attached its mouth parts to the host results in a reaction
by the parasite that causes intense pain. Something like a
venom injection, or a sting. Then as other vibes attach themselves and the process is repeated, the victim stops trying to
remove its attackers just to avoid stings, and once a certain
number of them have fixed themselves on a creature, it dies,
quite rapidly, as if, now, from a neurotoxin.

WILLIAMS: Yeah. But look! Some of them rats kept a-tryin'
to pull off the worms no matter *how* it hurt, and once they
got to hauling on about three, they died like they was shot.
I figured that out, in the first—well—it seemed an hour—it
was actually maybe ten minutes.

SNIGGINS: Ten minutes? From when to when?

WILLIAMS: From when I see that low bow wave, like, hit the
riprap till there ain't a rat movin'. Just a million worms on

the bodies and the rest slowly moving up the lawn, like acting careful, as if they never been in grass afore. Well, next thing, Amy Teetle comes around the palms to see what the screaming is all about. It's her day, or one of 'em, to open up an' air and clean the Kipper place. Amy's a blonde and real good-lookin', twenty-one, and about every guy from our town has slept with her from sixth grade up, because she purely adores to bex . . . excuse me.

SNIGGINS: A nymphomaniac.

WILLIAMS: Amy ain't no maniac of any sort! She don't *charge* nothin, Doc. She just loves to furnish poontang around, is all. She broke in a lot of the winter folks' millionaire boys, too. She's *real* friendly. Generous. And she can do things make a old hooker look like a beginner!

SNIGGINS: Go on. The—vibes—in the lawn? Did they see her? Sense her, somehow?

WILLIAMS: I been trying to *say!* I seen Amy afore the vibes did a thing. And I yelled at her to go back to the house fast and either drive away or lock herself in. I tried to say all about the rats and vibes. But she's under them palms they planted to hide the house from the water, I guess, and there's this breeze, so she can't hear good and keeps coming closer, realizing I got *something* to say important, by the way I was a-hollering and a-waving.

SNIGGINS: And then?

WILLIAMS: Gimme a little time. This is a girl, *lady now,* I *know.* One I *like.* One I often—used often—to—well—

SNIGGINS: Take it easy, son. I know it's hard—

WILLIAMS: Hard? Hell. Then? Before a single person had *died?* I didn't *imagine* Amy was in any real danger, more'n me. Just . . . I knew she was squeamish-like, on some things, and hated slimy critters, snails, like. She comes halfway down the lawn an' I begin to get across to her there's a whole flock of rat-eatin' worms right ahead of her, a hunnert feet about, and she don't see nothing so she keeps coming to us. Curious. Or think it's some gag to get her to mah boat. The reason she sees nuthin' is, old crumb Bentum has the yard work for Kipper and he is supposed to mow every week, but who's to know, and what harm anyhow, if he skips every other week and just cuts higher grass? Good for lawns to grow some, he says. So the grass is right tall and the worms kinda—halt, anyhow.

SNIGGINS: If you don't want to talk about what followed—

WILLIAMS: I don't mind all that much. It's real nasty. But I'm getting money for just flapping the jaw. Anyhow, the vibes get wise, somehow, to Amy. I can see 'em, here an' there, o' course. Know what to look for. White, slick, shiny, maybe slippery, spaghetti, like. One atop of another and so on, if they feel hurried. The grass finally starts to bend and wiggle with a grass bow wave, sort of, and I tell Amy to run. These damn vibes can go good and fast if they want. Land or water. Sprint a bit, anyhow. So the grass shows 'em sprinting at Amy. Maybe they got leaders, or extra-fast types, among others, like ants, bees; same varmint come in several styles. Whatever it is, a vibe gets Amy while she's just ready to scram. She's wearin' sandals and she looks down in a sudden way an', I guess, sees a worm's borin' into a toe. Up comes the leg and she stands there, staring at the thing, balancing on the other foot, and in a half second she gets a handkerchief out from between her boobs, excuse me, and wraps her hand in it—being chicken about slippery-type varmints— and she grabs the worm—vibe—pulls—and lets out a yell you could hear in Pompano.

SNIGGINS: It hurt her, the sting, or whatever, very badly?

235

WILLIAMS: It sure to hell did! She may be chinchy about slimy critters but Amy's no sissy. I seen her old man beat her to beyond bloodshed an' old Amy never even moaned. Now she's whopping and shrieking. And some vibes get the foot in the grass. More. And she changes feet and tries to tear them off. And that *does* it. She panics! Kicks and stomps and runs in a circle and flails at her rump when she sees one there and then she starts racing for the house. But she only gets halfway back to the palms and goes all woozy. Topples. Jerks a few times. Then the follow-upper types arrive and you can't see nothing, no dress, even, for the white wriggling mess is all over her.

SNIGGINS: You believed she was dead?

WILLIAMS: I plumb *knew* she was. Or else I'd have come up on the sea wall and lawn and tried to get her to my boat. I already figured by then, though if four-five vibes could sting a rat to death, fifty, a hundred, could kill a person. And by then she had a million on her. Well—thousands. How many would it take to cover a fair-sized woman, maybe a hundred-thirty pounds, worms all nose down and tails up straight and stiff? Each one size of an angleworm, say? Thicker'n quills on a porcupine, side to side, covering the whole girl's body. Anyhow, it starts to stink a little, in no time, up there.

SNIGGINS: Stink?

WILLIAMS: Why, sure. What're they doin'? Suckin her blood out, anything else liquid. Then eatin' into the tissues. Skin they don't like, vibes. Bone they can't eat. Or hair! No nourishment, I suppose. Everything *else*—it goes and fast!

SNIGGINS: You had observed that speed so soon?

WILLIAMS: Did I say I had? No. I said I saw the worms start to sink down an' I could smell they were eating her whole. But I didn't know *what* they ate, what got left, till later.

236

Tide came in and some rat corpses floated out and I poked 'em with a oar and see how there's nothing left but hide and bones. No eyes, even. No faces, much. And caved in like Amy—guts gone. Right then, I'm sort of stunned, personally. Not panicked but worried. I see they will eat people. I see they can climb a cement wall, wet or dry, an' rush across grass, so I wonder why haven't they come aboard? They went right *under* me, in billions.

SNIGGINS: You hadn't realized you were in danger?

WILLIAMS: Not till they got Amy.

SNIGGINS: You pulled away?

WILLIAMS: Like hell! I stayed *right there*, mister, in the middle of my leaky oil slick because I figure if they didn't come for me that first pass, it *must* of been the kerosene an' oil an' gas around the boat. It's a big oval, with that rainbow tinge oil on water has. I figure, when Amy's smelling before my very eyes, they're like mosquitoes. You don't get that? *Look*. You put a little oil on a pond full of mosquito wigglers, and, *bang*—it spreads clear over the pond—and no wigglers keep wiggling. That's what come to me at the time, see?

SNIGGINS: Fortunate thing you made that guess.

WILLIAMS: It ain't guessin', Doc, at all. *Common sense.* What have I got to protect me that Amy didn't have? A oil slick, is what. So I figure to stay in that slick till kingdom come, till, I mean, I figure a way to get back to my own dock, or till somebody comes out for me with, maybe, a fast boat—too fast for them vibes.

SNIGGINS: But no one came.

WILLIAMS: Not that day, nobody did. Want more o' this? Okay. Once I catch on it's the slick saves me, I look into things. Got over four gallons of kerosene. Nearly one of white gas. Can of engine oil. Two peanut butter and Surinam cherry jam sandwiches. Pair of oars. Waterproof gloves. Boots, rubber and knee-high. Bailing can. Some old rags. An' I'm about standing steady in the lee of Elysian Fields Island. Been standing up quite a time so I sit, amidships. Check the oil scum on the bay to be sure there's no gaps in it. Later on, soak a rag in the engine oil an' wipe the gunwales and sides to the waterline, near as I dared.

SNIGGINS: You could see—vibes—in the water? Didn't dare put in a hand?

WILLIAMS: In the water around Lauderdale you couldn't see a searchlight, two inches down. Well, hardly. Or, say, usually. *Nope.* I just ain't takin' chances. I want plenty of oil around the boat and more on the sides, in case they try climbin' up for me. See? Right! By this time, maybe ten minutes after Amy got hit, the vibes have moved on and I also realize around then there must have been other schools—swarms—whatever—because I hear some yelling on the island. Not too many people there, o' course. But there's some men and women on jobs—and I get the word of where they are being hit, more or less, by where the screaming comes from. In a while the island's quiet. It's a offshore breeze, southeast when I shoved off, but it starts to die out. I felt hungry, or needed moral support, like, around then, and opened a sandwich. That's when—I'm eating—I hear this other kind of noise, from the mainland. Like a jet flying low, sort of. But it doesn't change the way it would with a jet—having to keep moving. I listen and listen and by Gawd! I'm that slow it is a *half hour* and the sound's getting *fainter before it pops into my noodle* that what I'm a-hearin' is, like, *thousands of folks screamin' together*—men bellering—women, kids.

SNIGGINS: Then what? You seem—suddenly embarrassed. No need.

WILLIAMS: Then what, is right. Embarrassed too. Then what, is, I shit my pants.

SNIGGINS: Oh. I see. Understandable.

WILLIAMS: Maybe to you. Not to me. I been scared a lot of times, Doc, like when I stepped over a log onto a big rattler that didn't strike but couldn't move off easy. Did I shit myself? No. I waited till it tried to crawl, *quit* raising up to stare at my leg—and laid down flat—an' I jumped clear. This time, though, in the boat, *proooooong!* Out it came! Because if you know all of a sudden that worms are eating everybody else but you, all around, you figure who in hell will be left to rescue you? You wonder how long your oil will keep the worms off. What'll happen when it's dark? Such things, like. And that scared me shitless, no mistake.

SNIGGINS: And then?

WILLIAMS: Hell of a question. *Then* I got my jeans off, stepped out of my boots, got out of my underpants, chucked the clothes overboard and started stirrin 'em with a oar to wash 'em, best I could. Bein' careful to keep the oar handle greased. I see vibes tryin' to eat the clothes, makin' passes, but it's no problem, till I get the stuff clean enough to haul aboard. Then—there's vibes latched on my drawers and I have to be real careful, dunking and dunking till they drop off—from hatin' the oil—and finally, shipping the laundry in and setting it to dry.

SNIGGINS: From what notes I have here, you spent the rest of the day and the night and most of the day after in the rowboat, anchored by a rock on a line in a cove nearby.

WILLIAMS: What else would anybody do? Start rowing for the dock, the shore, any land—and row right out of your slick? Go farther out on the bay on any course and the chop maybe

239

washes your boat clean? Then up come the vibes! I anchor, sure, and sit tight in a cove where the tide's slow. To hold my oil slick. Afternoon goes by. Twilight comes. I hear nobody. When it gets dark to where I should see house lights and cars with headlights on the roads, I see nothing. I can't sleep—boat's got inches of water so I have to bail her out regular. So I sit. Morning, and I see a few planes but they are high. I had me a jug of water to drink but that's getting low. I decide that, before it's dark again but when I can see enough still, I'll grease up the oars and boat and head for open water. Maybe, out there, there won't be vibes. Maybe they're all busy inland—moving inland, that is. But just about when I am set for the trip, this helicopter makes a pass and spots me and lands on pontoons. See, they already know you oil up anything, pontoons, for instance, and you're okay. They drift up and the copilot talks and it takes awhile for him to decide I can step from my skiff to a pontoon and then aboard, without bringing no vibes along. That's what I done, and then we have to fly over the goddamn Everglades to Sarasota, believe it or not, because Miami's gone, all Dade County and most of the east coast halfway to Jax. Jacksonville. But the vibes ain't in the Glades, yet, and they ain't showed on the Gulf side of Florida, so that's where we set down. And once I get fed, a lot of big bugs come to the airport and start asking a zillion questions. Doctors, scientists in white coats, cops, state police, a mayor, reporters, TV people, the whole kaboodle. I tell them what I been telling you, but not as fully, and not so—well—start-to-finish like. Get things out of order. I'm tired, see, and I need to sleep, and I didn't get my jeans clean so they stink, and I think folks'll think I stink like that always, so I wasn't about to pose and yak and so on, forever, and they finally took me to a hospital, for Christ's sake, to sleep!

SNIGGINS: A hospital, Oliver, because you'd been subjected to very intense trauma. To check you over. And then on here for more checking. I must say, your behavior was perceptive, fast, analytical, productive, controlled, deductive, inventive, experimental, in fact, *exceedingly intelligent* and under the most harrowing conditions. There are several things you did that not one grown man per thousand of whatever high grade intelligence would manage, I'm certain. Your school records have you down as a high-grade—never mind the technical term—

WILLIAMS: High-grade moron. They told me when I had to get papers to work. So, what's your big deal here, Doc? Can't even us high-grade morons do a little common-sense figuring? You must realize I been charter-boat matin' since sixteen? I like fishing, sports or for food, fresh water or Gulf Stream. School—they had nothing *to* like particularly since they didn't like me. I'm too truancy-prone, when the weather's good. What I mean, Doc, I am school dumb, no doubt about it, but *not* outdoors dumb, 'cause if I was I wouldn't be here.

SNIGGINS: What are your plans?

WILLIAMS: Well, maybe I can get work, matin' on some boat out of here. If things get steadied down so people will be willing to sports-fish again—
A muffled scream tore out on the tape. Sniggins' voice muttered "Miss Wissett?" or a name with that sound. Running feet were audible, followed by a female voice, tightly hysterical, apparently that of the "Miss Wissett" who'd cried out.

MISS W.: Dr. Sniggins! Dr. *Sniggins.* Run for your life! They've just sighted vibes in the bay.
Again, on the tape, faintly, a siren—air raid, perhaps.

WILLIAMS: Before we run, Doc, we better stop by the room you people got me. Pick up my ten gallons of kerosene. Okay?

SUMMARY OF EARLY DATA:

Of course, not all the people in the first areas of attack were slaughtered. The vibes could not force themselves around well-fitted doors. But the sheer horror was bad enough! Their terrestrial-predatory period was from ten to fifteen days, when a return to water was mandatory, that or death. Their inability to survive with an oil film on their bodies became known in hours and was broadcast nationally in a few more hours.

Their first waves moved into rivers or bays near to large population centers. Their numbers were reckoned in trillions. Using waterways or even moving on land for miles at a speed of a fast walk, they devoured all mammals they overtook.

Their mouth parts and glands were perfectly adapted to their needs—and to produce the three effects young Oliver Williams had so quickly deduced. A fine proboscis-like instrument was entered into skin or hide with an accompanying minute droplet of anesthetic material, which swiftly deadened to all feeling an area of dermal, subdermal and deeper tissue ample to allow the outer mouth parts to bore ahead till blood was reached. Then, instantly, microscopic, stiff hairlike processes were extended in the tiny wound, to hold the creature fast. Any attempt to dislodge it, mash it or even scald, burn or otherwise destroy it resulted in the injection of a second substance by the same organ but from a second gland, venomous, and immensely painful to the victim. The third substance of the "sea leech"—its common name among those too snobbish to use "vibe"—is not understood entirely. Either it consisted of the venom and some *additional* toxin, or perhaps it was merely a full dose—the whole gland content—of the one venom. And, as again the keen young Oliver Williams so speedily and accurately observed, a sufficient amount of this third (or the second) substance acted as a neurotoxin, producing rapid debility, nerve-signal failure and resultant loss of muscular control, followed by "sleepiness"—a cerebral blacking out prior to death.

It has been difficult, thus far (September 4, 1989), to capture and make laboratory or animal tests with the predator as their continuing viability (and the stability of their metabolic products) depends on an extremely unusual but doubtless sensory-governed neuromechanism. So long as a specimen seems to "believe" its mission is feasible it will proceed even through areas intensely hot, over ice, through many strong acids and alkalis and, indeed, until it is physically damaged beyond movement. Petrochemical products alone, so far, seem to be its nemesis. No pesticide disturbs it. Since it consumes mammalian flesh, blood, soft parts and fluids entirely it cannot easily be test-fed poisons. But its sense of selfless forging ahead while it seems to have a "hope" of success is extinguished the instant the animal "decides" it cannot reach its prey. Captured specimens died quickly. And, when dead, they seemed to go into a swift state of auto-decomposition, of tissue disintegration, down to the molecular level.

On the same summer as the Florida strike, two young lovers, both in medical school and residents of Leningrad, walked out on a bridge over the Neva and exchanged kisses. It was a bright night with full sun, though the hour was nearing eleven—on one of Leningrad's famed "white nights." The approach of a policeman on his bicycle led them to break their embrace and feign a very intense interest in the dirty water of the river below. A moment later they were shouting to the officer to return.

Their reason was good. They had seen that rolling "bow wave" of a land-bent mass of vibes and knew from headlines in *Pravda* and *Izvestia* the curse that had descended on USA along its east coast some time before.

What they saw, and what all three watched with frozen terror as it moved up the concreted embankment, was not *Negeedulatia Cornuta horribilis* but its related species, *N. C. boreas*, a second "vibe" better adapted to much colder water and weather than *horribilis*. All three bridge-spotters escaped the invasion but they were among Leningrad's most fortunate three per cent. About a month later *N. C. boreas* appeared at Vladivostok, the first evidence of either species in the Pacific.

When, in late September, *horribilis* hit Los Angeles, considerable means for resisting the dreadful leech had been prepared. Wherever the white carpets came ashore, covering several acres even that first year, floods of crude oil blocked their paths as fast as men could manage. Fire departments sent out their pumpers, hoses fixed en route to tanks of crude oils diluted with lighter ones, and these engines effectively stopped the inland movement where terrain and buildings allowed.

The following spring, Calcutta was first to be hit. Other coastal cities of India followed at the rate of from one to three a day. Without sufficient oil supplies and lacking sophisticated equipment deploying available stores, India suffered even more than China was to do, later in the season. Japan managed fairly well, its population already reduced to a tenth of its peak by the Rice Blast.

That summer the vibes came up the Mississippi. Oily river surfaces did not stop the massive ascent of the writhing, "fish-belly-white" hordes till they had reached so far up small tributaries their shallows compelled oil contact. Some cities, such as Cincinnati, where it was believed the invasion could not occur, were hit at night and virtually depopulated before dawn, amidst scenes of incredible panic and rout.

A note follows from the book, *Years of the Vibes*, by Dr. Candley Mason, an eminent biologist:

"We did not recognize this animal at first as one with known relatives, however distant. Then it was noted that the two species were somewhat like certain Indian Ocean leeches. It was next announced by various biologists and others that the so-called 'vibes' might account for several mysterious events in far places, during the past century or more. Thus, a tiny Amazonian-basin Indian tribe was located by Wilson Kollade, of the Smithsonian Institution, in 1906, people who claimed they had been reduced from a 'mighty race,' living on remote tributaries of the Amazon, to we 'few, poor people' who lived far inland, in caves. These Indians spoke a language their nearest neighbors understood poorly. They translated the local claim that their great tribe was cut to near nothing by the 'worms that eat people'—a rendition to which Kollade paid scant attention and mentioned only in a personal letter.

"Other similar reports of a worm blanket crawling out of the sea and leaving nothing of a village in some remote spot, Tasmania, Ceylon, elsewhere, have been turned up by students of mine, but these were mere paragraphs in newspapers in distant cities and presumed mere fables to feed credulous appetites. Several strange oceanic events may perhaps have had such causes, one of which, the tale of the *Mary Celeste*, will come to every mind. And the *Mary Celeste* is by no means the only ocean vessel found abandoned, without a sign of the reason for departure or an explanatory note in the log.

"But by far the most shocking fact now known about this grisly destroyer is that its explosive multiplication is indirectly

THE END OF THE DREAM

man's fault. The larval form of both N. C. *horribilis* and *boreas* was preyed upon by innumerable small fishes and molluscs, by squids, octopi and certain protozoans, in particular. However, not only the widespread reduction of small fishes, squid, and so on, but the *total extermination of the protozoans* that chiefly kept the 'leech' in check was the real cause. Owing to chemical contaminants in the seas which those particular protozoa could not tolerate, the control predators on *horribilis* and *boreas* dwindled, while their chief consumers, several protozoa, have been *wiped out* by man's sea pollutants.

"Certain manufacturing processes used world-wide in the making of cheap dyes for paints, enamels and the coloring of plastics generate—army term—thousands of tons of specific wastes that were dumped in rivers and estuaries. They were neither acid nor alkaline; they mixed readily with salty water but were not toxic; they produced no discernible harm to aquatic life, algae included, though not enough protozoa were tested for effect; the materials were inert, apparently harmless to sea life forms of human interest from oysters to fish . . . the conclusion was foregone. Wastes of that elaborately proven 'harmlessness' needed no treatment before being let into rivers or the sea.

"And those compounds, over the decades, spread through the oceans till they reached some fraction of maybe one part per billion of ocean water, or per million. At that concentration, so low we have not yet established it exactly, it was fatal—but only to a dozen or two species of protozoa, protozoa of no great interest to science, it would seem. Out went the species which till then had kept our ultimate nemesis at low numbers, such very low numbers that what we know of them from the past is largely found in hints of strange happenings in alien and remote villages, and in certain legends. So this truly miraculous being, instead of dying in quadrillions in the larval stage, *matured*. Some hundreds of millions of us became victims of their 'population explosion' which we made possible. It was one of fantastic magnitude, even though nature provides staggering abundances in many life forms.

"Several puzzles relating to the vibes still remain undetermined. One question is: What warm-blooded mammals were the chief foods of these quasi leeches in their pre-population-explosion past? That one is now quite well understood. In view of their immense larval toll and owing, then, to their scarcity, the vibes preyed on porpoises, seals, possibly even small whales, a single large animal sufficing for a small school of, perhaps, a hundred individuals. Thus in the vastness of the seas, this long uncommon and widely scattered predator may not have been observed at his ghastly feed, or, if so, the sight was misunderstood at any distance.

"The fact that *horribilis* and *boreas* finally took to charging upon centers of dense human occupancy must be in part owing to their sudden and gigantic numbers-increase. Also, in the past decades, man has reduced oceanic mammals greatly, with many whales extinct and porpoises suffering from recent, intense hunting in the period after the Rice Blast. Some marine mammals may not have been acceptable food for this model engine of parasite efficiency. Sea otters, for example, should have been eradicated—and seem untouched. We are using them in hopes of finding they have, or exude, a vibe-repellent.

"Finally, the curious but truly wondrous (to a biologist) being seems formerly to have made his land incursions for food at dawn or dusk. There's a wealth of little-sifted yet maybe relevant material from the coasts of Africa. Tales of lions, various antelope, hyenas, even some elephants, come upon by natives freshly dead, yet 'boiling with great maggots' and with sorts never seen on animal or human bodies. Again, how many natives have vanished, without the fact reaching ears outside the tribe? How many white men, for that matter, hunters, explorers, biologists, have become 'lost' and never found, in areas not too far from the seashore or a riverbank?

"Once such rare and scientifically missed species grew to be near numberless, cubic miles of sea ranges packed with them, how long would it take them to readjust and make shore forays in brighter daylight? No time at all, as other species indicate to be possible! We have now enjoyed a full year in which their depredations have been virtually nil. And our many expeditions at sea are not finding them in such vast masses as they did only months ago. *Why is that?* Very recent evidence tends to confirm early speculations. The first assumption must be that, for whatever reason, they died off almost as explosively as they multiplied.

"Why should they die off, without controls—their normal predators being extinct? New methods of biochemical analysis point to the probable cause. Once their numbers became astronomical, and also, perhaps, mutants in a slight way but enough to alter their prey-animal target somewhat, and to stimulate their land invasions a little more, they consumed man in hundreds of millions, along with man's domestic animals and pets. But in all *such* prey they consumed the *pesticides* stored in those beings at levels far higher even than those in oceanic mammals. Whatever the reason, it is quite sure that *Negeedulatia Cornuta, horribilis* and *boreas*, are perishing in quintillions, or whatever the ordering number may be, and that they are not reproducing either.

"Man's industrial wastes brought this super-biblical plague into being. But eating man, and his pets and domestic animals, was a dismal solution for the two species. For an individual human being, or even rat, is far more toxic, by weight, than porpoises are. That being the case, the horror story of the vibes has a double moral." Theirs and ours.

VII
The Search for Energy

One problem that faced technical man as early as the middle of the last century was where to find adequate sources of energy. This problem was complicated by the fact that such sources as were drawn on up to the middle of that century were often remote from where their products were in demand. As long as coal provided the major fuel for industry it was largely the home demand (for gas, electricity) that presented difficulties of long haul or piping. For industry tended to establish itself in places where both iron ore and coal were nearby.

Soon, however, that situation changed. Petroleum for vehicles meant that oil or its refined products had to be moved by rail, by truck or in pipes to its places of use, and these were all places in civilization. The soaring need or demand for electricity also meant that generating plants would rise in every area, whether near a fossil fuel source or not. Transcontinental railways and pipelines multiplied. Natural gas was carried to generators a thousand miles and more from the wells.

Ships built to carry petroleum, "tankers," moved that fuel from one corner of the earth to another. During the Second World War the Fascist powers actually sank by submarine so many tankers bringing oil from the Gulf of Mexico and

South America to the American east coast that gasoline had to be severely rationed.

It was expected after the war's end that nuclear power would be rapidly developed and end the growing fuel dearth. In fact it took many years to develop the earliest and most primitive reactors, and these were more costly to operate (as well as to construct) than the optimistic scientist-engineers had predicted.

By 1970, it will be remembered, enormous tracts of forest and woodland were being "strip-mined" for coal. "Known petroleum reserves" were estimated as adequate for some decades. Oil sands were being worked and a huge store of petroleum in oil shales was looked on as an eventual source.

Another untapped wealth in coal was known to exist in Antarctica. Seams visible in cliff faces were reported and some of these were nearly thirty feet wide! But Antarctica was largely buried beneath mile-deep glacial ice. It was thousands of miles from the places where the energy demand was greatest and floating ice made it difficult to reach.

Meanwhile, nuclear reactors using both "enriched uranium" and then "enriched plutonium" breeders multiplied as their cost of construction and fuel became competitive and soon cheaper than any fossil fuel used for generating electric power. In Part II of this book we have seen the result of that reactor proliferation. Radioactive krypton and argon as well as tritium appeared in massive amounts in stack and coolant effluents. The necessity of storing "hot" plant wastes and the radiated metal of such plants created an ever greater congregation of "tank farms" where the material boiled constantly and had to be kept cool by condensing systems and other expensive machinery. Also, no long-lived material for these storage vessels could be discovered or invented so that every huge, cooled and closed-system container had to be abandoned and its vast contents transferred, by remote-controlled machines, to new vessels.

By 1970 "small leaks" had been found in many such tanks. In the years to follow, bigger leaks occurred. Earthquakes, on several occasions, split open the tanks on entire "farms" with terrifying results. Several rivers received the hot deluge from shattered tanks, killing thousands in nighttime flushings and forcing the removal of all persons from riverbank areas for periods of years.

Before these major accidents had occurred, there had been a rising protest against the amount and rate of radioactive nuclides being added to the air, seas, fresh waters and land. Medicine had for some years warned that existing "hot" isotypes were affecting humanity. Local effects of specific sorts in large areas around places where nuclear accidents had occurred were, admittedly, sometimes caused by radiation. But for years the nations supporting reactors, with industry and other interests related to the reactor programs, had convinced the masses that the danger was nil, or nearly so, save in those few and rare instances of known sorts which, the civilized world was officially promised, would be avoided by new procedures.

When such propaganda, such outright lying, was shown to be just that, the "atomic crisis" followed, as has been told. By then, the incidence of stillbirths, of the births of "monsters" or deformed babies, along with the evidence of a world drop in life expectancy, together with literally hundreds of illnesses and especially of cancers attributable to no other possible cause, brought on the period of atom panic.

The world, at that time, had lost about two billion five hundred millions of human beings owing to the direct result of the Rice Blast, the vibes and the disease and conflicts caused by these disasters. But the victims were in general the people who used the smallest amount of electricity so that their erasure did not greatly relieve the ever growing demand for more and more energy.

Meanwhile, several technical advances made it feasible to begin to draw on Antarctic coal. Superconductors in inert gases or vacuums, heavily shielded gases, alloys, were run along the sea bottoms to bring massive kilowattage from the ice-clad continent to demand-areas. First, huge plants using the coal for fuel rose in that distant region. Soon, however, methods were developed by which coal was burned where it lay, underground, and under the ice, which was melted for water to raise steam; electricity thus generated was borne by the efficient, new, submarine "pipes" to the rest of the world.

When petroleum was also discovered in Antarctica it, too, was exploited swiftly, and for a short time the "advanced" nations truly believed their energy requirements would be served indefinitely, even at their ever escalated rate.

The exploitation of these new resources was the work of many nations, each claiming or trying to claim a slice of the icy continent for its own use. Moreover, the way men rushed to exploit both the coal and the oil was reminiscent of the many past plunderings of natural resources by other generations. No effective international controls could be established. And, fairly soon, events predicted by many knowledgeable experts occurred. The "fire-mining" process, the burning of coal in situ to raise steam, led to "runaway" fires. And the fires of one nation's seams of coal encountered the fires of others.

By the middle nineties, considerable alarm over "industrial abuse in Antarctica" was being expressed. How vast the coal and petroleum reserves might be had never been estimated. Most of the continent carried such a load of ice that its land surface had been depressed as much as five thousand feet. Only the outer rim of that great bowl was being exploited for fuel and no adequate means for determining the petroleum and coal masses in the greatest area, that under a mile of ice, had been developed. Geologists differed greatly and often violently in their appraisals, some claiming the oil-coal "lodes" were peripheral entirely, while others stated the continent had gone through the past eons in which coal and oil were deposited before being ice-covered and then depressed so enormously by that glaciation and icing.

But from the early nineties other factors caused unease. The pit-firing means of generating high-pressure, superheated steam and so electricity for the power-avid Northern Hemisphere created masses of soot, sulphur oxides and other impurities, especially particulate matter of a very fine size but containing heavy metals, and this unchecked air pollution was not, as had originally been promised, confined by circulating in the circumpolar currents but entered the worldwide atmosphere. Soot, to be sure, was then blackening the ice of the continent. But pollutants from the inefficient, rude procedures in use were also measurably entering the global atmosphere.

Between 1992 and 1996 "runaway fires" increased in numbers and reached awesome magnitudes. Then, in May and June of 1996, Antarctica entered a period of vulcanism. Erebug, an active volcano, had been discovered by early expeditions. The great furnace under the ice created a madness among scientists, that dwindling brotherhood restricted to nations with sufficient coherence, government, educational systems and funds for the maintenance of science and scientists. These, in the mid-nineties, still numbered more than twenty, and though their efforts were then largely confined to searching for means to undo the major and more general harms of past years, more and more of them turned to study the Antarctic Gehenna, a fire mixed with lavas and ice that would have satisfied Dante.

The program was of too great a magnitude and too complex for the experts. It involved too many unknowns and reliance on declared "knowns" that weren't completely understood. Increased mixing of the heavy polluted polar air mass with the air to the north, in all directions, occurred quite soon after the bigger installations began to operate. Public alarm was considerable. True, the power flow was prodigious; the whole world—that is, the surviving parts with adequate technologies—used electricity like something almost free and infinite, too. The inhabited portions glowed at night as if chunks of the sun lay on them. Vast engineering undertakings were made simple by the quantity of power available and, of course, by the rapidly refined and gigantically enlarged engines fabricated for all purposes.

Very fast submarines began to bring incredible amounts of ice to Temperate Zone cities, and these cubic miles of pure, fresh-water bergs, when cleansed of their soot coatings, were melted into upland riverheads and renewed whole watersheds, filling creeks, then little and large rivers with clean clear water, and allowing massive restorations of fish and other aquatic populations. Forests began to grow in these areas, and game to return.

But the world-wide joy over these blessings was short-lived. The atmosphere below the Equator commenced to darken seriously. In a few years this dismal pollution crossed the Equator and reached north to the Arctic Circle, then beyond. In any three-month period the increased murk could be noted. Cloud formations changed. The jet streams went haywire. Before the end of the nineties USA, like all nations in that latitude, lay under a perpetual roof, a smoky air mass from which soot and fly ash steadily fell.

Then, in 2003, the great quakes began in Antarctica and these spread around the Pacific. Cities collapsed and hundred-million death tolls recurred. Starvation followed as sea transport broke down, owing to unpredictable but devastating counterwaves that rebounded from shores hit by titanic tsunamis.

In the winter of 2004 (summer, at the South Polar region) the satellites reported what was at first but suspected (and anxiously though covertly told northern governments): the polar smoke had taken a new ring formation, possibly a vortex configuration. Smoke from inland, from mines generating power, from runaway fires, smokes caused by volcanic eruption and by numerous lava flows, were being sucked away from land into the rapidly spinning ring, offshore. That soon led to the exposure of the subcontinental surface to sunshine round the clock, save where smoke trailing outward caused shadows. The ice was now largely free of cloud or cover of any kind.

This phenomenon had never been recorded or anticipated, though there had been periods of brief sunshine on Antarctica's ice fields, here and there. These ice fields were now sun-bathed—and now uniformly covered with black soot. The result was that heat from the sun was absorbed at a rate never conceived of, and, in fact, regarded as impossible, since it was supposed the smoke dome would forever keep the sun from reaching the surface. The enormous melt of that summer raised the seas seventeen inches. But, as autumn came in the Southern Hemisphere, the melt strangely continued. The giant smoke ring had dissipated in that autumn, dissipated almost explosively, and its outflung contents, concentrated and heavily burdened with contaminants, descended on lands below the Equator, suffocating or poisoning unknown myriads there. The residue crossed the Equator and invaded the Northern Hemisphere with the coming of summer, attenuated but still unpredictably hazardous. Worse effects gave more concern to those in the Northern Hemisphere.

255

The sea kept rising!

The smoke soon returned to its prior circuits and covered Antarctica with its former "dome." But the "Polar Cities," where the huge power-generating stations were located and their personnel lived, began to suffer from violent quakes, from lava flows of unprecedented volume, avalances of ice and floods that came with no warning. Satellite observation was again difficult, owing to the dense smoke "shield," and to the temperature variations indicated on the land, that is, on the ice, largely. These thermal readings were deemed "errors" because they could not be shown as logical in cause. The earth convulsions increased and it was reluctantly found that enough ice had been melted from the central mass by the soot-absorbed sun rays and the lesser heat sources to reduce that continental load sufficiently so that the mile-down rock surface of the continent was, in lay terms, "springing back," that is, heaving upward, or rebounding.

Not only was that process, more accurately recorded when special monitoring instruments were designed and orbited for the purpose, titanic in scale, but also the upheaving rocks often split deep into the strata beneath, and through those cracks magma, hot matter from deep in the crust, welled up into ice crevasses made as the rocks split. In places where the ice-load thickness of five thousand feet was still near that—and in others, where the summer melt had removed hundreds of feet of ice—magma often rose to the ice rims and spread out its blackened surface for scores of miles. The spring-up and cracking were accelerated as this lava melted more ice. The increments of water ran off toward the seas and caused more loss of overburden, which triggered more rebounding of granitic, basaltic and sedimentary rocks that had been ice-buried for eons and to a depth of a mile.

By 2010 the seas had risen more than two hundred feet,

causing the submersion of all port cities and all inland areas of altitudes less than two hundred feet. Meanwhile, the atmosphere, staggering under a cloak of coal-mine-fire pollutants, began to deposit a rising volume of toxic compounds produced by volcanic activity. The rare mineral riches of Antarctica were never exploited for profit. Instead, the veins and lodes were netted, vaporized, pulverized and blasted into the planet's air. At that point Miles decided to abandon Manhattan, the offices of the Foundation and his apartment, which for some time had been reached only by motorboats.

The Faraway installations were by then complete.

By then, too, the population of the world was perishing rapidly, owing to the terrible fact that the darkling daylight was now often swept by storms in which toxins were concentrated at deadly levels. Complete body cover and independent breathing tanks were essential for all outdoor movement. These "suits" had warning monitors that rang bells when the air was likely to become unbreathable.

So we made our way to Faraway—those who were assigned there, and their families. Some, of course, failed to arrive. At Faraway we had a small, short-term fusion plant and, so, ample power for a time. The settlement was domed with a new plastic and the air beneath kept clear, clean and safe by chemical means that removed CO_2 and many other compounds, and by an oxygen-replacement system that extracted the vital gas from the rock of the Adirondacks. Contact with other habitats gradually diminished, and for two years, 2013–15, we assumed we might be the only living human beings left on the planet. But once the Antarctic vulcanism began to die down and the atmosphere to recover, we found the small but glorious degree of our mistake—as radios began furtive operation. Soon our joy at having company was marred. We turned to bloody ways, as some other survivors found and attacked our settlement.

Our canopy was repeatedly destroyed in those battles.

Finally the day came when we found we need not erect a new "bubble" over our community. And the day also came when we began to get radio messages of constructive sorts from many regions.

EPILOGUE

To Dr. Miles S. Smythe
Director, District Two, Area Six
Member Congress
New Plaza Athenee

Important! Rush! Read instantly, please:

The last part of a massive amount of material began coming in at Ax Station, Paris, at 2:00 A.M. as arranged.

A much longer last chapter was expected and time for it was open. With the page (transcript) herewith, the Center City transponder, your District Two, Area Six, stopped abruptly.

The standing on air beam quit.

The secondarges did not take up work or respond to queries or emfgt restart effort from here.

An hour passed, time allowed to get secondary plant in operation. No secondary power on. We then queried, as per standard procedures, three stations within a 300-km. radius. All responded. None aware of Center City cutoff. Awaiting orders to dispatch party (overland, trucks only, those points) if desired.

This is a situation without any recent analogue. Any of seven generating plants or diesels should be able to power tower and come in here clearly. No signals yet.

Should fast planes be dispatched or should we wait another 85 minutes (now 1300 hrs) when satellite photo can be shot, results beamed here for TV scrutiny?

Await orders.

MAJOR PAUL COULEL, NIGHT CHIEF
CENTRAL OPERATIONS CONTROL
PARIS, DISTRICT ONE, AREA TWO

261

Miles was wakened and read the dispatch. He then turned to Will's last-sent part page. Will was by no means finished with the last chapter if he had said a long one was due. And Will hadn't stopped sending when he had allotted time, hard to get.

Miles phoned Major Coulel and suggested planes be readied but held for the satellite shot.

He was not, usually, upset even by very dire realities. The present one seemed some power and technical foul-up but the French expert thought that was hardly possible. What, then?

He ordered coffee, paced, tried to read the top inch of stuff that bellied his brief case, realized he'd gone over four reports and not assimilated anything about even one.

The time dragged. Five minutes after satellite transit the major rang. His report was alarming as his ultracalm instantly revealed. "The satellite shot was made in clear weather at an excellent angle. The whole Adirondack area is dark for twenty miles around Center City—your gorgeous Faraway. Not a light there. Nothing. No fires. No haze. No more detail possible with on-board equipment. The place is pitch-dark. Whether the people are there or not, who knows?"

Miles said, "Send the ships. Armec, of course. Have them start reporting when an hour from target area."

That wait couldn't be worn out by striding.

Miles had coffee, skipped breakfast, attended a meeting, and took his place at the half-circle table on the dais with the other district directors who were also the equivalent to the World Government's "Senate."

The Nemo-Caedmons should be talking in another hour, Miles believed. He got wrist-watch fever. Neighbors noted that and grinned a little. What could get Smythe that riled— a date with a woman?

A red-uniformed guard stepped to the podium, bowed, asked and was given the Director General's permission to speak to Miles. Miles saw from the man's face that the plane news was bad and stepped down, into a small room behind the draperies shielding the half-round podium.

There was a Communications man there.

"Jules Reveneau," he said. "Communications commandant. An honor."

Miles exchanged handclasps, bowed at the "honor" attached to meeting him, and waited.

The hour message was fine. Weather fair. On course. No problems. Half an hour later, as ordered, the lead ship reported from a former Albany area. Of course, sunny, nothing wrong.

"As my three fighter-bombers moved to some ten thousand meters from the lake—Enigma—at your Faraway—Center City of Two, Area Six, the pilot started to say some French words of astonishment. Nothing more. We flashed back. Called the other ships. They are silent, lost, clearly, sir.

"A strange thing, yes?"

Miles nodded. Faraway—out. Dark in night hours. Will got nothing through. Three of the fastest and toughest warplanes —wiped out while a stupefied pilot said two or three astonished words before he reported, which, then, he couldn't. All ships must have been crashed, somehow.

The man at his side was tense. "There has to be an explanation!"

Miles nodded. "Not one that occurs to me. If Faraway's gone, what's next? We must interrupt the regular meeting. Gather the experts and set them to thinking, data-collecting, what they will do, once they get the mystery.

"My God. Faraway! And—" Miles collapsed in a chair which almost broke under that heavy load and covered his eyes with his mighty hands.

"It could be the last one. The one too many. The one we

brewed but never tracked to the brewery. It wouldn't take much, now, to whisk away the hangers-on, would it?"

The French war hero, Communications commandant, his chest medal-heavy, sighed. "No, my brave and admired American, not much."

Miles shrugged. "Well, get your people locating the ones who answer. Maybe a chart of that would show, not what must be it—but which way it's coming. We could be next, last, or escape. Or something different and unguessable could have occurred."

"As it often has. We still live." The commandant bowed and then saluted and turned. "While there's life, hope exists?"

"A man can run out of hope and not be dead yet," Miles replied.

Alone. Briefly, he wept.

He'd forgotten even the feeling.